MOURNING GLORIA

SUSAN WITTIG ALBERT

THORNDIKE
CHIVERS

This Large Print edition is published by Thorndike Press, Waterville, Maine USA and by AudioGo Ltd, Bath, England.

Copyright © 2011 by Susan Wittig Albert.

A China Bayles Mystery.

The moral right of the author has been asserted.

Thorndike Press, a part of Gale, Cengage Learning.

Thorndike Press® Large Print Mystery.

The text of this Large Print edition is unabridged.

Other aspects of the book may vary from the original edition.

Set in 16 pt. Plantin.

LIBRARY OF CONGRESS CATALOGING-IN-PUBLICATION DATA

Albert, Susan Wittig.
  Mourning Gloria / by Susan Wittig Albert.
      p. cm. — (Thorndike Press large print mystery)
  ISBN-13: 978-1-4104-3617-7 (hardcover)
  ISBN-10: 1-4104-3617-9 (hardcover)
  1. Bayles, China (Fictitious character)—Fiction. 2. Herbalists—Fiction.
3. Arson investigation—Fiction. 4. Murder—Investigation—Fiction.
5. Texas Hill Country (Tex.)—Fiction. 6. Large type books. I. Title.
PS3551.L2637M68 2011b
813'.54—dc22   2011006984

BRITISH LIBRARY CATALOGUING-IN-PUBLICATION DATA AVAILABLE
Published in the U.S. in 2011 by arrangement with The Berkley Publishing Group, a member of Penguin Group (USA) Inc.
Published in the U.K. in 2011 by arrangement with The Berkley Publishing Group, a division of Penguin Group (USA) Inc.
U.K. Hardcover: 978 1 445 83702 4 (Chivers Large Print)
U.K. Softcover: 978 1 445 83703 1 (Camden Large Print)

Printed and bound in Great Britain by the MPG Books Group
1 2 3 4 5 6 7 15 14 13 12 11

For Peggy Moody —
She Without Whom Nothing Happens

Mille phantasmata e daemonum obversatium effigies circumspectarent.

This description of the hallucinogenic effects elicited by the Aztec "magical" preparation ololiuqui [morning glory seeds], was recorded by Francisco Hernández, personal physician to Philip II of Spain. He carried out extensive investigations on the flora and fauna of Mexico during the years 1570–75. [His report] contains a detailed description of the preparation and use of ololiuqui, and he notes that: "When the priests wanted to commune with their gods and receive a message from them . . . they ate this plant; and a thousand visions and satanic hallucinations appeared to them." This is one of the earliest written accounts of the use of a hallucinogen, and it provides cogent support for the belief that primitive cultures employed psychoactive plant extracts to gain access to the supernatural rather than for pleasure.

John Mann
Murder, Magic, and Medicine

A NOTE TO THE READER

Used with care and in the proper context, many drug plants *do* confer advantages on the creatures that consume them — fiddling with one's brain chemistry can be very useful indeed. The relief of pain, a blessing of many psychoactive plants, is only the most obvious example. Plant stimulants, such as coffee, coca, and khat, help people to concentrate and work. . . . There are psychoactive plants that uncork inhibitions, quicken the sex drive, muffle or fire aggression, and smooth the waters of social life. Still others relieve stress, help people sleep or stay awake, and allow them to withstand misery or boredom. All these plants are, at least potentially, mental tools: people who know how to use them properly may be able to cope with everyday life better than those who don't.

Michael Pollan
The Botany of Desire:
A Plant's-Eye View of the World

Those of us who cultivate herbs sometimes get into the habit of treating them like well-mannered pets. We find them useful in our food, cosmetics, and medicines; we enjoy growing them and using them to decorate

9

our gardens and our homes; and we take delight in their taste, scent, and form. Where herbs are concerned, we like to think that we're always in charge.

But sometimes we're not as much in charge as we might think. In this book, I want to tell a story built around plants that have power over us, changing the way we feel. These herbs contain phytochemicals that may enhance our moods (such as the bolstering caffeine in coffee and tea that keeps us awake; or the esters, ketones, and aldehydes in lavender that have the ability to ease us into sleep). Or they may stimulate and relax us at the same time, like the nicotine in tobacco, which produces simultaneous feelings of calmness, alertness, sharpness, and relaxation, as well as enhancing concentration and memory. Plant chemicals may also create feelings of euphoria and awareness of sensation (chile peppers, chocolate, marijuana); feelings of alertness and physical and sexual energy (cocaine, derived from the coca plant); and powerful hallucinations (the seeds of certain morning glories, for instance). Plant chemicals may also narcotize us and dull all sensation (morphine and codeine, derived from the opium poppy) — useful painkillers when we need them.

I'm not encouraging you to experiment with the more powerful of these mood-altering plants. But I do think we need to understand that many of the most common and familiar plants have the ability to influence our perceptions and behaviors. Imagining all herbs as warm and fuzzy "feel-good" plants is a mistake. Used unwisely, even mild-mannered plants can pack an unexpectedly powerful punch, especially when they are combined with prescription drugs. Before you ingest any plant, consult with the appropriate professionals, do your homework, and use your common sense.

Mourning Gloria is fiction, and all of the incidents, people, and places (yes, even Pecan Springs, and isn't that too bad?) are fictional or used in a fictitious way. For me, stories derive a particular meaning and resonance from particular places, and the Texas Hill Country is a favorite nonfictional place of mine. The summers are always hot and often dry; the winters are mild and sometimes wet, especially in El Niño years. I hope you'll come for a visit in April, when the spring wildflowers are in bloom — in bloom, that is, if the winter has been wet enough. Gardeners will understand.

As usual, thanks go to the herbalists and researchers who have compiled the various

11

books and monographs I rely on, and to the many friends around the country who support this series. I am also grateful to Alice LeDuc, who checks my botanical references, and to Gina Mondello, the winner of a "cameo character" raffle for the benefit of the Story Circle Network. Gina agreed to come in on short notice and work in China's shop for a day. Thanks, Gina!

Susan Wittig Albert
Bertram, Texas

PROLOGUE

The TV weatherman had forecast thunderstorms for the evening but clear skies and plenty of sunshine and warm temperatures for the coming weekend, so Gloria tossed a pair of khaki shorts into her duffle bag and followed them up with her red bikini and a tube of suntan cream. The patio at home was totally private, and she could lie on a longue and bake in the sun as long as she wanted, with or without her bikini — all day if she felt like it, with a pitcher of iced tea at her elbow and her iPod and music. She'd get all nice and toasty brown, and there'd be time to do her hair and take long baths and work on her nails. A makeover weekend. A serious boost to her morale.

Which she needed, definitely. A boost to her morale, that is. If she stuck to her plan, the week coming up was going to be the purest hell. She had to get her head straight so she could deal with all the crap that was going to get dumped on her. She was confused about a lot of things these days, but one thing was perfectly clear. She was *not* going back to Mexico. She was going to the cops, instead. And once she went to the cops, that was it. That was the end. Cross that line, and she could never go back.

Of course, if she were totally honest with herself, she would have to admit that she had already crossed too many lines, and that every week of the past month had been hell, too. The past couple of months, come to that, ever since she'd let Matt talk her into
—

She shuddered. *Do not go there,* she reminded herself sternly. She had to put that out of her mind and concentrate on the perfectly ordinary thing she was doing, getting ready to spend a long, lazy weekend at her mother's house in Seguin. She didn't have classes on Monday, so she could stay until Tuesday. Nobody — not Matt, not Stu (if he cared, which he might or might not) — had to know where she was hanging out. Her mother was up in Dallas getting Grandma settled in one of those ritzy residential villages where they warehoused selfish old people who wanted to keep their kids and grandkids from inheriting their money. Her dad was in Alaska, working on the pipeline — she hadn't heard from him in months, except for the checks he sent for tuition and books and the new laptop, which she was grateful for, naturally, even if he was doing it only because she had made him feel guilty for abandoning his wife and daughter for that bottle-blond slut in Anchorage.

In fact, that was the beauty of going home. Nobody in the whole wide world would know where she was. She'd be all alone and safe, with free access to the drinks cabinet, the well-stocked freezer, her mother's steaks and pizzas and ice cream, and as much TV as she wanted. No phone calls, no threats, no harassment, and by the time she got back to Pecan Springs, she'd be psyched up to do what she had to do. The weekend would give her time to get things under control, at least in her own head. Give her time to come up with a good story for the cops. Yes, that's what she needed — a believable, plausible-sounding story that would protect her and allow her to deal with the inevitable aftermath, which needn't be so bad if she kept her wits about her. If she came up with the right story, maybe they'd even let her into the Witness Protection Program. Well, why not? She was a witness, among other things. She definitely needed protection.

But most of all, she needed to put all that bad stuff — bad choices, bad people — behind her. She needed a fresh start.

Oh, is that right? scoffed the snarky voice in her head, the voice that sounded a lot like her mother's. *And just who do you think you're kidding? There's no way to get a fresh start after what you've done, Gloria, and you know it. Admit that you're in way over your head and there's no way out. No easy way, that is. You'll end up in jail — or worse.*

She forced herself to shut out the voice and turned, catching sight of herself in the full-length mirror on the back of her closet door. Medium-tall, narrow hips, great boobs, if she did say so herself. She turned to admire her profile, lifting her shirttail so she could see her flat stomach. Good nose, flirty eyes, nice mouth, reasonable hair — not bad-looking, all things considered. But those boobs were extra-special — full and firm, like two ripe melons — and she knew how to show them to best advantage. Those boobs caught guys' attention and held it. They had caught Stu's attention, hadn't they? They had made him want the rest of her — want her badly enough to drop Shannon and focus all his attention on her.

She made a face at her reflection. Yeah, well, those boobs were just about all she

16

had. Without them, she'd never get noticed. She turned away from the mirror. She had no special talents, no special interests, no special skills, no special hopes or dreams. She had drifted through undergraduate school with Cs and a few Bs, compiling a GPA that was barely high enough to get her into grad school, which she had wanted not because she aspired to do anything special with a master's degree but because another two years of school would allow her to postpone the rest of her life. And since her dad was so eager to pick up the tab, why not let him? It was a small price for him to pay, considering all the pain he had caused. It made her feel like she was getting even, and that felt good. Getting even always felt good.

She turned in a circle, surveying the messy apartment bedroom, clothes strewn everywhere, magazines, makeup. What else should she take on her makeover weekend? Oh, God, yes, her laptop. She giggled half hysterically. She wouldn't survive the weekend without her Facebook friends, who sometimes seemed like the only real friends she had, because they weren't in her face all the time. Her former roommate Vickie, for instance, who got to be such a pain that she had moved out. And Shannon, who was always mouthing off about Stu.

And then she sobered, thinking. No, better not post this weekend, or if she posted, better not say where she was. Don't say she was in Seguin, at her mother's place. Lie about it. Make up a story. Yeah, that was what she'd do. Make up this great story that everybody on her friends' list would be bound to remember. Like, tell them she was driving down to South Padre Island for a long weekend at the beach with a couple of girlfriends from high school that she hadn't seen since graduation. That they had reservations at the beach-front Marriott, where the blue-green ocean broke onto a strip of white sand under the Gulf-side balconies and the sun shone down on a jewel of a swimming pool, surrounded by swaths of green grass and swaying palm trees. That the three of them would slather on the sun oil and lie by the pool all day and spend all night bar-hopping at the foot of the island, dancing to hot bands until the last margarita was poured.

Sure. She could do that, easy, because if she had one single talent in the world, it was making up stories about herself. She would imagine the whole thing from beginning to end, a great adventure, and tell it bit by bit in posts, so if anybody came looking for her and thought to check her Facebook page, they'd be convinced she was at South Padre. What was it they called this in those true crime shows on TV? A cover story? Whatever, it was a brilliant idea.

And with that, she sat down at her laptop, brought the screen up, logged on to Facebook, and in five minutes had posted the first installment of her story, time- and date-stamped, 6:10 p.m. on Friday, today. According to her post, she was packed, the car was loaded, her friends were waiting for her in the parking lot, and they were heading for South Padre, aiming to drive as far as Corpus tonight, get a motel there, and start again early in the morning. Look for her next post from the beach. Smiling to herself, she logged off. A great weekend trip, sounded like a lot of fun. Too bad it wasn't true. But that was okay. Where she was headed was just as good. And free.

Five minutes later, she was in the parking garage, stowing her bag and her laptop in the trunk of her jazzy red Mustang convertible, which she had bought with her ill-gotten gains. She glanced out through the concrete arches at the sky, trying to decide whether to put the top up or down. Clouds were piling up in the east, dark blue on their heavy bottoms, rosy pink like strawberry whipped cream on top where the evening sun struck them. Lightning forked from cloud top to cloud top, and the pale leaves of the cottonwood at the back of the parking lot rattled like scraps of shiny metallic paper in the slight breeze. Seguin was only thirty minutes away, but from the looks of that sky, it was going to rain before she got to her mom's house, so she'd leave the top up. It didn't matter, as long as the weather cleared for the weekend. She was in the mood for some serious sun. A couple of days stretched out on the patio would do wonders for her spirits.

She shut the trunk, went around the car, and slid into the driver's seat. She was putting the key into the ignition when the passenger door opened and a familiar, softly pleasant voice said, "You weren't leaving for the weekend without letting me know, were you? I thought we were going to have a chance to talk this thing over." He slid onto the seat beside her.

A flash of fear, like forked lightning, seared through her. "Talk? Were we going to do that? I guess I forgot." She shrugged, trying to make her voice sound natural, aware that it didn't. "Anyway, I'm only going for a couple of days. Just for the weekend. We can talk when I get back. Okay?"

He smiled. "I'd rather not put it off. And to be honest, it bothers me a lot that you tried to get away without telling me, you know?" There was an odd light in his eyes. His voice hardened almost imperceptibly. "So let's go off by ourselves and talk for a while, and then you can go wherever you're going. How's that?"

A guy walked past the car, whistling. She bit her lip, thinking fleetingly that she had better get out of the car right now, while she still had the chance, and —

He put his hand over hers on the steering wheel and she was suddenly aware of his strength, his size, his physical presence — and something else, some sort of animal intensity she hadn't seen in him before. She had known him for months, and he'd always seemed easygoing and laid-back, so there hadn't been much attraction. But this was different. Guys who knew what they wanted and were ready to take it always turned her on. Part of her liked being in control, but there was another part that liked it even better when she wasn't.

His fingers tightened on hers. He smiled crookedly. "Hey," he said, teasing now, but firm. "I know you want to, so come on — let's go." As he pulled his hand away, his fingers touched her breast and she shivered.

He caught the shiver and threw her a knowing glance. Then he patted his shirt pocket, his dark eyebrows lifting. "Got some stuff here I'm pretty sure you'll like, and I'm ready for a little fun. And some talk, too. Okay?"

Her belly muscles tightened and she felt goose bumps break out on her arms. She hadn't planned this, but she was always one to take an opportunity when one presented itself. She thought of his fingers on her breast and shivered again. They could go somewhere and fool around for a while and have their talk before she drove on to her mother's place. A last little fling, so to speak, before she went totally straight.

"Okay," she said slowly. "Yeah, I guess." Then, "Where do you want to go? Your place? I'll leave my stuff in the car and —"

"How about if we go back out to the trailer? The place where you crashed when you were between apartments."

She shook her head. "I don't have a key. I gave it back to —"

"I do," he said, and grinned. He lifted his hand again, this time touching her cheek. "I've got a key." His fingers felt cold, but his voice was coaxing. "Hey. Just the two of us. It'll be fun. Then you can bring me back here and be on your way wherever."

She had got the car started and was backing out of the parking space when it occurred to her. She had just posted the perfect cover story. If anybody came looking for her, they'd start with her Facebook page, which would lead them to South Padre. Which would prove to be a dead end.

If anything happened to her, nobody would know where to look.

CHAPTER ONE

A morning-glory at my window satisfies me
more than the metaphysics of books.

Walt Whitman

Flowers really do intoxicate me.

Vita Sackville-West

Friday night's thunderstorm rumbled off to
the west and the Saturday sun rose on one
of those stunningly lovely June mornings
that seem to happen only in your dreams or
in the half-forgotten country of childhood,
when you spent summers with your favorite
grandmother — the one who never made
you help with the dishes. Sunlight slanted
through green leaves tender and innocent
as spring, not yet baked brittle by summer's
heat. Grasses glittered with dew, birds
danced light as a song on the cool morning
breeze, morning glories bloomed heavenly
blue over the arbor — a lovely day to spend

in the garden, once the dew had dried.

Caitie and I had been out there for an hour already, picking and tying up bunches of fresh dill, rosemary, sage, parsley, cilantro, thyme, and basil and stowing them in the big picnic cooler. As a general rule, it's best to pick herbs after the dew has dried, but I was making an exception this morning. Today was Saturday, Market Day, and these dew-fresh green bundles would be snatched up by eager customers before the morning was half over.

On an ordinary Saturday, Brian would have been in the garden with us. But on Monday, he'd left for a two-week session as camp counselor at Hill Country Kids' Camp. He'd hoisted his duffle over one shoulder, tucked his laptop under his arm, and pecked my cheek with his familiar good-bye kiss before he sauntered out to the van that had come to pick him up, a self-confident young man on his way to his first job. I'd made him promise to email us while he was gone, but I wasn't worried that he'd get homesick. His longtime girlfriend Jake was working as a girls' counselor at the same camp.

Howard Cosell and I (Howard is Brian's elderly basset hound) had watched the van drive off. I don't know about Howard, but I had a largish lump in my throat and a film of tears in my eyes. Brian isn't my biological child. He's Mike McQuaid's son by an earlier marriage, but he's been an important part of my life since he was a little boy. It's hard to believe that he's on his way to a life of his own, separate from ours — a separation made even more emphatic by the fact that he now holds his learner's permit. He's a responsible kid, but kids in cars are always a worry.

Since this was Saturday, McQuaid might also have been in the garden, except that he was away, as well. My husband (whom I have called by his last name ever since we met in the courtroom where he was testifying against a woman I was defending) is a helpful sort of guy and has been known to lend a hand when he's nicely invited. But in addition to a part-time appointment as an associate professor in the Criminal Justice Department at Central Texas State University, McQuaid is a private investigator. He left for Memphis on Thursday to do some work for Charlie Lipman, a local lawyer. He wouldn't be back until Monday or Tuesday.

So it was just the two of us this Saturday, picking and packing in the early-morning sunshine. Caitlin, eleven, is my niece, my half brother Miles' daughter. She's been with us for less than a year, but it already feels like a lifetime. And there's an irony here. For decades I cherished an independent and solitary life, putting off marriage to a man I loved while I stubbornly hung on to my freedom. Now, improbable as it often seems to me, I am married. I am raising two children. Life is full of surprises.

After a quick breakfast, Caitie and I loaded the cooler into the car and headed for town. Along Limekiln Road, we could see banks of cheerful daisies, drifts of gaudy yellow and red Indian blanket, winecups the color of rich burgundy, the delicate white blooms of prickly poppies, even a few tardy bluebonnets. In Pecan Springs, the gardens along the streets blossomed with June exuberance and the courthouse square was festive. Vinca, marigolds, and zinnias spilled out of the wooden half-barrels the Chamber of Commerce has installed on the street corners, and our green Farmers' Market banners — brand-new this spring — fluttered from the lampposts.

This is the market's first full year, and we have high hopes for its success. Especially me. I'm China Bayles. I own and manage an herb shop called Thyme and Seasons, located at 304 Crockett, just a few blocks east of the square and right across the street from Dos Amigas. The market is held in the restaurant's parking lot from nine to one on Saturdays, from May through early November.

Hosting the market is smart business thinking on the part of Janie and Janet, the two women who recently bought the restaurant. Smart, because it allows them to buy their produce from the vendors and advertise that they are serving farm-fresh, locally grown vegetables. Also smart because when customers finish shopping at the market, they can have lunch at Dos Amigas. The neighboring merchants benefit, too, since the customers drift across the street to shop at my Thyme and Seasons or Ruby Wilcox's Crystal Cave and enjoy lunch in our tearoom, Thyme for Tea, where we specialize in great veggie sandwiches, salads, and quiche. Then they can visit the quilting shop and the yarn shop at the Craft Emporium, next door at the corner of Crockett and Guadalupe. Or the Hobbit House Children's Bookstore next door on the other side.

Got the picture? On Market Day, everybody wins, customers and merchants alike. Green isn't just the color of fresh vegetables or environmentally friendly this-and-that, much as we value these things. Green is also the color of money. I don't want to sound crass about it, but money is what keeps our small businesses alive and thriving. If the Farmers' Market stays healthy through the heat of summer and into the fall, the enterprises in the 300 block of Crockett will be healthy and very happy.

Caitie and I had left home an hour before the market opened so we'd have time to set up before the customers flooded in. She's small for her age, with dark hair and the largest dark eyes I've ever seen — and sometimes the saddest. I often think that a child should never have such sad eyes. But there's a reason. She is still fragile from her mother's drowning three years ago, her father's murder last summer, and her aunt Marcia's death from cancer earlier this year. A heavy weight of tragedy for a child.

But while she will always wear indelible scars, Caitie is a survivor. She has found friends and activities that keep her busy. She does well in school, enjoys photography and soccer, and has fallen in love with the violin my mother Leatha gave her at the beginning of the previous school year — a three-quarter-size violin, somewhat scarred, that has been in our family for several generations. When I was Caitie's age, Leatha made me take lessons. These went on with increasing painfulness until it became clear (first to me, then to my teacher, and at last even to my mother) that I was utterly lacking in talent and even more deficient in interest. Happily, the violin survived my carelessness. It just fits Caitie, who seems to have a talent for it and enjoys practicing so much that the school orchestra teacher suggested private lessons. As it happens, Sandra Trevor, a regular customer at my shop, teaches strings at CTSU and supervises graduate students in music education. Sandra recommended one of her grad students, a young woman named Brenda, and every Monday afternoon, Caitie eagerly goes off for her violin lesson.

I unlocked the front door of the shop and stepped inside, Caitie behind me. I glanced around warily, remembering what had happened a couple of weeks before Christmas, when I was surprised by an early-morning intruder. We fixed the window where he broke in, but that doesn't mean it can't happen again. I'm always on my guard.

Caitlin took a deep breath. "Mmm," she said appreciatively. "Smells yummy."

And so it does, as you'll notice the next time you visit the shop. The sweet, spicy, flowery scent comes from the baskets of handmade pomanders and sachets that sit

31

on the counter beside the cash register, the bunches of tansy and yarrow that hang from the ceiling, the ristras of red chile peppers and braids of silvery garlic that decorate the walls, and the wreaths of artemisia, sweet Annie, and delicate dried flowers that bloom in every nook and cranny.

If you like natural fragrances, you'll see displays of essential oils and fragrance oils, bottles of herb tinctures, and large jars and heavy stoneware crocks full of dried herbs. Enjoy cooking? You'll find all the herbal seasonings, vinegars, and jellies you need to bring a new and tasty zip to any dish. You're a reader? Books line one wall in a cozy reading corner, beside the door to the tearoom. Or maybe you'd like to find out what your horoscope has to say about your future, or buy a set of rune stones or a book about how to indulge your Inner Child or some herbal incense that will help you get in touch with your Higher Self. Just go through the door that leads to Ruby's Crystal Cave, and you'll find all the New Age lotions, potions, and notions you need to satisfy your soul.

And maybe you'd also like a bite to eat — food for the body, as well as the spirit. You're invited to Thyme for Tea, the tearoom that Ruby and I own and manage, with the indomitable Cass Wilder staffing the kitchen. With luck and good weather, the tearoom would do a brisk business this afternoon, and so would the shops.

And the weather did look good, not just for today but for tomorrow, when it was supposed to rain again — which was certainly okay with me. A rainy Sunday doesn't make everybody happy here in the Texas Hill Country. Lots of people like to go boating on the Highland Lakes or tubing on the Guadalupe River or swimming in Barton Springs, which averages a chilly 68 degrees year-round, even when it's 102 in the shade. But rain pleases the farmers and gardeners and ranchers. They don't care what day of the week it rains, as long as it *rains*.

I grinned at Caitie as Khat, the shop Siamese, jumped down from the windowsill and rubbed against her ankles. "First order of business, feed Khat. Can you handle that while I get things organized for the market?"

"Sure," Caitie agreed happily, picking Khat up and hugging him. But Khat is an imperious creature, and not very huggable. He jumped out of her arms and trotted off in the direction of the kitchen, casting a look over his shoulder to make sure she was following him. He knows which shelf his kitty liver lives on and which dish he eats it from,

33

but he can't open the refrigerator door or turn on the microwave to heat it up.

While Caitie was fixing Khat's breakfast, I got busy organizing the items for the booth. The evening before, I had loaded the metal five-shelf plant cart with trays of four-inch pots of the most popular culinary herbs: thyme, basil, sage, chives, dill, lavender, rosemary. There were a couple of dozen larger potted plants, as well — Powys Castle, my favorite artemisia; several salvias, much loved by hummingbirds; and Texas tarragon, *Tagetes lucida,* also called *yerba anise.* It's a coveted substitute for French tarragon, which sulks in the hot, humid summers here in Central Texas.

I balanced our two folding tables and our portable shelves on the red garden wheelbarrow and trundled the load across the street to our usual shady spot on the east side of the parking lot, under the chinaberry tree. Caitie followed me with the plant cart. We pushed the plant cart into position, set up the shelves and the tables, and covered the tabletops with a red-checked oilcloth (easy to wipe off spilled dirt). I left Caitie to arrange the shelves and put out the bundles of fresh herbs while I went back to the shop for another load: packages of dried herbs and potpourri, handcrafted soaps and lotions, some homemade herbal jellies, packages of herbal teas, a few of the best ristras, wreaths, and swags, and books on growing and cooking with herbs, including a dozen copies of my own book, *China Bayles' Book of Days*. Oh, and the large painted Thyme and Seasons sign, and business cards and copies of our tearoom menus, as well as brochures for Cass' Thymely Gourmet and Ruby's and my catering service, Party Thyme. Ruby, Cass, and I are big believers in what Ruby calls our "multiple profit centers." I call it our three-ring circus, complete with clowns. But don't get me wrong: I'm not making fun of the concept. All three centers may not show a big profit every month, but they do bring in business. I can live with that.

Back at the shops, Ruby was getting ready to open — she would manage both the Cave and the herb shop until I closed the booth. That's the advantage of having side-by-side businesses: one of us is always around to keep an eye on things. In the tearoom, Cass and Lisa, a young woman who comes in to help with the lunch crowd when we're busy, were setting the tables. And at our booth, the shelves were filled, the tables were nicely arranged, and everything looked attractive. I brought over the cash box and the credit card machine, Caitie and I put on our Thyme and Seasons aprons, and we were open for business.

If you've been to an outdoor market or visited a farm stand, you'll feel right at home at our Farmers' Market. A couple of area farms (CSAs, or community supported agricultural enterprises) had set up large booths and were displaying a gorgeous array of organically grown vegetables: bouquets of fresh lettuces, spinach, and bok choy; baskets of pea pods and green beans; bunches of orange and yellow carrots and red and white beets; paper bags filled with potatoes and tomatoes; trays of early cucumbers and zucchini.

The Mistletoe Creek Farm booth, run by my friend Donna Fletcher, was especially attractive. Donna and her volunteer helper, Jessica Nelson, were already at work, filling customers' shopping bags. When I whistled and waved, they both waved back. Mistletoe Creek Farm is about ten miles south of here on Comanche Road, in the direction of New Braunfels. Donna and her sister Terry used to grow flowers there, but Terry was still serving a prison sentence (a complicated, unhappy story). A couple of years ago, Donna moved from flowers into market gardening, selling farm memberships that provide subscribers with a basket of fresh produce every week during the growing season, along with opportunities to pick their own. She also supplies Cass with vegetables and eggs for the tearoom kitchen, and her wreaths and dried flowers are always big sellers at Thyme and Seasons.

Other booths feature strawberries, figs, and luscious heirloom tomatoes that you'll never see in a grocery store. As the summer goes along, there'll be melons of all shapes and sizes and bushels of fresh Fredericksburg peaches (wonderful!), and in the fall, ripe pears and apples. Home-baked breads, too, and pies and cakes, as well as cheese from Hill Country goats, honey from local bees, and even locally brewed beers. The idea, of course, is to encourage people to develop a taste for local vegetables and fruits, instead of lettuce from California or apples from New Zealand or cheese from Switzerland.

As the morning went on, the crowd got bigger and bigger. Friends stopped by to say hello and buy a few items. Janet came from the Dos Amigas kitchen for a bunch of fresh dill (they'd just run out), and Cass sent Lisa for some basil for the quiche. Bob Godwin, owner of Beans' Bar and Grill, stopped by and bought four bunches of cilantro, which features prominently — way too prominently for my taste — in his tortilla soup. But I'm not a cilantro fan. Maybe you are. Next time you're eating at Beans', order the soup and see what you think.

I was hunting for more cilantro among the bundles in the cooler when Stuart Laughton paused at the table to remind me that the Hill Country Local Food Society was meeting at Mistletoe Creek Farm the next evening. Stu is tall and broad-shouldered, a personable, easygoing guy with brown hair, an engaging grin, and a teasing, flirty manner. He teaches horticulture at CTSU and is a passionate advocate of homegrown foods, farmers' markets, and local agriculture. He and his wife Margie have written a book about the small-farm movement in America — not a research study, but a book designed for a popular audience — that will be published next month. I've read an early draft of the book, which is titled *Small Farms, Sustainable Food, and the Future of the Land.* It's good. Sustainability is a hot topic these days. The book should do well.

This morning, Stu had his eight-year-old twin girls in tow. Margie, he said, was at another booth, buying tomatoes for her secret-recipe pizza sauce, which everybody loves — although it won't be a secret much longer, since the recipe is included in the book.

"You're coming to the meeting, I hope," he added, dropping a casual arm around my shoulders. "Looks like we're going to have a great turnout. Everybody's bringing food, as usual."

"Can we come, too, Daddy?" one of the girls asked, and Stu said, "Yeah, sure, sugar. It's a family thing. A picnic." To me, he added, with a squeeze of my shoulder, "We're bringing pizza." He waggled his eyebrows at me. "Love to share some with you, sweetie."

I ducked out of his embrace. Stu doesn't mean anything with his flirting, but he can sometimes be a little physical. I'm not comfortable with it and I hate being called "sweetie." I was glad to see him with the girls, though. I'd heard that he and Margie had been having a few problems and that she had taken the kids and gone to stay with her mother. But it apparently wasn't very serious — just one of those things that happen in a marriage from time to time. Whatever the difficulty, they had patched things up and Margie and the girls had moved back home.

I promised Stu I'd be at the meeting. I don't promise, though, to be a committed, uncompromising locavore — that's the name that's given to people who eat only locally grown food. I agree that it's a waste of fossil fuel to tote a tomato fifteen hundred miles from its native field to my eager fork. But I doubt that I'll ever be willing to give up coffee or tea or smoked salmon. Neither *Coffea arabica* nor *Camellia sinensis* enjoy our Texas climate, and while it's possible to take a catfish out of the Pecan River and a nice striped bass out of the Highland Lakes, you'll never find a salmon around here.

Stu had just made off with some fresh basil and thyme for Margie's pizza sauce when Sheila walked up — Sheila Dawson, Pecan Springs' chief of police, out of uniform on her day off and looking comfy in jeans and a denim shirt, her ash-blond hair pulled back in a bouncy ponytail. With her, on a leash, was Rambo, a Rottweiler and the K-9 star of the PSPD.

It doesn't much matter what Chief Dawson wears, actually. Uniformed, sloppy-casual, or dressed for a party, Sheila is unfailingly drop-dead gorgeous. Her friends call her Smart Cookie and wish we could all look just like her. We could just as easily call her Tough Cookie, though. She may be a dish, but she's an experienced officer, savvy, street-smart, and tough as a horse-shoe nail. Since she took on the job of chief, she's been remaking our local police force into something resembling a professionally trained organization. Her methods don't always please the good ol' boys, or even those on the city council who have an investment in the way things were. They like to imagine that Pecan Springs is still a cozy, comfortable place where the only criminals are jaywalkers and double-parkers. But those of us who live in the real world are plenty happy about Sheila's retooling of the police department.

"Hey, China," Sheila said, with a warm smile. "How are you this morning?"

"Pretty well," I said, "considering that I was in the garden at dawn." I came around the table and stroked Rambo's ears. "Hey, Rambo," I crooned, putting my face down to his. "Good to see you, old buddy. Caught any crooks lately?"

With well-bred restraint, Rambo licked my cheek. When I first met this dog, he frightened the bejeebers out of me. Big, burly, savage-looking, he's everybody's nightmare of the junkyard dog who would dearly love to take a bite out of your right leg, two bites of your left, and work his way up from there. But when his owner (Colin Fowler, Ruby's Significant Other) was killed and Rambo came to stay at our house, I learned that he had a sweet heart and an amiable disposition. When he also proved to be an expert drug-sniffer and crook-catcher, Sheila asked if she could take him. Howard Cosell voted yes (in fact, he voted yes three times), so Rambo went to live with Sheila.

I kissed Rambo on one ear and straightened. "You doin' okay, Smart Cookie?"

Sheila gave me a conspiratorial grin. "Got something to show you." She held out her left hand, her nails beautifully manicured, a sizable chunk of diamond blazing in the sun.

I blinked. "Wow," I said feebly, suddenly aware of my grubby hands. I stuck them into my pockets. "Gosh. A ring. That's beautiful. Blinding, but beautiful. I guess I should say congratulations, huh?"

"Good guess," said a deeper voice, and Blackie Blackwell snugged an arm around Sheila's waist. Blackie is the Adams County sheriff and McQuaid's fishing and poker partner, a friendship that goes back to their student days at Sam Houston State. Blackwells have worn the Adams County sheriff's badge for decades. Blackie's grandfather was sheriff back when the biggest criminals were cattle rustlers and bank robbers, and his father kept the peace for another thirty years after that. Blackie, who has been elected to multiple terms as sheriff, is carrying on the family reputation. He looks the part, too: muscular build, square shoulders, square jaw, regulation haircut, regulation posture. He's a by-the-book man, but he has the intelligence and the wisdom (the two aren't always the same thing) to know when to put the book aside.

I matched my grin to theirs. "I am so glad, guys. When's the wedding?"

They exchanged glances. Sheila spoke first. "September, maybe. We haven't decided."

"Definitely September," Blackie said firmly. He scowled down at Sheila. "Got that, woman?"

This requires an explanation. You see, Blackie and Sheila have been engaged before, in an on-again off-again way that drove their friends crazy. Both of them are really great people, and they look like a perfectly matched pair: two experienced, dedicated law enforcement professionals. They have their work in common, and there's obviously a strong sexual attraction between them, as well as a strong bond of respect and affection.

But while Blackie has never had any

doubts, Sheila has had plenty. It wasn't their relationship that was the problem, she told me the last time she broke the engagement, almost two years ago. It was their careers. "Two cops in one family are one cop too many," she said firmly. "In fact, even one cop in a marriage can be one cop too many."

I know where she's coming from. McQuaid was a Houston homicide detective when I met him, and his career was a big factor in the demise of his first marriage. Whether it's the long hours or the necessary risks, divorce is an occupational hazard among police officers. Some reports I've read put it at sixty or seventy percent above the national average. Does that mean that with two cops in one family, the risk of divorce is a hundred and forty percent higher?

Blackie gave me a crooked grin. "Definitely September," he repeated. He tightened his arm around her neck in a mock stranglehold. "And this time, she's not getting away."

Sheila elbowed him sharply and slipped out of his grip. Rambo stood up, growling deep in his throat. He's Sheila's Rotti now, and fiercely protective. But she laughed, and Rambo relaxed.

"Okay if I tell McQuaid?" I asked. "He'll

44

be so pleased." Of course he'd be pleased. But like me, he'd also be apprehensive. Neither of us want to go through that on-again, off-again angst again.

"Tell McQuaid, tell the world," Blackie said grandly. "We're even going to get Hark to put an announcement in the paper. We're doing it the old-fashioned way. With a couple photo."

"We are?" Sheila asked, surprised.

"We are," Blackie answered, and I wondered if he was insisting on the announcement to make it more difficult for her to break the engagement again. "I'm calling the photographer myself." He tweaked her nose with his fingers. "If I leave it to you, Chief, it won't get done."

"Hark will be devastated," I said. That's Hark Hibler, the editor of the *Pecan Springs Enterprise.* He's had a crush on Sheila for years.

"I thought Hark and Ruby were hanging out together these days," Blackie said.

"Doesn't keep him from having a crush on Sheila, too," I replied. But it's true that Ruby is seeing Hark on a fairly regular basis, for which I am glad. Hark is solid and substantial, the kind of stability that Ruby needs in her life — in my opinion, anyway.

"Hark can have his crush," Blackie said

generously. "I've got the gal. Come on, babe." And with a wave, the two of them, with Rambo, wandered off.

As I expected, the bundles of fresh herbs had disappeared by ten o'clock, and the four-inch pots of herbs were pretty well picked over by eleven. I sold (and signed) the last *Book of Days* about that time, too. The other items moved a little more slowly, but when the market closed at one o'clock, Caitie and I didn't have much to lug back to the shop. We made it in one trip.

After all the unsold stuff had been put back on the shop shelves, I gave Caitlin a hug, thanked her for a good morning's work, and handed her twenty dollars.

She held the money in her hand and tilted her head to one side, considering. "I've been thinking about this," she said. "My teacher told us that child labor is illegal in Texas. Maybe I should ask for more money, huh?" She gave me a cagey look. "To keep my mouth shut."

"You could try," I replied cheerfully. "Except that you wouldn't get it. Want to know why?"

She nodded doubtfully.

"The Texas Labor Code, Chapter 51, specifically allows the employment of a child in a nonhazardous occupation, under the

46

direct supervision of a person having legal custody of the child, in a business owned by the custodian." I grinned. "I have legal custody of you, and I own the business. Blackmail will get you nowhere, kid. You're out of luck."

Caitlin sighed and pocketed the money. "I think I'll be a lawyer when I grow up, Aunt China. Like you."

She might've said, "Like my dad," but she didn't. She doesn't talk about her father, or her mother, or her aunt. It's almost as if they never existed, as if she didn't have a life before she came to live with us. I don't think this is altogether healthy, but now wasn't the time to work on it. I gave her a quick hug.

"Well, let me tell you, child, real-life lawyering is nothing like the TV shows. Long, boring days with the law books, tedious months of pretrial, hours and hours in stuffy courtrooms — and not a minute for yourself."

I know what I'm talking about. I spent more years than I care to count as a criminal defense lawyer in a large Houston firm that mostly represented big bad guys with bankrolls — until finally, I just couldn't do it any longer. I had already given up the idea that our legal system actually works to serve justice. I was sick of the company I had to keep, exhausted by the hours I had to put in, and worried that I'd never find the time to have a real life, real friends, a real lover (as opposed to those who drifted casually in and out of my life). I cashed in my retirement fund, left the firm, moved to Pecan Springs, bought Thyme and Seasons, and . . .

Well, here I am, minding my own business, with friends, a husband who loves me, and two great kids, one of whom has just tried to blackmail me.

Caitie hugged me back. "I was just kidding, Aunt China. Okay if I go next door and buy a book with some of my money?"

"Absolutely," I replied. When I see Brian or Caitlin reading a book, they almost always get an automatic pass on whatever chore I was about to assign. I'll be delighted if they grow up to be the kind of people who can't stay out of bookstores and libraries.

Caitie headed for the Hobbit House and I went to work behind the cash register. The tearoom had done well during the lunch hour. There were still quite a few people around, including some who thought that the market was open all day and were disappointed to find that it was already closed and the vendors had packed up and gone home.

But not all the vendors had left. The door opened and Donna Fletcher came in. Brown-haired, slender, but built like an athlete, Donna always wears jeans — today, topped with a green T-shirt that invited everybody to Grow With Us at Mistletoe Creek Farms. She wore leather sandals, and her taffy-colored hair was braided and topped with a yellow baseball cap. She leaned her elbows on the counter, a morose expression on her sun-browned face.

"You're unhappy?" I asked in surprise. "It looked like you were doing a brisk business this morning."

"I'm unhappy," Donna replied. She spread her square hands. Her nails are even grubbier than mine, but then, she's a farmer, with acres of vegetables and olive trees and Christmas trees to tend and goats and chickens to take care of. Compared to her, my gardening efforts are small-time.

"You'll understand, when you hear why," she added glumly. "Terry's back in town."

She was right. I understood.

CHAPTER TWO

Shka Pastora, the Leaves of the Shep-
herdess [*Salvia divinorum*], grows in small,
hidden glades in the upland moist forest
of the Sierra Mazateca. The plant seems
to propagate itself from nodes of the fallen
stems, perhaps with the help of humans
who tend their private patches. It is specu-
lated that the species diminished its ability
to set seed through centuries of human
tending. And perhaps this highly sensitive
species — growing in light-speckled seclu-
sion in such a small region of the world —
would have long ago disappeared, had it
not been for its lovely *medicina* and gift to
human consciousness. Each healer's
patch is a family secret, and the spirit of
the plant is known to have a personal
relationship with the one who cares for her.
Not just anyone can pick her leaves and
derive benefit from her medicine. One's

purpose must be clean and clear.

Kathleen Harrison
"Roads Where There Have Long Been Trails"
Terra Nova: Nature & Culture, Summer 1998

"Terry's back?" It was Ruby Wilcox, coming through the door from the Crystal Cave. She sounded surprised. "When, Donna?"

"Two weeks ago." Donna straightened. "Terry's my sister, and I know I shouldn't feel this way. But I do, damn it. Life is complicated enough, trying to manage the farmwork and keep up with Aunt Velda's various weirdnesses. Things were going along pretty well, though." Her mouth twisted. "Until Terry showed up again, more Terry than ever."

"Well, we're not all a hundred percent perfect," Ruby said sympathetically. She put an arm around Donna and gave her a quick hug. She had to lean over to do this, because Ruby is six feet plus in her sandals and Donna is five feet two in hers. And since Ruby was entirely dressed in yellow today (yellow cropped pants, yellow top, yellow floaty scarf tied around her frizzed carroty hair), it was a little like Big Bird cuddling a munchkin. I would have smiled at the sight, but the news about Terry was sobering.

"Where Terry's concerned, I'd settle for twenty-five percent perfect," Donna replied wryly. "Or even ten." She made a face. "I know I promised to be here for her when she got out of prison, but she's not making it easy. Between her and Aunt Velda — well, I'm about at my wits' end."

To tell the truth, I couldn't much blame Donna. Her sister had been sentenced to prison in California for selling dope, but she served out the last part of her term in Texas on an arrangement with both states, since she had what are euphemistically called "supportive ties" in Texas. In Terry's case, these ties were her sister and her aunt.

Ruby may look like a certified dingbat, but she has a practical soul. She spoke with her usual common sense. "Terry's got a green thumb. She'll be able to help with the farm, won't she?"

I refrained from saying that it was Terry's green thumb that sent her to prison in the first place. She had been extremely successful as a market gardener — growing marijuana.

"Yeah, she could help." There was an edge of bitterness in Donna's voice. "For instance, she could have been around to help this morning, instead of taking the farm truck yesterday and going off God knows where. It was a good thing Jessica came out to give me a hand with picking and loading. Good thing Roger loaned me his truck, too. Otherwise, I'd have missed today's market."

"I'm sorry to hear that," Ruby said compassionately. "You've got enough to worry about without Terry running off with the truck."

"Yeah." Donna looked down and lowered her voice. "I'm sorry, too. I don't know why I'm spouting off to you guys. There's nothing you can do. Best I can hope for is that Terry will find a job and get another place to live. The way she's acting, it's clear that she doesn't like staying at the farm. She's even ticked Aunt Velda off, and that takes a heckuva lot of doing."

"How is Aunt Velda?" I asked. Donna's elderly aunt is a character, to put it mildly. She was abducted by extraterrestrial aliens a few years ago and taken on a long sightseeing excursion around the galaxy. She might still be up there somewhere, lost in space, but she says that her hosts got tired of her sass and dropped her off at home. The last time I saw her, she was wearing the purple "I Am a Klingon" badge the aliens had pinned on her shirt. She says it's her ticket to the next space voyage. She's packed and ready to go whenever they come for her.

"Aunt Velda?" Donna frowned. "She's mostly okay, although Terry's causing her grief. Terry keeps pestering her for money — and not in a very nice way, either."

"Uh-oh," I said.

"Oh, dear." Ruby sighed.

"Right. I really hate it when Terry is mean to her," Donna said regretfully. "Aunt Velda is a big help, in spite of her age. She just keeps on truckin'." She sighed again. "Speaking of truckin', I'd better go. Jessica's waiting to take me back to the farm. I just dropped in to remind you that the local food folks are meeting at the farm tomorrow evening. Hope you'll be there."

"Stu reminded me," I said. "I'm planning on it."

Donna turned to Ruby. "Why don't you come, too, Ruby? Stuart and Margie have promised to hand out copies of the first chapter of their book." She looked proud. "My farm is in it, you know. Maybe we'll get some good publicity when the book comes out. Oh, and we're having pizza — with Margie's secret sauce."

"I'd love to come — if China doesn't mind picking me up," Ruby replied. "Amy's using my car tomorrow to drive to San

Antonio." Ruby isn't a convert to eating locally, but she's interested, and she and Margie Laughton are longtime friends. She took a flyer from the counter and handed it to Donna. "Could you post this at the farm? It's an advertisement for the lecture China is giving in my shamanic garden in a couple of weeks, for the Pecan Springs Garden Club. The public is invited."

If you've already met Ruby Wilcox, you know that — in addition to owning the only New Age shop in Pecan Springs — she teaches classes in astrology, Tarot, the I Ching, and runes. She's also a grand master of the Ouija board. It's no surprise that, earlier this year, she decided to plant a shamanic garden.

Donna held up the flyer, reading aloud. "Magical, Mystical Plants. Come to Ruby Wilcox's Shamanic Garden and learn about some of the many mysterious plants that have taken people on magical journeys. Tobacco, morning glories, datura, wormwood, *Salvia divinorum,* and many others. Garden talk by China Bayles. Guided garden visit by Ruby Wilcox." She raised her eyebrows. "You two aren't offering drug trips, are you?"

"Of course not," Ruby said, pulling herself up indignantly. "People are forever asking about plants that have been used for divination in different cultures. I thought it would be fun to plant a shamanic garden, and China agreed to help. And then Alison Hart — she's president of the Garden Club — heard about what we were doing and asked if the club could visit."

"The garden is in Ruby's backyard," I put in. "We thought it would be safer there."

At first, Ruby had suggested planting it at the shop, where there are plenty of other herb gardens — culinary, medicinal, dye plants, and so on. But I pointed out that security might become an issue. If some of the local teens heard that we were growing psychoactive herbs, they might stage a raid. After consideration, Ruby agreed that the garden would be safer inside her backyard. If any unauthorized persons tried to climb her fence and score a big one, Oodles would sound the alarm. Oodles, who belongs to Ruby's next-door neighbor, is a miniature poodle. He's about the size of a four-legged football, but he has the bite of a snapping turtle and the heart of a pit bull. Bark for bark, he can shout down Rambo.

"Right," Ruby said. "And China's talk is entirely academic, all about how the plants were used by shamans in traditional societies. Then we'll walk around the garden and look at the plants themselves. There's no experimenting — and every plant is legal and can be grown right here in the Hill Country."

"Really?" Donna wrinkled her nose. "It's legal to grow *Salvia divinorum* in Texas?"

Salvia divinorum has gotten a lot of media attention lately, most of it negative. Unlike other garden-variety salvias, this species is highly psychoactive. Mazatec shamans, as part of their religious practices, used the plant to produce trance states and visions. You can eat it, drink it, smoke it, or take it as a tincture and it will make you high — although you can't prove that by me. I use plants in all sorts of ways, but getting high isn't one of them. I've never even smoked tobacco, which is one of the most mood-altering herbs available.

"Of course it's legal," Ruby said huffily. "You don't think I'd grow a prohibited plant, do you?"

"It's legal until the Texas legislature gets around to adding it to the Controlled Substances list," I amended. "The proposed bills I've seen control only the sale of the plant, though. They're not planning to make it illegal to grow the stuff — as long as you don't harvest it."

Donna laughed shortly. "And just how do

our good-doing legislators plan to enforce a no-harvest rule?"

"Not a clue," I replied. "I guess we'll have to post a lookout for the garden police."

"The garden police?" Ruby opened her eyes wide, alarmed. "You don't really think —"

"Just kidding," I said hastily. "We don't have anything to worry about, Ruby."

"That's a relief." Ruby turned to Donna. "You'll post the flyer, won't you?"

"Sure." Donna sighed. "Terry will probably want to come to your program. She was saying she needed to find a supplier who could get her some pot."

"Uh-oh." Ruby frowned. "Now, *that's* illegal."

"Yeah," Donna said sourly. "It would be all I'd need, wouldn't it? Aunt Velda taking another trip around the galaxy and Terry getting busted — again — for possession. Why couldn't I have *normal* relatives?" There was a honk outside, and she lifted a hand in a good-bye wave. "That's Jessica, wanting to get back. On my way, girls. See you tomorrow evening."

When she had gone, Ruby turned to me. "Amy called a few minutes ago, China. She and Kate are cooking out tonight and invited Hark and me to come over for supper. I told her that you're batching it this weekend, and she wondered if you and Caitlin would like to come, too. I hope you don't have plans already."

"If we did, we'd cancel," I said. "I'd love to come. And you know how crazy Caitie is about Baby Grace. She'll probably lobby for a sleepover."

In case you're new to our little group, Grace is Ruby's eighteen-month-old granddaughter — a real cutie-pie. Her mother Amy is Ruby's wild child, and Kate is Amy's live-in partner. To Ruby's eternal credit, she didn't bat an eye when Amy announced, before Grace was born, that she and Kate Rodriguez were a couple and had decided to live together. From the outside looking in, I'd say that Kate has had a distinctly calming effect on Amy — or maybe Grace has had a calming effect on both of them. Whatever, it's always a pleasure to see the three of them together.

The door opened and two women came in. "We're looking for some fennel plants for the garden," one of them announced. "Do you have any?"

"I think so," I said. "Let's take a look."

While I was supplying them with potted fennel (dearly beloved by the swallowtail butterfly caterpillars in our area), somebody else came in, looking for ideas for planting a culinary garden. I showed her the display garden, gave her a plant list, and she ended up buying two or three pots of every culinary herb I had in stock.

The rest of the afternoon zipped past, with plenty of traffic in the shop and in the gardens. Caitie came back from the bookstore in time to help close, and when I cleared the register and made up the bank deposit, there was a gratifying wad of cash and an equally gratifying bundle of checks and credit card slips. Ruby reported that the Crystal Cave had done well, and the tearoom had been busy until after three o'clock. A successful Saturday all around. The Farmers' Market was good for us. Good for the bottom line, too.

I hummed a tune as Caitlin and I drove to the bank.

Amy and Kate live in a neat little house on Dallas Drive, on the east side of town. When Caitlin and I got there, everybody was already out in the backyard. At the grill, Kate was cooking hamburgers, hot dogs, and sweet corn. At the nearby picnic table, Amy was arranging bottles of ketchup and mustard and a tray of lettuce, pickles, and sliced tomatoes and onions. Ruby (who had changed into a swirly red-and-brown tiered skirt, a red spaghetti-strap top, and red cowgirl boots) was pouring lemonade. Hark Hibler, an orange UT Longhorns gimme cap pulled down over his eyes, was observing this domestic activity from a comfortable lawn chair in the shade of the willow tree.

"Yo, China," Hark called, tipping up the brim of his cap and raising his lemonade glass in greeting. "Got that article finished yet?"

I plopped the big bag of non–locally grown potato chips (my busy-day contribution to the picnic) on the table and stuck out my tongue at him. Hark is my boss — at least, he likes to think he is. I write a garden column and edit the weekly "Home and Garden" page in the *Pecan Springs Enterprise* in return for free newspaper ads. In my opinion, this is a very fair trade. Hark gets local garden writing for the newspaper and the shop gets great exposure.

"I'm working on it," I replied. "Don't worry. I've never missed a deadline yet, have I?"

I hadn't told him that next week's piece was about Texas plants that have psychoactive properties. I had helped Ruby with the research when we planted the garden early last fall, and I thought it would make a good topic for a column. I wasn't sure Hark would be pleased, since the "Home and Garden" page usually showcases relatively harmless herbs, vegetables, flowers, and landscape plants. I'll probably get a few letters from uptight readers who object to a feature about plants that have been used for mind-altering purposes, rather than feeding us or making our yards look good.

On the other hand, maybe Hark will like the column. He says that a little controversy boosts circulation, and he's always looking for more readers. Since he bought the *Enterprise* from the Seidensticker family several years ago, he has been trying to fetch it into the twenty-first century and make it at least as relevant as yesterday's TV news. Which is definitely a change from the previous editorial policy. Until Hark came along with a journalism degree from the University of Houston and an insistence on covering all the news, good, bad, or indifferent, every story was pasteurized before it was printed, which left Pecan Springs looking like the cleanest, coziest little town in Texas.

This was an entirely fictional portrayal, of course. Pecan Springs is picturesque and pretty, but on a per capita basis, there's just as much insatiable greed, unbridled passion, and downright bad temper in this town as there is in any other small community on the outskirts of a modern big city. And since the town is halfway between San Antonio on the south and Austin on the north and crime tends to flow in both directions along I-35, we get the spillover from both cities. We also get some of the bad stuff that seeps north from the border counties, which are engaged in an escalating war with the drug cartels in Mexico and the coyotes who haul illegals across the border. Peek under our cozy cover, and you'll get a glimpse of our darker side.

Under Hark's editorial direction, the *Enterprise* shines some light into this darkness. He tries to avoid the merely sensational, but he prints the stories that matter — and tell the truth about who we are. The recent corruption case on the city council, for instance, and the meth labs that Blackie closed down in the outlying county, and the chemical spill in the Pecan River. Naturally, this does not please those folks, like the Chamber of Commerce, who would prefer to portray Pecan Springs as a town so clean it squeaks. They'd like to see the Fire Department's Taco Breakfast Fundraiser above the fold on page one, or the annual First Baptist Charity Rummage Sale. But

Hark is stubborn, journalistically speaking. He tells it like it is.

"No, you've never missed a deadline," Hark said, patting the chair next to him. "Come sit beside me, China."

I sat. Hark is a Garrison Keillor kind of guy — rumpled dark hair, heavy build, sloping shoulders, soft speech, shambling gait. You wouldn't exactly call him exciting: he goes to work at the *Enterprise* every day, shows up at softball games, and covers the Elks Club picnic and the Fourth of July parade. His only vice is an occasional game of pool, so far as I know, anyway. But while an electric personality may have a certain appeal in the short run, it seems to me that reliability, trustworthiness, and comfort count for more in the long haul. And where intellect is concerned, Hark is one of the sharpest guys I know, and definitely the most curious.

Hark and Ruby have been dating since before last Christmas. She's finally begun to pull herself out of the spiral that sucked her down after Colin died, and for that, Hark deserves some of the credit. For all of her adult life, in every relationship I've known anything about, Ruby has loved the guy more than he has loved her. With Hark, it's the other way around. He cares more than she does. Unfortunately, Ruby has gotten into the habit of thinking that unrequited love is the only kind of love there is, and I'm not sure she'll settle down with somebody who seriously loves her. But for now, she seems content to hang out with Hark, he seems happy, and I'm glad.

"What's up?" I asked. "Anything exciting on the journalistic horizon?" Hark has two staff writers who handle the local news, plus one or two interns from CTSU and the usual gaggle of unpaid "correspondents" from various clubs and organizations. But as he often says, reporters can't make the news — all they can do is report it.

"Exciting?" Hark chuckled wryly. "This town is as dull as a bachelor bull with no cows in sight. Just to show you how bad it is, the Farmers' Market is gonna be the headline in the next issue." He eyed me. "Unless you can come up with a thriller of some sort. Got any good ideas?"

"How about a prepublication review of the Laughtons' new book on the importance of small farms?" I offered helpfully. "Stu is speaking at tomorrow night's meeting of the Local Food Society. Margie is making the pizza sauce. I could do a write-up."

"Whoopee," Hark said. "A real thriller. Anyway, it's already assigned. Jessica is covering the meeting. Writing the review, too."

Jessica Nelson is a grad student in the CTSU agricultural journalism program and a summer intern at the *Enterprise*. I met her at Mistletoe Creek Farm last summer, where she was getting some hands-on experience in the operation of a market farm. I liked her because she has a lively enthusiasm for her work, and over the following few months, she began to hang around the shop. She also helps Donna with the Farmers' Market and volunteers with the Local Food Society. From Hark, she is learning how a small-town newspaper operates, with the hope that one or two rural newspapers will still be hiring when she finishes her master's degree. I hope so, too. Jessica is smart and nosy and stubborn, three traits that make for a good reporter. She's the kind of writer we need these days. At the rate newspapers are going under, though, she may have to look for another line of work.

"Jessica will be here a little later," Amy told us, on her way to the table with a plate of shortcakes. "She's bringing strawberries." To Hark she added, "I met her when she was writing that story on that awful puppy mill over in New Braunfels." Amy, an animal lover, is a veterinary assistant at the Hill Country Animal Clinic.

"Jessica is a hard worker," Hark allowed. "She has a tough time staying objective, but that's something you learn over time. And once she sinks her teeth into a story, she's ruthless." He shrugged. "Of course, there haven't been a helluva lot of stories worth the effort lately. Not so good for a competitive reporter who wants to make her mark in the world of journalism. I tell her it's not too late to move her internship to San Antonio or Houston, where things are happening."

I grinned. "How about turning her loose with a romantic scoop? 'Local Police Chief and Adams County Sheriff Plan September Wedding.' "

"Again?" Hark pulled his dark eyebrows together. "I'll believe it when I see folks tossing rice after the ceremony."

"They don't toss rice anymore, Hark. It's not environmentally friendly. They toss birdseed. Or grass seed."

"Whatever." He paused. "Do you really think they'll do it? Sheila and Blackie, I mean."

"Dunno," I said thoughtfully. "They certainly seemed happy enough this morning. She was showing off her diamond, which is big enough to choke a horse. He was looking smug."

"Breaks my heart, you know," Hark said with an exaggerated sigh.

I patted his hand. "Poor Hark. Love lost, and all that."

"Tell Ruby she needs to help me take my mind off Sheila's defection."

"You tell her."

He made a wry face. "She doesn't listen to me."

"She doesn't listen to me, either." I pointed to where Ruby was holding a yellow buttercup under Baby Grace's chin in the age-old childhood game, to see if she liked butter. The little girl, her hair as red and curly as her grandmother's, was giggling and snatching at the flower. "There's our competition. Ruby is totally besotted with that child. You and I might as well be on the moon."

"Well, it could be worse," Hark said in a resigned tone. "It could be another guy. Where Ruby's concerned, I'll take what I can get."

We sat there for a few companionable minutes, indulging in our feelings of mutual neglect. Then Ruby brought Grace over and put her on Hark's lap, and Caitlin came over and asked me if she could stay over-night.

"Have Amy and Kate invited you," I asked in my sternest mom-tone, "or have you invited yourself?"

Amy was using a pair of tongs to turn foil-wrapped ears of sweet corn on the grill. Over her shoulder, she said, "We invited her. Say yes, China. You know how Caitie loves to read stories to Grace. They're working on *The Velveteen Rabbit.*"

Amy is a younger edition of her mother, tall, slender, freckled. When I first met her, she looked and dressed like a punk rocker, but now that she's a mom, the wild child seems to be settling down.

"Say yes, China," Kate commanded, put-ting a platter of hamburgers and hot dogs on the table. "We love to have her."

Kate Rodriguez owns an accounting ser-vice and does the taxes for many local firms, including Ruby's and mine. She is tall and sturdily built, with a quiet dark-haired beauty passed down to her by generations of Mexican ancestors. She and Amy make a striking couple.

"Pretty please, Aunt China?" Caitie wheedled, leaning on the arm of my chair. "Kate says they'll bring me home in the morning."

"Okay," I said. "But no solo babysitting until she's at least thirteen," I reminded Kate, in case they were planning to go out later. Caitlin may think she's old and wise enough to cope with baby emergencies, but I don't.

"Boo-hoo," Caitie pouted.

"Your mom makes the rules," Amy said to Caitlin. "But when you're thirteen, you're hired." She took Grace from the long-suffering Hark. "Come on, cutie. Time for a change."

"You said it," Hark muttered, peering down at his lap.

A light, cheerful voice interrupted my response. "Hi, everybody! Sorry I'm late. I stayed at the farm to help Donna feed the livestock — and pick a few strawberries."

I turned to see Jessica Nelson, the summer intern at the *Enterprise.* She's in her early twenties, a lively young woman with boy-cut blond hair and freckles across an upturned nose. Cute and sassy, she has an easygoing manner and a soft Southern voice that's at odds with the watchful, intent expression in her brown eyes. On the surface, she's just another young journalism student learning a profession, but I have the feeling that there's a great deal more to her than that. Maybe it's because I sometimes see myself in her — myself when I was her age, unwilling to take no for an answer and eager to get on with the pressing business of becoming the best and brightest lawyer the world had ever seen.

"Hey, Jessica," Amy said. "You brought the strawberries for the shortcake?"

"Ta-da!" Jessica said, pulling the cover off a plastic container and holding it out. "Fresh out of the field. And I've brought real whipped cream! None of that squirt-out-of-a-can stuff."

"Milked the cow, too, did you?" Hark inquired dryly, and Jessica stuck her tongue out at him.

He grinned. "Just checking. Some folks carry this locavore business to extremes, y'know. Figured maybe you were one of those."

Kate picked up a fork and rapped a glass. "Time to fill plates, everybody. Food's getting cold."

Caitlin came over and took my hand excitedly, tugging me out of my chair. "Come on, Aunt China, I'm starving. Let's eat!"

We gathered around the picnic table, helped ourselves to good food, ate and talked, and talked and ate some more. The corn (picked the day before, bought at this morning's market) was delicious, slathered with herbed butter, wrapped in foil, and grilled. The hamburgers and hot dogs and toasted buns were summertime perfect. The potato salad was just the way your grandmother always made it, and Jessica's fresh-picked strawberries, heaped on homemade shortcakes and topped with real whipped cream, tasted as good as they looked. After that, none of us could eat another bite.

Hark and I took over at that point, and the two of us and Caitlin managed the kitchen cleanup — only fair, since the others had done the cooking. When we finished, we all sat around for a while, talking idly, until Ruby announced that she and Hark were going dancing at the Long Shot Saloon (which was why she was wearing her twirly dance skirt and cowgirl boots). I looked at my watch and discovered that it was after nine. I gave Caitie a hug, said my thanks and good-byes, and followed Hark and Ruby to our cars.

Ruby paused beside Hark's old green Subaru. "Want to go out to the Long Shot with us?" She grinned. "I'm sure you can find a cowboy or two to dance with."

"No cowboys for me," I said, without regret. "I'm a married woman, remember? Anyway, I was up before dawn and out in the garden, not to mention working the market all morning and the shop the rest of the day. I'm heading for home, a bath, and bed. Have to feed the dog, too." Caitie and I had gone straight to Amy's after we stopped at the bank. Howard Cosell's supper was going to be several hours late. I hoped he wouldn't mind.

"Don't say we didn't ask," Ruby replied. "What time are you picking me up tomorrow evening?"

"Is six okay?" I asked. "The meeting starts at six thirty."

"Sure. See you at six." She waved goodbye and I got into my Toyota, turned the key in the ignition, and started for home, thinking that Howard was going to get his late dinner in less than twenty minutes.

As things turned out, however, he was going to have to wait a couple of hours longer.

CHAPTER THREE
JESSICA NELSON

Jessica stayed for a half hour after China and Ruby and Mr. Hibler left, drinking another glass of wine and enjoying the pleasant company of Amy and Kate. Then she said good night and drove home through the warm, starlit evening. Since January, she had been living in an older house on Santa Fe, a residential street in the hilly area north of campus, not far from the river. She'd be alone tonight, because Amanda, her current roommate, had gone camping with her boyfriend, which was just fine with Jessie. In fact, she had been looking forward to going home to an empty house, happily aware that it was hers for the entire week and that she could do whatever she pleased — invite people over, have a party, whatever. She probably wouldn't, though. She had a few friends, but she was basically a loner. When she had time to spend at home, she'd rather be by herself.

But the bottom-line truth was that Jessie didn't think of any place as home. She and her twin sister Ginger had been Army brats. Their mom and dad had dragged them from one military post to another, until they used to joke that home was just a pillow on a bed, a closet for their clothes, and a shelf for their stuffed animals. Which had been okay, as long as she had Ginger, as long as they were a family.

But then the unthinkable had happened. Ginger and their mother and father had died when their Georgia house burned ten years before. Jessie had escaped because she was on an overnight school trip, and when she got home, everything and everyone she loved was gone. She had mourned inconsolably, writing interminable entries in her journal, crying over photographs of herself and Ginger and Mom and Dad in happy times.

But the happy times were all gone, vanished like the smoke from the killing fire. After a year, Jessie stopped writing in her journal, put the pictures away, and forced herself not to cry. It had been hard to stop grieving, but it had actually been a relief, she realized afterward. You couldn't mourn forever, or blame yourself for being alive while all the people you loved were dead.

You had to put the bad stuff behind you and get on with your life; that's all there was to it. So she had tried. Unfortunately, all the willpower in the world couldn't put an end to the fiery nightmares that woke her nearly every night, drenched in sweat and shaking with fear — the fear of being burned alive.

After the funeral, Jess had gone to live with her grandmother — her mother's mother — in a small town outside of Monroe, Louisiana, where she had spent her last year of high school. That place was no longer home: Gram had died the previous summer and Jessie had sold the house to finance graduate school. There'd been no real homes in her college years, either, for she had moved from dorm to apartment and from one apartment to another, and finally to this house, which she rather liked because it was at the end of a dead-end street and had a large backyard where she and Amanda had planted a vegetable garden, although she was the one who took care of it. Unfortunately, there was Butch, who lived next door. She sighed. She might have to leave here, too, if the situation didn't improve.

But Jessie really did love Pecan Springs, had loved it from the moment she had arrived as a CTSU freshman. She was naturally athletic, thin and agile, with an abundance of physical energy, and she had enthusiastically flung herself into all the outdoor activities she could find time for — tubing on the Pecan River, sailing on Lake Travis, swimming at Barton Springs in Austin, hiking in the Hill Country. And since she was hungry for what she thought of as real culture, she indulged herself in everything the eclectic university community had to offer — plays, music, ballet, foreign films. She even went to most of the football and basketball games (that first year, anyway), since sports were a huge part of the campus culture.

Turned out that she'd been hungry for real men, too — that is, for males who were older and more experienced than the local boys in that small Louisiana town. So she indulged herself in them, as well. Not promiscuously, of course, but with her usual intensity, her usual insatiable appetite for new adventures. And not for love or even for sex, either, although sex (in which Jessie indulged enthusiastically) was a bonus. She had gotten involved with a basketball player, and after that, with a graduate student from Nigeria, then with a Mexican national who worked at Mistletoe Creek Farm, and most recently, with a faculty member who had told her that he and his wife were separated and planning a divorce and that he was free.

But it turned out that the separation was only temporary and divorce wasn't in the picture and the guy wasn't as free as he'd said he was. Anyway, things got uncomfortable when somebody told his wife that her husband was sleeping with one of his graduate students and she threatened to leave him. The good thing about it was that his wife didn't know who the graduate student was — at least, Jessie didn't think so. She had broken off the relationship anyway. She didn't consider herself a terribly moral person, but she was no home-wrecker.

Unfortunately, the guy couldn't seem to get the message. She still had to see him at school and in a few other places, and he still called her, wanting them to get together "just to say good-bye." That was out of the question, of course. As far as Jessie was concerned, when a relationship had to end, a clean, sharp break was the only way to do it. So she was moving on (the story of her life). In fact, she was thinking that maybe it was time to take a vow of chastity, at least for a while, and forget about guys. She could focus on her internship at the newspaper. She could pour herself into her work there, instead of being distracted by a relationship that could only cause her grief.

And Jessie loved to pour herself into things. She was an intense sort of person, very Type A, and when she got excited about something, she really got excited. Working in a newspaper definitely suited her, although Pecan Springs wasn't very big and the *Enterprise* was a kind of slow-motion place. So far, her most significant assignment had been covering the recent city council meeting, the one where the council unloaded on the chief of police for overspending the overtime pay budget. She was on the lookout for a real story, where she could practice the investigative journalism skills she was supposed to be developing. And she'd have to start looking for a job before long. She needed a story that would separate her from the rest of the competition, make her stand out. Make editors look twice at her work, let them know that she was worth hiring.

Jessie parked her car in the drive, unlocked the back door, and went into the quiet kitchen, savoring the silence. No loud TV, no blaring music, no Amanda sprawled bulkily on the sofa or entertaining the (also bulky) boyfriend in her bedroom, their frenetic activity punctuated by the rhythmic banging of the bed against the wall. The silence was something to celebrate. Jessie went to the fridge, found the full bottle of cold Chablis she had left there (no Amanda to help herself), and poured a glass of wine to take out into the backyard, where she sat in the swing, looked up at the starry sky, and listened to the summer serenade of friendly crickets and cicadas.

But not for long. She had been enjoying herself for only a few moments when she smelled Butch's cigarette and heard the chink of his beer can hitting the fence on the other side of the straggly hedge. Her insides clenched and she felt the skin on her shoulders prickling with irritation and (she had to be honest here) apprehension. It was their creepy next-door neighbor, sitting on his back porch steps, not five yards away. Who rode a Harley as loud as a freight train and worked in a warehouse and always seemed to be holding a muttered conversation with himself. Whose weird friends dropped in at all hours of the night — or maybe they weren't friends at all, but customers, like he was dealing, maybe. And who leered at Jessie through the hedge and had actually spied on her through her bedroom window, which was just across the driveway from his bedroom window, until she threatened him with the police if he ever did it again.

But then she forgot to close her blinds one evening and he did it again. Steaming, Jessie was picking up the phone to call the police and file a complaint when Amanda asked her not to. The problem was that Butch's mother (who lived in San Antonio) owned both houses, the place Butch lived in and the one Jessica and Amanda were renting. Their lease had expired in May and they were on a month-to-month and Amanda was afraid that if they complained to the police about Butch's peeping, his mother would throw them out. (Of course, that was easy for Amanda to say. Butch wasn't peeping at her, either because her bedroom was on the opposite side of the house, or because she was fifty pounds overweight. Or maybe because her boyfriend was even bigger than Butch.

Jessie (by now almost as angry at Amanda as she was at Butch) had pointed out that sometimes window peeping escalated into stalking and other nasty stuff, and if anything, Butch's mother ought to be glad that his problem was caught before it got him into serious trouble. Still, she had to admit that Amanda had a point about the month-to-month, and in the interests of good relations with her roommate and their landlady, she had reluctantly given in.

But last week, she had caught Butch peeping again, watching her through the hedge as she lay in her bikini on a beach towel on the grass. And tonight, she could hear him muttering to himself and smell that infernal cigarette. He wasn't doing anything she could legitimately complain about, at least not at the moment. He was . . . well, he was just being Butch. He was *there,* damn it.

Somewhere in the distance, a dog barked. The wind stirred, lifting the leaves, and the night sounds no longer seemed quite so comfortable and friendly. Jessie picked up her empty wineglass and went back inside, thinking angrily that life was too short for this kind of crap — for guys like Butch, watching her every move. She still had some of the money from the sale of Gram's place. It wasn't much, but enough for a couple of months' rent in advance, and there was her share of the rent she and Amanda had paid in advance here, which she was supposed to get back when she moved out. And this time, she would find a place by herself, even if it cost more money. She had outgrown Amanda, definitely. Time for a clean break there.

But that would have to wait until tomorrow, or next week, or maybe even longer than that. Tonight, right this minute, Jessie was unsettlingly aware that Butch knew that Amanda was gone. She was all alone in the last house on a dead-end street, with a nutcase for a neighbor.

She shivered. Then, one after another, she went to each window, checked the lock, and drew the blind.

CHAPTER FOUR

Alcoholic beverages are a favorite means of altering moods. Take gin, for example. The word is an English abbreviation of *genever,* the Dutch word for juniper, for the predominant flavor of this popular alcoholic drink is derived from juniper berries (*Junipers communis*). In Holland in the 1580s, British troops fighting in the Dutch War of Independence found a juniper-flavored spirit. They drank as much as they could to give themselves what they appreciatively called "Dutch courage." Soon, gin was being consumed everywhere, at any time. For textile mill workers in northern France, for instance, a slug of gin in coffee (a *"bistouille"*) was a popular breakfast drink.

In addition to the predominant juniper, gin may be flavored with citrus (lemon, lime, grapefruit, and bitter orange peel), as well as anise, angelica root and seed, orris

root, licorice root, cinnamon, cubeb, sa-
vory, dragon eye, saffron, baobab, frankin-
cense, coriander, nutmeg, and cassia bark.
China Bayles
"Mood-Altering Plants"
Pecan Springs Enterprise

McQuaid and the kids and I live twelve
miles west of town, just off Limekiln Road.
If you make the drive in daylight, there's
plenty of entertaining scenery: hillsides
pocked with clumps of yellow-blooming
prickly pear cactus and white prickly poppy;
rocky ridges clad with dark green juniper
and lacy mesquite; high limestone bluffs;
clear, shallow creeks. White-tailed deer graze
with cattle; roadrunners dart after lizards
among the rocks; buzzards perch on the
tops of trees and utility poles, waiting for
the next roadkill.

At night, though, unless there's a bright
moon, you can't see a thing beyond the
headlights of your vehicle. Along some
stretches, rocky embankments fall steeply
away into the blackness; along others, the
trees close in like shadowy rows of sentinels.
The road dips down, rises up, and twists
and turns unexpectedly, like a snake slither-
ing through a rock-strewn meadow. It's
treacherous when there's ice on the road,

and the low-water crossings can be deadly during rainstorms. (*Turn around, don't drown* means just what it says.) In any season, the best way to stay out of trouble is to drive slow and be alert.

To give myself credit, I wasn't driving fast and I'd had nothing to drink but a couple of glasses of iced tea. It was a warm evening, and I rolled the windows down to enjoy the cedar-scented air. There was no moon, and I was cruising along one of those snaky, up-down segments of road, just past the clanky old iron bridge over Cedar Creek, about seven or eight miles from town. I was watching for deer, which have a nasty habit of jumping out in front of you and causing much grief, for themselves and for you. A solid hit or even a swerve can cause you to lose control of the car and end up off the road or smashed against a tree. In fact, I was so focused on potential deer disasters that the first orange flickers off to my right and up the hill barely registered. But then the road went around a sharp curve and the trees opened up to a rocky hillside. I saw the flames and smelled the smoke at the same time and jammed on my brakes.

A single-wide house trailer was perched on the side of the steep hill, a couple of hundred yards off the road, mostly hidden behind a screen of trees. I had driven past the place twice a day, five or six days a week, noticing the trailer but not really seeing it. Back in late April or early May, it looked like the renters had moved out. Trash was piled in the garbage pickup area beside the mailbox and there was a new For Rent sign near the road, with a yellow Students OK banner posted across it. Sometime in the past week, though, the sign had come down. Maybe it was rented again.

If it was, the occupant was in trouble. Almost half of the trailer was engulfed in flames, the fire leaping twenty, thirty feet into the sky, showering the surrounding junipers with sparks. I pulled over to the side of the road, as far as I could get off the pavement, just past the narrow gravel driveway that climbed diagonally up the hill. Hurriedly, I fished my cell phone out of my purse and flipped it open. The signal is spotty along Limekiln Road — in some places I can get three or four bars, in other places nothing. Tonight, here, I had one bar. Not much of a signal, but enough, I hoped. I thumbed 9-1-1 and got the Adams County emergency dispatcher.

"Fire!" I exclaimed. "There's a trailer on fire on Limekiln Road! Get a truck out here, fast!"

"Address?" The dispatcher's voice was flat, clipped, professional.

Address, address. I looked up. The lights of my Toyota caught on the mailbox just ahead, four painted numerals barely visible. "Limekiln Road, Eighteen-eleven. One-eight-one-one. Just west of the old iron bridge. On the right, up the hill."

"Casualties?"

I stopped breathing. "Casualties?"

"Anybody injured in the fire?"

"I don't . . ." I swallowed. "I haven't tried to look."

Damn, what was I thinking? There was no car in front of the trailer, but the For Rent sign was gone and it was possible that the place was occupied. Maybe somebody was in there, burning to death, while I was jabbering on the phone. I opened the car door.

"Don't put yourself in danger," the dispatcher said sharply. "Keep away from the fire. There's nothing you can do. You by yourself?"

"Yes." I was suddenly very glad that Caitlin had stayed at Amy's. After all her trauma, she didn't need to see this. Especially if somebody was —

"The truck is on the way," the dispatcher said, adding sternly, "Stay with your car. And stay on the line with me. You hear me?

Stay on the line. I need to know what's —"

But I was already out of the car and running, the cell phone in my hand. I headed straight up the hill, which was totally stupid because it was steep and littered with ankle-turning loose rocks. I fell and grasped at a bush to keep from sliding backward, gouging a deep scrape into my forearm, knowing I should've gone up the drive — farther to go but easier, faster. Picked myself up and began to scramble again. By the time I made my way through the trees and reached the trailer, I was gasping for breath and there was a sharp pain in my side.

The flames had already eaten their way from the eastern end of the trailer almost to the center. They were as loud and fierce as a windstorm, lunging and roaring and snapping like something alive. I could feel the heat of the fire on my face and the air was thick with choking black smoke, but I ran up the three steps to the door, and twisted the knob. Hot. The door was hot and the knob wouldn't turn.

I banged on the door. "Anybody in there?" I shouted. "Anybody there?" No answer. I tried again. "Anybody in there?"

I was turning away when I heard it. "Help! Help me!" A panicky cry, high-pitched, shrill with terror. A woman or a kid, maybe even a teenaged boy. "I can't get out. Help, please help!"

Frantically, I twisted the door knob again and put my shoulder to it. Nothing doing. It wouldn't budge. But there was a window just to my left. If I could find something — a heavy club, a tire iron, a rock — I could break it. A rock! That was what I needed. I turned and took a step down, looking for a big, heavy rock I could heave —

WHOOOMPH!

The window exploded outward and a fiery fist shoved me off the step, slamming me to the ground in front of the trailer. My forehead hit a rock and I saw stars, but I struggled to my knees, groggy. There was another explosion, louder this time, and I turned to look. The entire structure was engulfed in a sunburst of flame, so bright and hot that it burned my eyes. The heat seared my face and singed my eyebrows and hair.

"Hello, hello!" I became aware that I was still holding my cell phone in my left hand. The dispatcher was shouting at me. "Caller, what's going on? What happened? Talk to me!"

"It blew up," I said groggily. My right knee was bleeding through a rip in my jeans. My right forearm was bloody. "The trailer just . . . it just blew up." I sniffed. "Smells like something I . . . smells like camp stove . . ." My voice trailed off. "Camp stove fuel," I managed.

"You're okay?" the dispatcher was asking urgently. "Caller, you're okay?"

"I'm okay," I said, and then I remembered. "But there's somebody inside, yelling for help!" I cried, getting to my feet. "A woman, maybe, or a kid. I heard it. Just before . . . before the trailer blew up."

"Sending an ambulance," the dispatcher said crisply.

With a heavy metallic sigh, the roof slumped inward, like a cake falling in the center. I shuddered and broke the connection. Whoever was in that trailer wouldn't need an ambulance.

The trucks from the nearby local volunteer fire department got there first. A white-painted tanker truck (there's no city water out this far, and no hydrants) pulled up in front of the trailer. Two guys in T-shirts and jeans jumped out, turned on the pumps, pulled out a hose, and began pouring water onto the burning structure. A couple of minutes later, a red ladder truck roared up the drive and stopped behind the first. Working deliberately, the driver climbed out and pulled a hose off the truck, hooked it to the tanker truck, and began pumping. Two men, already suited up in bulky gray fire-fighters' garb, jumped down.

By this time the water from the tanker truck had put a damper on the trailer fire, turning it into pillars of steam and black smoke. The suited-up firefighters were pulling on helmets. I ran over to them.

"There's somebody in there," I rasped. "I could hear her crying. Or maybe it was a kid. I couldn't really tell. I tried . . ." I looked at my right hand. There were blisters forming on my palm. "I tried to get the door open. But there was an explosion. Like a bomb going off. And another explosion after that."

"Where's the victim?" one of the men asked. He pulled a heavy ax off the tool rack. "Which end of the structure?"

"I was at the front door when I heard her." I looked at the ruined trailer. The metal skin was crumpled and blackened, the door buckled in. It would be a miracle if anybody was still alive in there.

Working deliberately, with practiced skill, the firefighters were fastening masks over their faces and adjusting the packs on each other's backs. "I'll go first," one said, and stepped up the stairs to the twisted front door. He shoved it with his gloved hand and it fell in, huffing out a thick cloud of acrid smoke. The second firefighter was right behind him. The tanker truck continued to pour water onto the flames.

My hand was beginning to throb, but that was a small thing. Somebody had just burned to death in front of my eyes. I bent over and threw up into the weeds.

The ambulance was next, a wailing siren announcing its arrival before the vehicle pulled up the drive and stopped behind the second fire truck. A uniformed medic jumped out just as the two firefighters came out of the trailer.

The first firefighter pushed up his face mask. "One fatality," he said tersely to the medic. "Nobody's going in for recovery until the guys get the place cooled down." He looked at me. "Somebody you know?"

Mutely, I shook my head. I could still hear the voice, frantic, frightened. *Help me! . . . Help, please help!* I swallowed and tried to find my voice. "I was just driving past and saw the fire. The place went up so fast. It just exploded."

Another siren. I turned to see an Adams County brown-and-white sheriff's car braking to a hard stop along the side of the road, behind my Toyota, the siren cutting off with an abrupt yelp. A moment later, Blackie was standing beside me. He was wearing a blue plaid cotton shirt and neatly pressed khakis, and I wondered if the fire had pulled him away from an evening with Sheila.

"I thought that was your car," he said. "What's happened here?"

"I was driving past when I saw the flames." I was ridiculously glad to see him. Sheriff Blackwell almost always has that effect on me. He's tough, stern, capable, utterly dependable, enormously compassionate. I coughed hard, tasting the vomit, and the tears came to my eyes. Blackie put a friend's hand on my shoulder.

"You okay, China?" he asked gently.

"Yeah. But there was somebody in there."

All sheriff now, Blackie dropped his hand and turned to the firefighter. "Dead?"

The firefighter nodded. "Smoke's still bad. We'll bring the body out when it clears a little."

Blackie turned back to me. "Do you know who it was?"

"No. I could hear her — I thought it was a woman, or maybe a teenager — but I couldn't get in." I looked at the trailer. If I'd been successful in breaking that window, I would've been inside when the place blew up. I'd be dead right now. My knees felt shaky.

Blackie sniffed. "Smell that?" he asked the firefighters.

"Yeah. Stronger inside," one said. "I'm thinking arson. Fire marshal's on his way."

Arson! I'd been so involved in what was happening that I hadn't caught the possible significance of the odor I had smelled.

"Okay, guys," Blackie said. "The body stays where it is until the marshal has a look." With a grim expression, he turned to assess the vehicles parked in front of the trailer and I knew he was thinking about tire tracks. It had rained the night before, and tracks were a possibility. But if there had been any, the fire trucks and EMS vehicle had likely obliterated them. He reached for the cell phone hooked to his belt. "I'll get the crime-scene team out here."

The crime scene team. I sucked in my breath. A murder had taken place here. Arson-homicide. And the victim was conscious until the awful, incomprehensible end. She knew what was happening to her. She knew there was no escape. Was she tied up? Injured? I shivered, suddenly cold. How could one human being do this to another?

Blackie clicked his phone shut and turned to me. "See anybody when you got here, China, or on the way? A vehicle, maybe?"

A vehicle. Did I remember a vehicle? Lights coming at me a time or two, but nothing specific, nothing I could identify. Anyway, the arsonist could have driven away in the opposite direction.

I swallowed, trying to firm up my trembling voice. "I don't remember seeing anybody on the road. This place has been empty. In fact, it had a For Rent sign out front until earlier this week. I really didn't expect to find anybody inside. I just banged on the door and heard —"

I was blathering. I closed my eyes. *Help me! . . . Help, please help!* I'd hear that plea until my dying day.

"Stay put for a few minutes, China," Blackie said. "I want to make sure you're okay." I opened my eyes to see him signaling to the medic.

"I'm fine," I said stoutly. "Don't worry about me."

The medic came up, eyeing me. "Looks like you got a little too close to the fire," he said. He took my arm, inspecting the scrape, and lifted the hair off my forehead, to see where I'd banged my head. "Come on over here. Let's clean you up and see what we've got."

I tried to protest, but not very hard. Ten minutes later, my face was clean, my forehead and knee wore Band-Aids, my burned hand was swabbed with a salve, and my arm had been treated to a stinging dose of antiseptic and a bandage. Then the kindly medic handed me a steaming cup of coffee, poured from a Thermos. He reached into a cabinet, produced a bottle of gin, and added a healthy slug.

"Dutch courage," he said. I didn't argue. Gin and coffee seemed like a great idea. I was sipping it gratefully when another, smaller truck came roaring up the hill, a cab-top light flashing. A team of four brush-fire fighters jumped out, grabbed equipment, and headed up the ridge behind the trailer. It didn't look like the fire up there was making much headway, but if it was, they'd take care of it.

Blackie had been walking around the trailer with a flashlight, making a careful visual inspection. I knew what he was looking for. Footprints, places where an accelerant might have been splashed, matches, a cigarette, an incendiary device. A little later, he was back.

"Feeling better?" he asked.

I nodded. "Find anything?"

"Maybe." He paused. "Any idea who owns the place?"

"No. Sorry."

He nodded. "I don't think we'll need a statement. Your 9-1-1 call establishes the time. If we want anything else, we'll get in touch." He glanced down at the bandage on my arm. "You going to be able to drive yourself home?"

"Of course. It's only three or four miles."

"Yeah. Well, I'll let you go home if you promise me you'll pour yourself a good stiff drink when you get there."

I knew that Blackie would be here for hours, until he finished his part of the investigation and was confident that he'd gotten all the information the site could yield. After that, he'd have one of his deputies canvass the neighbors up and down the road, asking if anyone had seen or heard anything suspicious. But it wouldn't be an easy investigation. Arson never is. I knew that from my days as a lawyer.

I nodded, trying not to think of what I had heard in that fiery hell. *Help, please help!* "I'll get that drink as soon as I fix Howard's dinner. The poor guy has been waiting for hours." It felt somehow trivial to talk about a dog, standing next to the place where a human had been incinerated.

Blackie chuckled. "Howard Cosell gets more regular meals than I do."

I took a deep breath, focusing on what we

were saying. Small talk, comforting talk. Talk about a normal world of everyday affairs. "That'll change after Sheila moves in."

He switched on a flashlight. "I doubt it. She doesn't have any more time to cook than I do. Two cops in the family — one's always gone when it's time to eat. Come on, China. I'll walk you down the hill to your car."

I took the driveway this time. I wasn't going to risk making a fool of myself by sliding down that hill on my butt.

I looked in my rearview mirror when I drove off. Blackie was sitting in his car, talking on the radio. My night was about to come to an end. His was just beginning.

Howard was waiting for me when I unlocked the kitchen door and went in. He wore a reproachful look (bassets are recognized champions in the canine reproach division), and thumped his tail accusingly on the floor.

"The sheriff says you get more regular meals than he does," I told him. He was not impressed. I apologized, made his dinner, and added a few slivers of leftover chicken to atone for my dereliction of duty. While he ate, I fixed myself a stiff gin and tonic, thinking that I could use a little more Dutch courage. Then I sat down in my favorite chair in the living room, put my feet up on the hassock, and called McQuaid.

"You found *what?*" he yelped, so loud that I might've been able to hear him without the phone, all the way from Memphis. "Jeez, China. Can't I leave you alone for three days without your looking for trouble?"

"I wasn't looking for it," I protested. "I was just driving along the road when I saw it. The trailer, just past the Cedar Creek bridge, on the right. Up the hill, behind the trees."

He paused. "Oh, yeah? I know that place." He sounded more reasonable now. "It belongs to Scott Sheridan."

I was surprised. "You know the owner?"

"Yeah, sure. Scottie owns A-Plus Auto Parts, just past the Dairy Queen on your way into town. That's where I get truck parts for the Beast." McQuaid's ancient pickup is affectionately named the Blue Beast. It's a genuine antique, but it still runs, thanks to a lot of tender loving care — and enough replacement parts for a full rebuild. "He asked me not long ago if I knew any students looking for a place to live. Said he'd just bought the place and evicted the pair that had been living there. They were into drugs. So what happened when you saw the trailer on fire?"

"I stopped and ran up the hill and banged on the door. That's when I heard —"

"Why the hell didn't you just call 9-1-1? You know better than to go running up to a —"

"Hush up and listen," I snapped, and managed to get the whole story out with only a couple more interruptions. I didn't exaggerate any of it, either. The situation was grim enough without trying to make it sound grimmer.

"You're okay, I hope," he said when I was finished. I could hear the relief in his voice and loved him for it. "You're back home?"

"I'm back home and I'm okay," I said. I got up and went to the mirror over the table in the hallway. It was the first time I'd seen myself since the fire, and my scorched face, looking oddly bereft, stared back at me. "Except that my eyebrows are gone. And my hair is singed."

"Thank God it wasn't worse," McQuaid said. "Was Caitlin with you?"

"She's sleeping over at Amy's house. She won't be home until tomorrow morning."

"That's good. The poor kid's had enough trouble." He paused. "You can take the day off tomorrow, can't you? Stay home for a change? Get some rest?"

I thought of the meeting at Donna's farm tomorrow night. I didn't want to miss it — and anyway, I'd promised Ruby I'd pick her up. "I'm sure I'll feel better." I paused. "How's the investigation going?" I asked, adroitly switching the subject.

"Not bad, actually." He began a lengthy tale about the day's activities, none of which sounded very dangerous. I've been uneasy ever since McQuaid first hung out his shingle as a private investigator a couple of years ago. He insists that he's only interested in investigative work — none of the shoot-'em-up, knock-'em-down action you read about in private-eye mysteries. But once a cop, always a cop. If trouble comes his way, he'll run to meet it. So far, though, his work hasn't involved anything very dangerous, for which I am grateful. So far. There's a first time for everything.

We talked a little more, then said good night. I went upstairs and was filling the bathtub when the phone rang again. I shut off the faucet and went into the bedroom to pick up. It was Sheila. She had talked to Blackie and he had asked her to pass along some news. Not for public consumption, but because I'd been the one who discovered the fire. He thought I'd earned the right to what little information he'd gathered so far.

I sat on the bed to hear what Sheila had to say. She was succinct, as usual. A search of the burned structure had turned up no bodies other than that of a woman on the sofa — on what had once been a sofa — under the window in the small living room. The foam cushions of the sofa had been highly combustible. The body would be difficult to identify from physical appearance, and no identification had been found. No purse, no wallet, nothing. And aside from some minimal furniture and the usual appliances, the place had been empty. No personal effects.

"The victim's hands and feet were tied and she was doused with an accelerant," Sheila added.

"Oh, hell," I said, under my breath. And that's what it must have been. A vast, unfathomable, fiery hell. I shuddered.

"One other thing," Sheila went on. "Blackie says he won't be sure until he sees Harkins' autopsy report." Tom Harkins, an MD at the hospital in Pecan Springs, is the new county coroner — an improvement over the previous situation, where Adams County autopsies were done in Bexar or Travis County. "He says it looks like she was shot. The shooter must've figured she was dead and set the fire to obliterate the evidence. The plan might've worked, too, if you hadn't come along."

Bully for me, I thought sourly. Sure, I'd come along, but too late to help the victim. "Any idea how the fire was triggered?"

"At first glance, it looks like a homemade setup at one end of the trailer," Sheila said. "Nothing fancy, but it would've given the arsonist four or five minutes to get outta Dodge. Something else may turn up, though. The investigation isn't finished."

Which reminded me. "Oh, hey, Sheila. Tell Blackie that McQuaid knows the owner of that trailer. His name is Scott Sheridan, at A-Plus Auto Parts. Sheridan bought the place fairly recently, apparently. McQuaid said he evicted the people who were living there. They were into drugs."

Drugs. That's probably what had happened tonight. A drug deal went bad, and a woman ended up dead. That kind of thing doesn't happen here as often as it does in the cities, and the arson-homicide was an unusual twist. But like everywhere else in the country, we have our share of bad drug deals.

"Scott Sheridan at A-Plus," Sheila repeated. "Thanks, China. I'll pass it on." She paused, and her voice became warmer, less official. "Sorry you had to be the one to discover this. I know it wasn't pleasant."

Howard appeared in the doorway, assessed his opportunities, and jumped up on the bed beside me. Bassets, even elderly bassets, are more agile than you might think. I didn't have the heart to make him get down.

"I just wish I'd happened along sooner," I said, low. "Maybe I could've gotten her out of there. Or caught the killer in the act. Or at least seen him driving off." How long before I showed up had he left? A minute? Five minutes? Ten? And why did I automatically picture the killer as a man? Women do drugs. Women kill. Women commit arson, too.

"Yeah, well, maybe you could've gotten yourself dead, too," Sheila said. "You did what you could, China. Don't beat yourself up. Forget about it — as much as you can."

"Thanks," I said wearily. "I'll try."

I said good night and clicked off. I guess I wasn't surprised to hear that the victim had been shot. Tied up and shot, which accounted for the fact that she couldn't get out of the trailer. I had read recently that arson-homicides were on the increase, and that in a growing number of cases, the victims were killed or left for dead before the fire was ignited. In fact, there had been a similar case in Florida not very long ago. A prostitute had shot the victim — another prostitute, a former friend — and set the fire in an attempt to conceal the dead woman's identity. The motive: jealousy, pure and simple. The victim had replaced the killer in their pimp's affections. Of course, the jealousy might have been compounded with an economic motive. The pimp was sending more traffic in the victim's direction.

I shivered, suddenly grateful for the safety and comfort of our house, the love of a good man and fine children, wholesome work, the kindness of friends, the safety — the relative safety — of a small town. What had happened tonight in that trailer was incomprehensibly vicious and ugly beyond words. But I didn't have to comprehend it or explain it or even describe it. Sheila was right. As far as I was concerned, the whole thing was over. Blackie and his deputies would do their usual competent work, and I'd hear all about the investigation when it was finished.

Howard pushed his cold nose against my arm, telling me he had forgiven me for not being home when it was time for his dinner. He added a raspy lick, expressing the wish that I'd allow him to sleep with me tonight,

106

since McQuaid wasn't there to take up half the bed.

I bent down and kissed one soft brown ear. There's something about a basset that makes me want to smile. And it didn't matter whether I "allowed" him or not, Howard would be sleeping with me. He considers it his right and his obligation to occupy the empty half of the bed.

But despite a luxurious hot bath (scented with the lavender salts Ruby gave me for Christmas) and a generous smear of aloe salve on my burned hand, I didn't sleep well. I dreamed that I was scrabbling up the hill toward the burning trailer, the shrieks of the dying woman echoing through the fire-torn night. It was one of those awful dreams where the faster you run, the slower you go. The harder I tried to scramble upward, the farther back I slipped, until at last a huge, volcano-like explosion ripped the sky, and the trailer vanished in a great gush of fire, showering me with searing flame.

I woke, crying. Howard was licking the tears from my cheeks.

CHAPTER FIVE

Coffee (*Coffea spp.*) is probably the most popular mood-altering plant in human experience. In the West, we've enjoyed a beverage brewed from this plant for only about three hundred years, but people in the Middle East began drinking it centuries before that. Legend has it that a Yemeni shepherd watched his goats nibble reddish-brown berries from a bush and then leap and dance, having a high old time — a caffeine rush, no doubt. The shepherd told his story to a monk, who (having fought off drowsiness during many all-night prayer sessions) knew a good thing when he heard it. He boiled the berries in water, and before you could say Starbucks, he was pouring cups of dark, rich mocha for himself and his fellow monks, who were also aware of the virtue of staying awake.

Whatever the truth of the legend, this

herbal beverage spread quickly from Africa through Arabia and Egypt, gathering converts wherever it was brewed. It was considered medicinal and used as a stimulant, diuretic, and a treatment for headaches, muscle aches, asthma, fever, colds, flu, constipation, menstrual cramps, congestive heart failure, and general what-have-you. Too much coffee can lead to nervousness, irritability, and the jitters. But most Americans couldn't get through the day without it.

China Bayles
"Mood-Altering Plants"
Pecan Springs Enterprise

The promised drizzle turned into a steady rain after breakfast the next morning, one of those sweet, gentle rains that do so much to refresh early summer gardens and restore the fields and pastures. At midmorning, Amy and Kate dropped Caitlin off and stayed for a cup of coffee and my report (brief, objective, and lacking in detail because I didn't want to alarm Caitie) of what had happened the night before. They had seen the burned trailer as they drove past and noticed several county vehicles parked along the road. Obviously, the investigation was still going on.

After they left, Caitie went upstairs to her tower room to practice her violin, carefully running a scale, slowly at first, then more rapidly, moving back and forth and up and down the strings in melodic repetition. When she made a mistake (there weren't many), she went back and corrected it. I could imagine her frowning, concentrating on her finger position and her bowing technique. It seemed to me that there was something intensely personal — sometimes reflective, sometimes playful — in the way she played the simple scale, searching for color and tone, making musical what might be purely mechanical. After a while, she stopped playing scales and began to practice the piece Brenda, her teacher, had given her — Pachelbel's Canon, much simplified, but beautiful.

I puttered in the kitchen, listening to Caitlin while I made several kinds of cosmetic vinegars — a big seller in the shop and something I could take to the market, as well. I was making lavender, floral, and mint vinegars in gallon jugs, which I would strain and rebottle into pretty glass containers when the herbs had steeped for a month or so. After I finished that project, I made a batch of carrot cupcakes to take to the Local Food Society meeting that evening. I had bought the carrots at the Farmers' Market and we had gathered the pecans under the tree by the creek and cracked them ourselves, so that much was local. The other ingredients, though — flour, sugar, cream cheese, vanilla, and so on — came from heaven-knows-where. The work reminded me that eating entirely locally would be a very difficult thing to do. However, I could add some of my own locally grown edible flowers, so I went out into the garden and collected enough blooms to decorate each cupcake.

Cooking doesn't require a lot of attention, giving me time to listen, think, and appreciate the space around me. Our house is one of those sprawling Victorians that you occasionally see around here, more often in town, though, than in the country. The former owners planned to turn it into a bed-and-breakfast and called it Meadow Brook, which — considering that the five-acre property includes both a pretty meadow and a spring-fed brook — is descriptively appropriate. It's close enough to the Hill Country tourist hot spots that a B and B might make good sense. The house is certainly large enough for that: two stories, five bedrooms, a turret at one corner, a wrap-around porch with roses and honeysuckle climbing the arbor. Every time the checkbook looks a little thin, I bring up the idea. But so far, we haven't tried to implement it, partly because we're all selfish about our personal space and partly because I'm not sure I want strangers in the house as long as the kids are with us.

There's plenty of personal space. McQuaid has a shop where he works on his gun collection and other projects, and he's converted what used to be the downstairs bedroom into his private investigator's office. (He points out that it could be awkward to mix clients and customers — another reason why a B and B might not be right for us.)

Brian, who plans to major in biology when he goes to college, has staked out the creek at the back of the property, where he collects frogs, lizards, and other amphibious creatures. They occasionally go AWOL from his bedroom and exercise free-range privileges around the house, showing up in unexpected places — behind the toilet, for instance, or in Howard Cosell's water dish.

I have a large garden area for plants I don't want to grow at the shop, and the screened-in back porch for crafts. Until Caitlin became a part of our family, I also claimed the turret as my getaway place.

Then, knowing that every little girl needs a magical place to call her own, I turned it over to her. She sleeps and reads and plays her violin there, and writes in her diary and does the other things that young girls do.

The rest of the day passed so pleasantly that I almost forgot what had happened the night before — or rather, relegated it to the status of a bad dream, like the nightmare that had awakened me. That is, I forgot until I was getting ready to go to Donna's farm for the meeting and looked in the mirror and saw that my eyebrows were gone and my face was reddened and splotchy. I repaired the damage with an eyebrow pencil and some cover-up, and asked Caitlin what she thought.

She put her head to one side and replied in her forthright way. "It's better than it was before, but you still look like you leaned too close to the barbeque grill."

"Oh, well," I said, and put away the eyebrow pencil. "It could've been worse. You sure you're okay about staying by yourself for a couple of hours this evening? Wouldn't you rather go to the meeting with me? It's at Mistletoe Farm." When Brian's home, I don't think twice about going out, because he can handle most crises. But Caitie is just eleven.

"Meetings are boring," she said, and ran her fingers through her short dark hair. "I like staying by myself, and I have a book to read. Can I make a sandwich?"

"Sandwich, milk, whatever," I said. "I've left a couple of carrot cupcakes. You can use the microwave if you want, but don't turn on the stove, please. The Banners are at home, if you need them, and their number is on the wall beside the phone." Tom and Maxine Banner live up the road from us and are on call if one of the kids has a problem. "Oh, and you've got your cell?" For a long time, McQuaid and I resisted getting Brian a cell phone, until we discovered how easy it is to keep track of a kid when he's got a phone in his pocket. Now, we view the phones as another of the costs of having children. The kids have to live without texting, though, and neither of them have Internet access. We're on a budget here.

She patted the pocket of her jeans, her delicate face sweetly serious. "I'll call you if I need to."

"And I'll call you every hour, so keep the phone handy." Maybe moms who have more practice than I do can go away and leave their daughters for an evening without worrying. I'm not quite there yet.

"Have a good time," she said, and hugged me. "You haven't forgotten about tomorrow, have you?"

I frowned. "Let's see — tomorrow, tomorrow. We have a dentist appointment?"

She rolled her eyes.

"Must be a haircut, then." I smoothed her dark pixie cut. "Nope, that was last week."

"I'll give you a hint," she said, and mimed bowing a violin.

"Oh, that!" I exclaimed. "Well, sure. Of course I haven't forgotten. Your lesson. Four thirty. "

She gave an exaggerated sigh of relief and giggled. "I knew you'd remember. With a little help."

"I'll tie a string around my finger," I said.

"Cool," she said. "Make it a violin string." One of her rare, brilliant smiles flashed across her face.

The rain had stopped by midafternoon and the sun had come out, turning the wet grass and trees to glitter and raising the temperature by about fifteen sultry degrees. As I drove into town to pick Ruby up, I had to pass the burned trailer. I didn't want to look, but I couldn't help myself, and the sight brought the whole scene back, hot and fierce. The trailer was a ruin, a twisted hulk of scorched, scarcely recognizable metal, and despite the rain, the fire had extended in a smudge of blackened trees and underbrush halfway to the top of the ridge. The area was marked with yellow crime-scene tape and the fire marshal's car was parked out front.

Resolutely, I turned my attention away from the trailer, toward the evening. Our Local Food Society meetings are pretty informal — I was wearing plain khaki walking shorts, a dark brown tee, and sandals. Ruby, when she finally appeared, was distinctly colorful. She came running out of her house breathlessly, dressed in red pedal pushers and a red-and-yellow draped top, carrying a tote bag.

I love Ruby. What's more, I admire her courage. To look at her, you'd never know that she belongs (as she puts it) to the tribe of one-breasted women. She had breast cancer surgery a few years ago, and refuses to get an implant. "No foreign bodies inside my body," she insists, and chooses her clothes with care. She says she'd rather have people looking at her face than her boobs, anyway, and she makes up accordingly. She's fond of colored contact lenses, well-defined eyes, glittery eye shadow, and bright red lipstick — not to mention that carroty hair, which she likes to wear frizzed. Today, it was held back from her face with red and yellow plastic barrettes.

"Vivid," I said appreciatively, as she got into the Toyota and put the tote bag on the floor.

"Thank you," she replied, settling in and fastening her seat belt. "Sorry if I'm late. It was Doris, of course. She had another . . ." She turned to me and her eyes widened. "Omigawd, China! What happened to *you?* It looks like you were torched!"

"An explosion." I shivered. "A trailer fire. Out on Limekiln Road. I was on my way home last night when I saw it." The rest of the story came tumbling out, uncensored and replete with the gory details, since I didn't have to worry about Caitlin listening in.

"Oh, gosh," she said, and touched my penciled-in eyebrow with her finger. "I'm so sorry, China. What an awful thing to have seen!"

"A damn sight worse for the woman inside the trailer," I said grimly, and started the car. "If I'd shown up three or four minutes earlier, I might've been able to get her out." I bit my lip, trying not to hear the echo of the frantic cry for help. "Even two minutes — that might've done it."

Ruby said the same thing Sheila had said. "You can't blame yourself, China. You did what you could, as soon as you got there. Have they found out who she is?"

I swung away from the curb. "If they have, I haven't heard."

To tell the truth, I really didn't want to know. The whole episode had begun to seem ugly and repulsive, too much like the sordid episodes of my former career. I didn't lead that kind of life anymore. I shoved last night's events into the back corner of my mind.

"You started to say something about Doris," I said. "What happened? Did she run away from home again?"

Unfortunately, something is always happening to Ruby's mother — or to be more precise, Ruby's mother is always making something happen. Doris lives in a senior care facility called Castle Oaks, about ten minutes from Ruby's house. In the past, we have made fun of her situation — among ourselves, of course, not in front of Doris. As Ruby and I would put it, her mom was one taco shy of a combination plate. Carrying on the food metaphor, Amy would say, "Gramma has been out to lunch for the past few months." Kate would add, "The poor old thing is a couple of eggs short of a dozen."

We've laughed at these lame little jokes, but sadly, for there is really nothing funny about Alzheimer's. It's a tragedy, nothing less, for the person who is afflicted and for family and friends. Still, what else can we do but chuckle at this business of being human and growing older and losing our grip on the dailiness of life? And everybody who knows Doris admits that, even in her worst moments, she can be very funny indeed.

"No, she didn't run away from home," Ruby said ruefully. "She got in a fight. She beat up on another old lady."

"Oh, my gosh!" I exclaimed, and my lawyer mode clicked in. "Assault and battery? Is anybody going to press charges? Is —"

"No, of course not," Ruby said. She was trying to smile, but not doing a very good job of it. "Things like that happen in the Alzheimer's wing all the time. They just patch people up and get on with it."

"But still . . ." I glanced at her. "What was the fight about?"

"They were in the cafeteria, having lunch, and the other old lady snatched up Mom's carton of milk and poured it into the fish tank. She was feeding the fish, she said. So

Mom plopped a wad of mashed potatoes down the back of her dress. The old lady slugged her with a pork chop. Mom knocked her down and sat on her." Ruby was smiling, but her eyes were filled with tears and I could hear the sob in her throat. It was funny, but it wasn't. "I don't think the episode lasted more than a minute," she added, "but it got everybody's attention. The nurses said that the old folks were all gathered in a circle, shouting for their favorites."

"Anything for a little excitement," I muttered. "Were you called in to referee or did you have to clean the fish tank? I don't imagine that the fish are very happy, swimming around in milky water."

Ruby wiped the tears off her cheeks with the back of her hand. "I was called in to bring Mom a pair of spare glasses. In the melee, hers got stepped on and smashed."

"Gosh, that's too bad," I said. "I hope the other old lady didn't get hurt." Doris is strong in her dotage. She went AWOL from Castle Oaks a few months ago, and it took a couple of burly cops to escort her back home.

Ruby giggled through her tears. "She lost her upper plate. When Mom jumped her, it popped out and got broken. But she told the nurses that she was glad to have an excuse for a new one, because the old one never fit just right."

I shook my head in amazement. "You and I should be so lively when we get to their age."

"I just hope I get there with all my marbles," Ruby replied.

"Yeah. Me, too. I want to be able to laugh at myself." I glanced down at the tote bag on the floor. "What's in the bag?"

"My famous Hot Lips Cookies." Ruby sighed. "Unfortunately, the only thing local about them is the habanero powder. I got it from one of the vendors at the market, who grows the habaneros on her deck. The rest . . ." She shrugged. "It's pretty difficult to bake if you have to restrict yourself to what's grown locally."

"You're right," I said. "Flour and sugar are a problem. Wheat and sugar cane are grown and processed in Texas, but the packages don't tell you where the stuff comes from."

"Oil and shortening, too," Ruby added thoughtfully. "And baking powder and baking soda. And salt — don't forget salt. It's a terrific idea, eating locally, and I'm all for growing lettuce and tomatoes and planting peach trees instead of crepe myrtles. But I don't know anybody around here who has a salt lick. Do you?"

"I read that the Indians used to get salt from seep springs over in Llano County, which is less than a hundred miles away," I replied. "And there are salt mines on the Gulf Coast."

"Well, maybe." Ruby shook her head. "But I'd hate to try and find my own salt. I can't even begin to imagine what would happen if we couldn't go shopping for what we need."

We were silent for a moment, contemplating our utter dependence on the grocery chains. At last I changed the subject again.

"So how was the Long Shot last night? Did you and Hark have a good time?"

Ruby gave a little shrug. "It was okay. Hark isn't much of a dancer." She brightened. "I danced with a cowboy who *was,* though. I mean, really."

"Hey." I frowned. "Aren't you supposed to dance with the one that brung you?"

Ruby was defensive. "Well, I would've. In fact, I wanted to, but Hark got involved in a game of pool. You know how he is when he gets a cue in his hand. He totally forgot about me." She sighed lustily. "I have to tell you, China — Jackson is a real cowboy."

"Jackson? A cowboy named *Jackson?*"

Ruby nodded. "He's the foreman at a big ranch in Llano County. Thousands of acres."

Hark doesn't look much like a pool shark, but looks are deceiving. And he's definitely much better at the table than he is on the dance floor. Still, he and Ruby were out on a date and he should have danced with her instead of playing pool. It was not the better part of wisdom to leave her to the tender mercies of the local cowboys, who are great dancers but play fast and loose with hearts.

"Hark should have been paying attention to you," I said sternly.

"You bet. Anyway, Jackson invited me to the rodeo on Friday night. He's riding bulls." Another giggle. "He's an outrageous flirt, China. And really cute."

I sighed. Ruby is capable of losing her heart on a moment's notice, and I fervently wished she would lose it to Hark. In my book, he's one of the good guys. He's been there for her when her current love affair has failed, and he doesn't deserve to be treated carelessly.

But even good guys occasionally have their bad points. For some, it's rodeo and bull-riding and outrageous flirting. For Hark, it's pool.

■ ■ ■ ■

To get to Mistletoe Creek Farm, you drive south from Pecan Springs to Comanche Road, which traces a twenty-mile loop off State Route 39. This area used to be farming and grazing country, but sprawling real estate developments and exclusive gated communities have gobbled much of it up, like angry locusts consuming the land. Without irrigation, farming has always been a chancy business here. If a creek or a stream crosses your property, you're lucky. If not, you have to irrigate with water pumped up from the aquifer, hundreds of feet below — and both the Trinity and the Edwards aquifers, which supply this part of the Hill Country, are seriously threatened by overpumping.

Donna is lucky. Her small farm straddles both sides of Mistletoe Creek, a shallow, fast-moving stream that flows into the Pecan River west of New Braunfels. When the fields don't get enough rain, she irrigates with water from the creek, so that her vegetables did fairly well, even during last summer's long dry spell. Her market farm is really taking off, energized by the community-supported agriculture movement that's gathering steam among folks like Stuart and Margie Laughton and the other members of the Local Food Society. And Donna herself is putting not only muscle power but imagination and mental energy into the farm. She's developed a website, a biweekly eletter, and offers subscriptions for the weekly delivery of seasonal vegetables. (If you want to subscribe, it's too late for this year — all the places are filled. But go ahead and put your name on her waiting list, and maybe you'll make it for next year.) She also has a booth at the Farmers' Market, where she sells what doesn't go to subscribers.

At this point, the farm has five acres in vegetables. That may not sound like much, but Donna practices organic, low-impact farming. Five acres are about all she can handle, along with the additional acres of olive trees and Christmas trees, not to mention the bees and the chickens and the goats (Nubians — she says they give the best milk) and the computer work that goes into managing the subscriptions and turning out the eletters. She has some help from subscribers who trade hours of labor for vegetables and from a few dedicated volunteers like Jessica. But when push comes to shove, Donna is the one who does most of the work. She might not welcome her sister back with open arms, but she (and Aunt Velda, too, I imagine) will likely be glad for whatever help they can get from Terry.

Ruby and I passed the Mistletoe Creek Farm sign at the corner of Comanche Road and turned down the narrow, bumpy lane, potholed from the recent rains. On the left, along the little creek, were the olive trees, green and lush. They were several years old now, and just beginning to bear well. On the right were the Christmas trees, twenty acres of pines, in various stages of growth. Ahead of us, at the end of the lane, stood the small house where Donna and Aunt Velda live. Behind the house was a substantial chicken coop (the sign on the door reads: Quiet, Hens at Work), and a red barn that houses the farm office, as well as the milking stations for Donna's goats. We were meeting on the deck in back of the house, under the shade of a large pecan tree. I pulled up in the graveled parking area, where a dozen cars were already parked.

As we got out of the car, Margie Laughton — a soft-faced, brown-haired woman in her early forties — hurried toward us, almost skipping. I've recently seen Margie wearing a forlorn expression when she thinks nobody's looking, and I've wondered if it was because of the problems she and Stu have been having. But just now, she was wreathed in smiles. She was carrying a copy of their new book, *Small Farms.*

"See?" she crowed, holding it up. "Isn't it beautiful? Don't you just *love* the front cover? Look — it's a photo of Donna's farm!" She turned the book over. "And on the back, there's a photo of Stu and me, with baskets of fresh veggies."

"It's gorgeous, Margie!" Ruby replied, and enveloped her in a hug so huge that Margie was almost pulled off her feet. "We're so proud of you!"

"And believe it or not, our publicist says that she's setting up an interview on *All Things Considered,*" Margie said, righting herself breathlessly.

"Wow," Ruby breathed, awed. "You and Stu — on *All Things Considered!* The national publicity will be great for you!"

"I want a dozen copies of the book for the shop," I said. "Where do I order it?"

"I'll get you the information — and of course, we'll be glad to do a book signing." Margie pulled us along. "Come on. Everybody else is here already. Let's eat."

The table was full, with homemade pizza with local-veggie toppings and Margie's sauce; a variety of greens from Donna's salad garden; and a half-dozen desserts. One person had brought cantaloupes from the Rio Grande valley, somebody had donated a dish of home-canned Hill Country peaches from the previous season, and another had come up with figs from the tree in her backyard. But the rest of the desserts were about as local as my carrot cupcakes and Ruby's cookies, so I didn't feel too guilty.

I was loading my plate when I felt a tug at my elbow. I turned to see Jessica Nelson, cute and perky in cutoffs and a green Mistletoe Farm tee. She leaned close and lowered her voice.

"I understand that you were the one who turned in the alarm on the trailer fire on Limekiln Road last night, China. It must've happened while you were on your way home from Amy and Kate's, huh?"

"News travels fast." I helped myself to two slices of pizza. "How did you hear about that?"

"Mr. Hibler got the word early this morning and called to tell me. I drove out and got a few pictures for the paper."

"Yeah. Well, I was the one who turned it in, all right. But if I'd only got there a few minutes earlier, the victim might still be alive."

"I seriously doubt it," Jessica said. "I talked to the sheriff just before I came out here, and he said —"

I didn't get to hear what Blackie had said, for we were interrupted. It was Stu, with a copy of *Small Farms* under his arm and a plate loaded with pizza.

To Jessica, he said, "Hey, aren't you Jessica Nelson, from the *Enterprise?* I'm Stu Laughton, author of *Small Farms.*"

I was surprised, because I thought Jessica surely knew him from the farm or the market. But I must've been wrong, because she replied, "Yep, that's me. Nice to meet you." She ducked her head, and I caught a glance that passed between them, a private glance weighed with a significance I didn't understand.

But the glance was gone in a flash, and Stu's tone was so casual that I thought I must have been mistaken. "Hark Hibler says you're reviewing our book for the *Enterprise.* Do you need a copy? I'll be glad to drop one off for you, if you'll give me your address."

"No need to bother," Jessica replied. "I'm all set. Your publicist sent me an advance reading copy and I've already written a draft of my review." Her expression became serious. "I'll tell you up front what I think, Dr.

Laughton. Everybody needs to know what's happening with our food — and they will, if they read the book you and your wife have written." She paused. "I was really impressed with the section on genetically modified crops."

Stu nodded. "Thanks for letting me know. Margie and I are hoping the early reviews will spark some interest."

"Spark some interest?" I laughed out loud. To Jessica, I said, "If you really want a scoop, Jessica, ask him about appearing on *All Things Considered*."

"No kidding?" Jessica's brown eyes widened. "*All Things Considered?* Now I *am* impressed."

"It's not definite yet," Stu said. But he was grinning that cocky grin of his. "Just a maybe, at this point."

"When it happens, it'll be an *Enterprise* banner headline," I said.

"For sure," Jessica agreed.

"Certainly hope so," Stu said, and made off in the direction of the beer.

When he had gone, I went back to the subject. "What was it you were saying about the sheriff?"

Jessica nodded toward two empty side-by-side chairs at a table on the far side of the deck, next to a wooden tub of patio tomatoes, the ripening fruit like bright red jewels. "Let's sit where we can talk."

"What's up," she said, when we were settled, "is that Mr. Hibler has assigned me to cover the trailer fire story. I'm going to get a byline on it, too." She paused. "I'd like to interview you, China."

I wasn't surprised that Hark wanted the story covered, although it was a little unusual that he hadn't taken it himself or assigned it to one of his staff writers, instead of handing it over to an intern. He probably wanted to help an ambitious girl reporter beef up her portfolio. But my role in the trailer fire was pure happenstance, and I hadn't been able to do anything constructive except phone 9-1-1. There's nothing newsworthy about that.

I said, "Well, I'm glad about the byline, Jessica. That's great. But the sheriff knows everything I know, and a heckuva lot more. Why don't you interview him?"

"I plan to, just as soon as he's available." Jessica's expression was serious. "But I really want to interview you, China. There's a strong human-interest angle to this, and I aim to give it my best shot." She gave me a crooked grin. "After all, this may be the only big story I get this whole summer. I don't mind telling you, I need it."

And want it, I thought, remembering what Hark had said about Jessica being competitive. "I can understand that," I replied reluctantly. "I hope you're not planning to do the interview right now, though."

She shook her head. "How about tomorrow? Lunch? Okay if I bring a tape recorder?"

"The tape recorder is fine, and so is lunch. The tearoom is closed on Mondays, but there's usually stuff for sandwiches and salad in the fridge. We'll have the place to ourselves." I grinned. "Unless you've got an expense account. In which case —"

"Expense account?" She snorted a laugh. "You've got to be kidding. Mr. Hibler is as tight as a tick when it comes to expenses. But I don't want to panhandle," she added hastily. "I'll pick up the tab."

"No tab when we're eating out of the fridge." I paused. "What was it you were saying before Dr. Laughton interrupted us? You mentioned that you had talked to the sheriff and he said . . ." I trailed off, prompting her.

She leaned toward me, her voice conspiratorial, her face purposeful. Her intensity reminded me of myself at her age. "He said that the victim was shot, China. Tied up, hands and feet, and shot."

"I know," I said, and was immediately sorry. Jessica had thought she had a scoop. I softened my tone. "Chief Dawson is a friend of mine. We spoke about the situation late last night. The sheriff had already filled her in, and she passed on the news to me."

Impatiently, Jessica threw up her hands. "This town. Everybody's connected to everybody else. Who the hell needs a news-paper?"

"I've often wondered that myself," I said ruefully. "Gossip travels at the speed of thought. Sometimes I think everybody is hardwired into some sort of central process-ing unit." I regarded her. "Did the sheriff say anything else? Anything about drugs, for instance?"

"Well, yes. Apparently, they found some drug paraphernalia in the place. I didn't ask him what, specifically."

"Could've been left by the previous ten-ants." I picked up my second piece of pizza, pondering the flavors in Margie's secret sauce. Basil — lots of basil. Thyme and maybe savory. And bay, of course.

She tilted her head, her glance sharpen-ing. "Previous tenants?"

I nodded. "According to my husband, the new owner — Scott Sheridan, at A-Plus Auto Parts — evicted them when he learned that they were doing drugs. I don't know whether he had time to clean out the place yet." I gave her a sidelong glance. Jessica — aka Lois Lane, Girl Reporter — was jotting down the information on her paper napkin. I had just made up for spoiling her scoop.

"Thanks," she said with satisfaction. "Scott Sheridan. A-Plus Auto Parts. I'll talk to him."

"Don't tell him I sent you," I cautioned. If my ex-cop husband knew I'd leaked that information to a reporter, he'd be annoyed.

"Don't worry," she said, with just a trace of self-importance. "I don't reveal my sources. Unless I'm subpoenaed, that is."

"Don't be," I said, beginning on my last slice of pizza. "Subpoenaed, that is. It'll probably happen sometime in your career, but you want to put it off as long as possible. It is definitely not fun."

"Right." Jessica stood up. "I've got to take a couple of photos for the story on this meeting, and then I'm heading for dessert. What did you bring?"

"Carrot cupcakes. Featuring locally grown carrots and pecans, plus wheat flour from America's breadbasket and exotic spices flown in from the far corners of the earth. I'd hate to calculate the carbon footprint of those cupcakes."

Jessica chuckled. "It's the thought that counts."

"Do thoughts have carbon footprints?"

"I'll try the cupcakes," she said, and left the table.

I had finished my pizza and was about to make my way to the desserts, when Donna appeared. She sat down beside me, took off her yellow baseball cap, and rubbed her face with her sun-browned hands.

"What's the matter?" I asked. As I know from my own gardening experience, it's always something. If it's not rabbits in the lettuce, it's vine borers on the squash or hornworms on the tomatoes. At least it hadn't hailed in the past few days — but there's always next week.

"It's Terry," she said bleakly. "She still hasn't shown up. Which means I still don't have a truck." She dropped her hands, her face hard, her mouth set. "When that woman gets back here, I am going to kill her. At the very least, I'm throwing her out. She can find someplace else to live. She can get her own vehicle, too, damn it."

I sat very still for a moment. "Remind me, Donna. When did Terry take off?"

"Friday. Friday morning." She sighed. "As in the day before yesterday."

"Did she say where she was going?"

"Are you kidding?" Donna shook her head. "Terry never tells me anything about anything. She's always been that way. Secretive, I mean. Drives me crazy — especially because of . . . well, her criminal record. I keep imagining all kinds of things. Like, she's off somewhere on a two-day high. Or she's gone to Mexico, intending to smuggle in some pot. Or something worse." She shuddered.

I hesitated. "Do you have reason to suspect she's out doing drugs somewhere?"

"Well, maybe." She sighed. "There were a couple of phone calls. Thursday night and early Friday morning — Terry wasn't there. From some creepy-sounding guy — he wouldn't give me his name or number. He said she'd know who he was."

"Did she return his call?"

"Not so far as I know." She paused, frowning. "Actually, she left right after I told her about that second call. She didn't even stay for breakfast, which really hurt Aunt Velda's feelings, because Auntie was making pancakes. She didn't ask whether I needed the truck, either. She just took the keys off the peg in the kitchen and bugged out. Not a word about where she was going or when she'd be back."

I spoke very carefully. "If Terry left on

Friday morning, that means she's been gone for over forty-eight hours." I calculated silently. "More like sixty hours, actually. Maybe you should report her missing."

"Missing?" She gave a short, brusque laugh. "Report Terry *missing?* That would mean the cops would be looking for her, wouldn't it?"

"Well, yes," I said. "That's usually what happens when people go missing. The cops look for them. They find them, too." Alive. Sometimes. But not always.

"Terry would *not* want the cops looking for her," Donna said definitively. "You know her. She tries to keep a very low profile. If I reported her missing, it wouldn't be me killing her when she got home. It would be her killing *me.*"

"I understand," I said slowly. "But under the circumstances —"

Donna spoke firmly, "I'm sorry, China, but there are no circumstances under the sun that would force me to ask the police to look for my sister. I'll just have to wait until she decides to come home, that's all."

I put my hand on her arm. I didn't want to say this, but I had to. "Donna, there was a fire last night, in a trailer out on Limekiln Road. I was driving by and saw it and turned in the alarm."

She looked at me, her head tilted, her eyes curious. "Sounds bad. But what does it have to do with —"

"A woman died in the fire. She couldn't get out by herself because she'd been bound and shot. I didn't get there in time to pull her out. Just as I was about to try, there was an explosion. The whole place went up."

"So?" she said, pulling her brown eyebrows together. "I mean, I'm sorry to hear it, but I don't know why —"

"The last I heard, they hadn't identified the woman."

She understood then, and pulled in a shuddery breath. "And you're thinking it might be —"

"I am not thinking anything specifically," I replied grimly, wishing I didn't have to do this. "I just thought you might want to give Sheriff Blackwell a call. He may be able to —"

But Donna had jammed her cap on her head, got up from the table, and was walking very fast toward the house. I didn't go after her. This was something she was going to have to deal with herself.

By the time I got to the dessert table, my cupcakes had disappeared, so their carbon footprints, whatever they were, were history. But by this time, I wasn't very hungry, so I skipped dessert and sat down to listen to Stu's presentation of the new book. It might have been very good, or maybe it wasn't — either way, you couldn't prove it by me. I'm sorry, but I wasn't paying attention.

I was thinking of the woman whose voice I had heard, the woman I couldn't save. And wondering if it was Terry.

CHAPTER SIX

Grown as an ornamental throughout the world, morning glory is a twining plant with bright blue, funnel-shaped flowers. Ololiuqui (pronounced oh-loh-LEE-ooh-kwee) was the name given to the seeds by the Aztecs, meaning "round things." The seeds were used in rituals for their LSD-like effects, inducing primarily a dreamy state with heightened sensitivity to light and sound. . . . Today, the people of Oaxaca continue to use the seeds as a source of spiritual help in times of trouble.

Chrissie Wildwood
Mood Enhancing Plants

The shops and the tearoom are closed on Monday. Being closed doesn't mean that Ruby, Cass, and I don't show up for work, of course. When you own your own small business, you never have a day off. It just means that we're not waiting on customers.

I usually spend Monday mornings in the gardens around the shop. Summer afternoons, when it's often too warm to work outdoors, I come inside to make orders, do some bookkeeping, and dust the shelves. (I learned the importance of dust a long time ago. If the customers see dust on an item, they immediately assume that it's been sitting on the shelf forever, forlorn and unwanted. They don't want it, either.)

This morning, I dropped Caitlin at her friend Alice's house to spend the day and got to the shop about nine. Ruby and I had planned to go over the handout for our program on psychoactive plants, so we took my laptop to a table in the tearoom, along with a freshly brewed pot of rosemary tea. (Rosemary is one of those mood-altering herbs that has an uplifting, tonic effect, welcome when you're working.) I had the feeling that the members of the Garden Club were going to be surprised by what they learned during our presentation, primarily because gardeners are a trusting lot. They don't like to think that their favorite plants might have a dark side.

Of course, there's been so much media coverage of *Salvia divinorum* in the past few years that lots of people are aware that the plant is psychoactive. They may even have heard that you can get high on morning glory seeds. But they probably don't suspect that their pretty, fall-blooming Mexican marigold (*Tagetes lucida*) was used by the Aztecs to calm sacrificial victims before they were put to death in a violent, gruesome ritual. Gardeners might guess that tobacco is mood-altering, or they may know enough about datura's psychoactive properties to warn the kids away from it. But wormwood? It has a dark side? Well, yes: this potent herb is the central ingredient in the notorious absinthe, which was reputed to be the downfall of the painter Toulouse Lautrec, among other imbibers of his generation.

Or lemon balm, which grows in almost everybody's herb garden. Chewed or brewed as a very strong tea, this mild-mannered herb is said to have a paradoxical effect, both calming and stimulating at the same time — lemon balm was an ingredient in absinthe, as well. And of course there's catnip, which can be highly psychoactive, if you're a cat with the right genes. If you're not a cat, well, not so much, maybe, although some people claim to get a buzz from smoking it, especially when it's mixed with tobacco.

Ruby isn't growing marijuana, of course, although we've included a photo of the plant and a paragraph about it in our handout. She's not growing *Poppy somniferum,* either. It's legal to possess poppy seeds (after all, they're a necessary component of poppy seed rolls, which are a necessary component of some traditional Yuletide celebrations), but possession of the plant is a different matter entirely. The Opium Poppy Control Act of 1942 doesn't discriminate between opium (a product made from the plant) and the opium poppy itself. Grow it — one plant or dozens — and you risk being charged with possession of a Level II narcotic. I didn't think it was likely that Ruby would get busted, but we felt it was safer not to tempt Sheila and the PSPD. Instead, Ruby has planted prickly poppy (*Argemone mexicana*), which is native to Mexico but now widely naturalized in the United States. It was known to the Aztecs as "nourishment of the dead" and is also a hallucinogen. Unlike its notorious cousin, it's entirely legal. Go figure.

For refreshments, Ruby had been consulting with garden club members about what they wanted to bring. They had decided on food flavored with some of the plants we'd be talking about — not to get club members high, but to show them a few of the many ways we use mood-altering plants and to demonstrate that some of our favorite plants have a different side to their personalities.

We don't turn the telephones off just because the shops are closed, so our discussion was frequently punctuated by phone calls. The answering machines took most of the messages, but when I heard Donna's voice on my machine, I got up and went to take the call. Ruby and I were finished, anyway. The program looked to be in good shape.

Donna was phoning from her car. She had just left the sheriff's office, and she wasn't making any effort to mask her apprehension. The night before, after I told her about the woman who died in the trailer fire, she had gone straight to the phone and talked to the deputy on duty. He hadn't been able to give her any more information about the identity of the victim, but he had asked her to come in this morning and take a look at the victim's few effects. Naturally enough, she had spent a long, sleepless night filled with a terrible uncertainty, imagining the worst — especially because Terry had neither come home nor called.

Unfortunately, Donna's visit to the sheriff's office had produced even more uncertainty. The victim's body was too badly burned for any attempts at visual identification, and she hadn't been allowed to see it. But she had been given some information about the gunshot wound and had been shown a shoe that had somehow escaped the flames, and a bracelet. The shoe, she thought, was similar to Terry's sneakers, although she couldn't be sure. It was the kind you could buy at Walmart, which meant that probably half the people in town owned a pair. She didn't recognize the bracelet, either, a silver-colored link bracelet with a flat panel engraved with the initials G.G.

And more uncertainty lay ahead. Terry's dental records would be requested from the prison, where she'd had some dental work done, and at the deputy's request, Donna had taken Terry's hairbrush to the office. Both the dental records and the DNA match would take some time. In the meanwhile, she had been persuaded to list Terry as a missing person.

"She's going to be furious with me when she gets home," Donna said. I could tell by her tone that she was trying to persuade herself that it wasn't Terry who had burned to death in the trailer. As for me, well, I couldn't be sure. I didn't want to remember the voice I had heard crying out for help, but when I tried, I had to say that it hadn't sounded much like Terry. But I had been panicked and the victim had been frantic, her voice unnaturally shrill and high-pitched. Yes, it could've been Terry.

But I didn't want to say that to Donna. Instead, I said, "How's Aunt Velda handling this? What have you told her about the situation?"

"She's not so good," Donna said glumly. "She's had a bad cold for a couple of days — that's why she wasn't at the meeting last night. To make things worse, she overheard my conversation with the sheriff's office last night, and I had to tell her about the trailer fire. She's in bed today."

"In bed?" That wasn't like Aunt Velda, who is one of the liveliest old ladies I know. I want to be just like her when I grow up. That is, I want to have her energy, although I'd just as soon skip her history of intergalactic space travel.

"Yeah. This definitely isn't good for her, China. It took a long time for her to recover from Terry's being sent back to prison. This time . . ." Her voice sank, and I could hear the desperation in it. "I don't know what I'd do if I lost Aunt Velda. That crazy old lady keeps me going when things get rough out here."

Sadly, there wasn't much I could say. I

made consoling noises and asked her to let me know as soon as she heard from her sister. Then I went to find my gardening trowel and headed out to the medicinal garden to do some serious weeding. I always think better with a trowel in my hand, and I had some serious thinking to do about Donna's call.

So now I was on my knees, weeding my way through the comfrey and wormwood and pondering the details that Donna had given me. I reflected on them as I dug up the tenacious root of a yellow dock that was intruding on the personal space of a bushy St. John's wort, gaudy with sunshine-colored blooms.

One was the bracelet. The fact that it didn't bear Terry's initials wasn't highly relevant to the identification — it could have been a remembrance gift from a fellow prisoner or a pen pal friend. The other was the fact that the victim had been shot in the chest with a small-caliber handgun — a Saturday night special, a gun that's cheap and easy to get. Which reinforced my sense that this had been a drug deal gone bad. Somebody trying to cheat somebody out of money. Somebody threatening to blow the whistle on somebody else. Somebody —

I yanked at a bindweed that was choking

the life out of a neighboring lavender plant. The possibilities were infinite. The information was scanty. There wasn't enough evidence to draw any sort of conclusion. We'd have to wait for the DNA report or the dental records, both of which could take a while. But maybe Terry would come home before then and that part of the mystery, anyway, would be solved.

And in the meantime, I reminded myself that — while I was deeply sympathetic to Donna's plight — this really was not my problem, and there was no sense in stewing over it. I had lots of other things on my mind, including the fact that McQuaid would be away longer than he had planned. He'd called the night before to say that he had wrapped up the investigation in Memphis but he'd uncovered another angle, and Charlie Lipman wanted him to follow up. Instead of taking a plane home this morning, he was on his way to Knoxville. So Caitie and I would be batching it until Wednesday, at least. Too bad. We were ready for him to come home.

"Hey, China."

I looked up, startled, squinting against the late-morning sun. "Oh, Jessica. Hi."

The intrepid girl reporter was wearing denim pants, a white blouse, and a red blazer, and carried a business-like leather bag over her shoulder. "I'll bet you forgot," she said in a tone that barely missed being accusing. "About our lunch, I mean."

"Oh, no," I lied, and scrambled to my feet. "I just got busy and lost track of time." But of course she was right. I had remembered our lunch date earlier that morning, but Donna's call had driven it out of my mind.

She hitched the strap of her bag higher on her shoulder. "Why don't we just go over to Beans' and get something to eat? Unless you've already made sandwiches, that is."

"I haven't," I confessed. I brushed the dirt off my knees. "Beans' is a great idea. The food is good, and we can sit in the back where there isn't much noise. Let's do it."

If you're looking for Beans' Bar and Grill, you'll find it in a tin-roofed stone building between Purley's Tire Company and the MoPac railroad tracks, across the street from the Old Firehouse Dance Hall. It's a Texas roadhouse of 1930s or '40s vintage, with a pressed tin ceiling painted white, a worn wooden floor, an assemblage of mismatched tables and chairs, and an antique mirrored bar that runs the length of the main room. You can go to Beans' to play pool, throw darts at posters of various politicos, sit at the bar and watch the Longhorns beat the bejeebers out of the Aggies on TV (or vice versa) while you pig out on a chicken-fried steak smothered in Bob Godwin's special cream gravy, with sides of deep-fried pickled jalapeños, beans, or coleslaw. You can also play "Boot-Scootin' Boogie" on the old Wurlitzer jukebox or carve your initials on the wooden Indian that stands just inside the door. And when you're ready to settle your tab, you can whistle for Bud, who will pick it up and take it to the cash register. Bud (short for Budweiser) has floppy yellow ears and wears a red bandana and a leather saddlebag with a side pocket for tips. He's Bob Godwin's golden retriever — so called, according to Bob, because he retrieves the gold.

Bob, a burly, red-haired Nam vet, has owned Beans' for the past five years or so. His furry red brows meet in the middle of a rugged, pockmarked face, and he sports a tattoo of a broken heart on one thick forearm and a coiled snake tattoo on the other. He lives in a trailer outside of town and raises goats, some of which occasionally put in a featured appearance on the menu. Bob's grilled cabrito kabobs — marinated with lime juice, soy sauce, and garlic and grilled with cherry tomatoes and chunks of onion, pineapple, and green peppers — are justifiably famous. His Drunken Goat Stew is even better, but he makes it only for special occasions. It's like Julia's *Boeuf Bourguignon,* only more so.

"I think I'll have the tortilla soup and a salad," Jessica said, when we had settled at one of the farther tables, away from the crack of pool cues and the wheeze of the ancient Wurlitzer.

"You might want to reconsider that soup," I said. "It's heavy on the cilantro." The four bunches Bob had bought on Saturday were enough to last ordinary people for a couple of weeks. Bob would go through them in a few days.

"What's cilantro?"

"It looks like parsley," I said. "But it has its own unique taste. It's used heavily in Mexican cooking." I was being evasive. I am not a cilantro fan, but I didn't want to prejudice Jessica. To each her own.

Jessica nodded carelessly. "The soup sounds fine."

Well, okay, I thought. "I'll have a burger." There's nothing not to like about Bob's burgers, which are thick and juicy and beyond reproach. He gets his beef from a local rancher over in Blanco County. Grass-fed. No factory-farmed animals.

A moment later, Bob himself was standing beside our table. "China Bayles!" He dropped an exaggerated kiss on my head. "Ain't seen you in a dog's age. What'cha been doin' with yerself?" He stepped back for a closer look. "And what'n the hell did ya do to them eyebrows, girl?"

"You don't want to know."

"Got too close to a bonfire, huh?" He chortled merrily. "Where's yer old man these days? Ain't seen him lately, neither."

I grinned. "He's in Knoxville, digging up dirt on somebody for Charlie Lipman."

Bob rolled his eyes expressively. "Prob'ly divorce dirt. Charlie makes a bundle off them divorces. Sure made a bundle off mine, years back." Bob was married to the woman who used to own the Resale Shop, until he caught her stepping out with an oil rig worker. For his friends and bar buddies, the episode rivaled *As the World Turns.* He tilted his head, regarding Jessica with a teasing leer. "And who's this purty little lady? You got a name, sweetheart?"

Jessica blushed. I introduced her, adding, "She's working as an intern at the *Enterprise* this summer."

I was impressed by the speed with which Jessica turned off the blush and switched to reporter mode, all stations alert. "Actually,

I'm covering the trailer fire out on Limekiln Road on Saturday night," she said. "Have you heard about it?"

Of course he had heard about it — probably two minutes after the fire trucks went out. He pulled his furry brows together. "Turr'ble thang, that fire, jes' turr'ble," he muttered. "Somebody said the girl that died was a student over at the college."

"Oh, really?" Jessica asked intently, leaning forward. "Where'd you hear that?"

Jessica probably didn't know this, but Beans' is one of Pecan Springs' gossip centrals, along with the Nueces Street Diner and the mayor's biweekly prayer breakfasts. When Hark wants to catch up on the news, he drops in here.

Bob stroked his chin. "Might've been Scott Sheridan told me. He was in here yestiddy afternoon. He owns the place — the place that burned, is what I'm sayin'." He took an order book out of the pocket of his grease-stained apron and a pencil from behind his ear. "So what'll it be for y'all? Them cabrito kabobs is really good today, if I do say so m'self."

We resisted the cabrito kabobs and gave him our orders. When he had gone, Jessica said, in a low voice, "I talked to Scott Sheridan this morning, China. He didn't

153

say anything to me about the victim being a student. In fact, he told me he had no idea who she was or what she was doing in the trailer."

"Maybe Sheridan was just blowing smoke for the boys at the bar," I said. "Or maybe it was somebody else who said it. Bob might not be remembering accurately." Or maybe Sheridan just didn't feel like giving an eager girl reporter something she could turn into a story. Me, I was impressed by the fact that Jessica had followed up with him. "Did Sheridan tell you anything helpful?"

"Well, yes, as a matter of fact, he did. At least, I think so." She took a reporter's narrow notebook out of her bag and leafed through the ruled pages, scanning her scribbles. "He said he bought the place because he thought the land was a good investment. The trailer was pretty run-down, but a couple of students were living there, a guy and a girl, on month-to-month. He would've let them stay on until the end of the semester, he said, but they were doing drugs. He told them he wanted to work on the place and get it ready to rent for the summer. He was planning to start repairs next week."

"Uh-huh," I said. That pretty much squared with what Sheridan had told Mc-

Quaid. "Did he give you the names of the renters he evicted?"

She flipped a page. "He couldn't remember the guy's name right off and was going to look it up for me. But the girl was . . ." She flipped another page. "The girl was Lucy LaFarge. He remembered, because it sounded like a name in an old B movie. The good thing about a name like that," she added, "is that it's easy to track down."

"Easy for a crack reporter, maybe," I said with a grin.

She was very serious. "Actually, I've already dug up an address for her. LaFarge has an apartment near the campus, 101 North Brazos. I don't know that she'll be able to tell me anything about the victim, but she can tell me what it was like to live in that trailer. That's the angle I'm after, you know. Human interest."

"Sounds like you're making progress," I said approvingly, as Bob brought the iced tea we had ordered and a plate of nachos we hadn't.

"Nachos are on the house," he said, and put a big hand on my shoulder. "You gotta come around more, China. You 'n' Mc-Quaid. Don't see y'all near often 'nuff."

"Thanks," I said, and smiled. Friends are one of the very nicest things about Pecan

Springs. You'll never catch a bar owner in Houston or Dallas giving away a plate of nachos just because he hasn't seen you in a while.

Jessica reached into her leather bag and took out a minirecorder. She put it on the table between us and flicked the switch. "Now it's your turn, China. I'd like to hear all about that night — the night you found the trailer on fire. Let's start with what you were doing earlier that evening and take it from there. Okay?"

"It's not a very appetizing mealtime story," I warned. I didn't want to go through the experience again, but I had promised. I made it quick and graphic. I was finished by the time Bob delivered my burger and Jessica's tortilla soup and salad.

But Jessica didn't notice the food. She was totally engrossed in what I had said. Her eyes were wide, her expression horrified.

"Omigod," she whispered, as she turned her tape recorder off. "I thought the shooter killed her. I mean, I heard that she'd been shot and I thought she died right away. Nobody told me she . . ." She gulped. "Nobody told me she was still alive when you got there. That you heard her scream-ing. That she *burned* to death."

"I'm afraid it's true," I said. I looked down

at my burger, which was thick and juicy and luscious-looking. But suddenly I was hearing the woman's voice again. And discovering that I wasn't very hungry after all.

"She must have been . . ." Jessica's voice dropped. "She must have been so . . . so frightened. Knowing that she was going to die, not being able to get out." She pulled her soup bowl toward her and dipped her spoon into it. She took a large swallow and wrinkled her nose distastefully. "Yuch. Tastes like soap. Soap and aluminum foil." She reached for her iced tea. "Is that the cilantro I'm tasting?"

I nodded, refraining from saying *I told you so.* "Lots of people love the taste. But for some, even a little cilantro is too much." I picked up my burger, thinking that Jessica most likely knew Terry Fletcher from her work at the farm, and wondering if I should tell her that Terry had been missing since Friday. I decided against it. There was no evidence, either direct or circumstantial, to tie Terry to the trailer fire. Her absence could be a coincidence. And for all I knew, she had already shown up back at the farm, in time for lunch. At least, I hoped so.

There didn't seem to be much else to say. Jessica abandoned her soup, focused on her salad, and finished off the nachos. I nibbled on my hamburger, and when Bud came with the check, I tipped him with a couple of fair-sized chunks of burger and a slice of dill pickle. Bud loves pickles.

We got into Jessica's green Ford two-door to drive back to the shop. I was planning to spend the afternoon alternating between weeding and dusting — two chores I can perform on autopilot — until it was time to take Caitlin for her violin lesson.

"So how are you spending the rest of the day, Jessica?" I asked, as we swung around the corner.

She answered my idle question with purpose. "I'm driving out to the trailer to take a few more pictures. On my way back into town, I think I'll stop at the auto parts place and interview Scott Sheridan again — I want to see if he's found the name of the guy he evicted. After that, I've got an appointment at the sheriff's office to interview Sheriff Blackwell and see the crime scene photos. Then I want to see if I can get Lucy LaFarge to talk to me. After that, I'm going home and write the story." Her face was serious. "I have the house all to myself this week. My roommate's gone camping — which may not be as good a thing as I thought. I'm having trouble with a neighbor. He's a real jerk. Last night, he . . ." She stopped. "But you don't need to hear about that."

I wasn't surprised to hear about her interview, but I'd bet that Blackie wouldn't let her look at the crime scene photos. I had no great desire to see them myself. They wouldn't be pretty.

"You're really digging away at this story, aren't you?" I remarked. What did Jessica want? Was she simply a good journalism student, trying to do her best? Or an ambitious reporter, eager to add a juicy story to her portfolio?

She shook her head, frowning. "Well, it started out being just a story. I mean, I wanted to do a really good piece. I *need* to do that, because there will be a lot of journalism grads out there looking for jobs. But when you told me what really happened — that made it even more real, China. More personal. The idea of that poor young woman, a student maybe, lying there on that sofa, knowing that she was about to be burned to death . . ." Her hands were clenched on the steering wheel, white-knuckled. "That's how I lost my twin sister and my mom and dad, you know. They burned to death. It happened ten years ago this month. I wasn't home that night — I was on a school trip. If I had been there, I would be dead, too. Like my sister, Ginger. Like the girl who died in the trailer."

I breathed out, appalled. Her family had burned to death? Her whole family? "Oh, God, Jessica — that's awful! How terrible for you."

"It was. It was unspeakable." Her voice was flat, expressionless. "It took a long time, but I'm okay now. You can't mourn forever." She gave a little shrug. "You have to move on, you know. Get over it. Get on with your life."

She was okay with it now? Somehow, I doubted that. It seemed to me like the kind of thing you'd never be okay with — that it would run like a sad, bitter current through every thought, every choice, every action. Some of the things I knew about Jessica were beginning to make a little more sense, now that I knew this. Her interest in this story was making sense, too. But it was worrisome. She had lost both her parents and her sister, her *twin* sister, in a fire — and now she was covering a story about another death by fire, the death of a young woman? It had to awaken all those awful memories.

"But doesn't that make writing this story a lot more difficult for you?" I asked, perturbed. "Are you sure you should be covering it? Maybe it would be a good idea to let Mr. Hibler handle —"

She turned on me fiercely. "Of course it's a good idea! I have been involved in a situation just like this one. I remember how it felt." Her voice was sharp and intense. "Which makes me exactly the right person to be writing this story. In fact, nobody else could cover it the way I can."

"Okay, okay." I backpedaled. "I just don't want you to get dragged into something that's personally hard to handle. You have to stay objective."

"Objectivity." Her mouth tightened. "That's what they teach you in journalism school, yes. But that doesn't mean that I have to stick to a just-the-facts-ma'am approach. This is a human-interest story." We reached the shop and she braked to a stop at the curb. "This is about the girl who died, China. I owe it to her to find out everything there is to know about her. Who she was, where she came from, what kind of person she was, what she was doing in that trailer, who killed her —"

"Whoa, Jessica," I said firmly. The red flags were flapping all over the place now. "You're a reporter, not a cop. Finding out who killed that woman is the sheriff's job. He wouldn't be very happy if you get in his way."

"I know all that," she said impatiently, and hit the steering wheel with the flat of her hand. Her face was grim. "And I sincerely hope the sheriff gets the sonuvabitch. Shooting that girl and leaving her to burn to death . . ." She shuddered.

"I hope they get him, too," I said, "but —"

"So I'm going to find out everything I can about the killer, as well," she went on, paying no attention to me. "I want to know why he did what he did, how he did it, what makes him tick . . ."

This was going too far. I opened my mouth to say so, but she barreled on.

"Have you ever read *In Cold Blood,* China? It's a true crime — the first true crime novel, really. It was written in the 1950s by Truman Capote, about a family that was murdered in Kansas. Capote interviewed everybody who knew the victims. He got really close to the killers. That's what I want to do. I intend to find out everything there is to know about the victim. Then I want to find out as much as I can about the guy who killed her. I want —"

I put up my hand, stopping her. There were two problems here, but I'd tackle the simpler one first. "A guy? What makes you think the killer was a man?"

She shot me a skeptical glance. "You really think a woman would do something like that? Shoot another woman and then burn her alive?"

Well, there was the prostitute in Florida, but that was beside the point. "Maybe. I don't know. I'm just saying that you can't jump to conclusions. There's something else, too." I tackled the other issue. "I know how Hark Hibler feels about keeping a story, any story, in perspective. If he were having this conversation with you, he would tell you to forget about using Truman Capote as a model. The way I remember it, Capote lost all objectivity on the Kansas murders. He wrote a very good book, a spellbinding book, but at a terrible cost to himself."

"Thanks." Jessica's voice had a sharp edge. "I'll remember about Capote. And I'll keep your warning in mind the next time I see a conclusion I'd like to jump to."

I sighed regretfully. I had alienated her, and I was sorry. But I wasn't sorry I had spoken. Jessica was so passionate, so determined, so *young*. When I was her age, I had been every bit as determined as she was. I had felt things as fiercely as she was feeling this. In fact, that fierceness was one of the reasons I had gone into law in the first place. I wanted passionately to see justice done, to stand up for people who needed someone between them and the brutally dispassionate and sometimes unjust law. But I had learned — the hard way — that it was important to keep my distance. It's dangerous to stand too close. You get scorched.

But Jessica was shifting impatiently in her seat, eager to get on with the things she'd planned for the afternoon, and I knew that nothing I could say would change her mind. I opened the car door. "Hey, thanks for the lunch. I enjoyed it."

She gave me a frowning glance. "No, you didn't. You gave your hamburger to the dog."

"Just a couple of bites. But I guess I lost my appetite." I smiled wryly. "You didn't finish your soup, either."

"I didn't like the cilantro. And I lost my appetite, too — after I heard that the girl was still alive when you got there."

Now I could finally say it. "I told you so," I said. "About the cilantro, I mean. Bob *always* puts too much in. And you were the one who wanted to hear the story while we were eating. I told you it was horrible."

"Yeah." She laughed. "I guess we're even, huh?"

"I guess we are." Impulsively, I leaned over

and gave her a hug. "Be careful, Girl Reporter. And keep me posted on your progress. Okay?"

She hugged me back, then held me at arm's length. "You're not just saying that, China? You really want to know what I find out?"

"Yes," I said firmly. "I really want to know." I really didn't, since I had already come as close to this story as I cared to get, and I had the scorched eyebrows to prove it. But it might be a good idea to keep tabs on Jessica. I didn't want her to lose her eyebrows, too — or worse.

"Okay, then," she said. "I'll phone you. And we'll have lunch together later in the week. How's that?"

"Good. Next time, we'll do it here, on me." I got out and closed the door. "Sandwiches and soup. Easy on the cilantro."

She waggled her fingers at me. "Maybe no cilantro at all," she said, and drove off.

I stood on the sidewalk, watching her turn the corner. Now, after it's all over, I wonder: if I'd had any idea what was going to happen, would I have let her go? But how could I have stopped her? She knew what she wanted to do; she knew what she was looking for. She wouldn't have listened.

But I didn't know what was going to happen, and neither did she. So we each went our ways, blindly, into the future.

CHAPTER SEVEN

In contemporary society, mild psychoactive stimulants containing caffeine (tea, coffee, colas, and chocolate) are considered to have a positive value, for they reduce feelings of fatigue and enable people to work harder, longer, and feel more alert. Caffeine is found in varying quantities in the beans, leaves, and fruits produced by some plants. The plants seem to have evolved the chemical as a pesticide, in order to paralyze and kill insects that might destroy them. Caffeine is usually consumed by humans in infusions brewed from the berries of the coffee plant and the leaves of the tea bush, as well as in beverages derived from the kola nut. Global consumption of caffeine has been estimated at 120,000 tons per year, making it the world's most popular psychoactive substance. Consider this the

167

next time you brew your favorite coffee.

China Bayles
"Mood-Altering Plants"
Pecan Springs Enterprise

Caitlin had spent the day with her friend Alice, who lives across the street from the Pecan Springs Library, where the kids' summer reading program meets every Monday. At four that afternoon, I drove to Alice's to pick Caitie up for her violin lesson. She was ready when I got there, cute as a button in her favorite yellow bib overalls and red-and-yellow-striped T-shirt, sitting on the front porch steps with Alice, her violin case and a bag of library books beside her. As we drove to CTSU, she chattered happily about the summer reading program (she had won a candy bar for reading twelve books last week, five more than anybody else), about Alice (her mom was getting a divorce because her dad didn't love them anymore), and about Alice's cute kitty (all white, like a baby bunny, with one black spot on his nose).

I listened, making appreciative mom-noises at appropriate points in the narrative and wondering how Howard would feel if a kitten moved in with us. In the past, he has expressed some very definite opinions about cats. I was also thinking that Caitie had changed a great deal in the past few months. She was on her way to being a happy little girl again. If her father could see her at this moment, he would definitely approve.

CTSU is a year-round campus, which means that parking is just as hard to find in June and July and August as it is during the rest of the year. I drove up Anderson and made a right at the top of the hill, stopping at the kiosk where a pleasant-faced uniformed guard used to check your parking sticker to make sure that you weren't wanted for any major crimes (unpaid library fines or parking tickets) and let you in or kept you out, accordingly. But the campus went high-tech last year, and while the kiosk is still there, the guard has been replaced by an electronic card-reader gizmo. Since McQuaid teaches on the campus, I have a card. I stuck it into the reader, various clickings and cluckings ensued, and the gate went up. I don't know why, but this always amazes me. I drove through quickly, before the gizmo could change its electronic mind and drop the gate on top of my car.

After some diligent searching, we got lucky and found an empty space behind the Music Education Building, where graduate students — as part of their training as teachers — use the practice rooms to give private lessons. Caitie grabbed her violin case, gave me a quick peck on the cheek, and ran into the building. I staked out a spot on the grass in the shade of a large live oak, overlooking the pretty little river that flows through the middle of campus. I had a book in my bag — Kinsey Millhone's latest mystery — and the place I'd picked out was close enough to the open window of the practice room so that I could listen as I read. Caitie was playing the Pachelbel Canon with her teacher Brenda on the piano. She had made a few mistakes the day before, but today she nailed it, at least to my untrained ear. I thought it was lovely, although that was probably a mother's pride.

But between listening to Caitie and thinking about my talk with Jessica, I didn't get much reading done. The longer I thought about what Jessica had told me about losing her family in that house fire, the more it bothered me. The story about the trailer fire was sure to stir up her feelings about the deaths of her sister and parents, and I didn't think it was a good idea for her to get involved any more deeply than she already was. But she wasn't going to listen to me, obviously. The only way I could stop her was to call Hark and give him a heads-up.

If I did that, though, it would look like I didn't trust Jessica to handle whatever came up, which might jeopardize her work at the newspaper. It was one of those damned-if-you-do and damned-if-you-don't situations.

I was still thinking about this when Caitie finished her lesson and came out to where I was sitting, Brenda with her. "Alice's mom gave me some bread for the ducks on the river," she informed me. "Okay if I go feed them?"

"I'm sure they'd appreciate that," I said with a grin. "Ducks can never get too much bread." She put her violin case on the grass beside me, took out a plastic bag, and skipped off.

Brenda plopped down on the grass beside me. She's a heavyset girl with brownish, disheveled hair and owlish plastic-rimmed glasses, in the last term of her master's program. The week before, she told me that she has a job lined up in Corsicana, her hometown. Come September, she'll be teaching music in the high school there.

"Could we have a conversation about Caitlin?" she asked in a serious tone.

"Is she doing okay?" I was trying not to be anxious. "I mean, she sounds fine to me. And she practices a lot. A couple of hours a day during the summer." I paused. Maybe she was overdoing it. I sometimes have the idea that Caitie is hiding inside the music, using it as a place to go when she doesn't want to be a part of the family. Using music instead of words, as a way to express her feelings. "Maybe we should encourage her not to —"

"She's doing very, very well," Brenda broke in. She pushed her glasses up on her nose. "But I've asked Dr. Trevor to take her for lessons for the rest of the summer, instead of me. I told Caitlin about it this afternoon."

"But why?" I asked, bewildered. "Don't the two of you get along? She really seems to look forward to coming here every week." I gave a rueful laugh. "I know the difference, believe me. When I was her age, I hated the violin. Hated my teacher, too. My mother had to drag me to my lessons. But Caitie is always eager to come. I'm sure she loves it."

Brenda turned to face me. "And I love working with her." She pushed her hair back, pulled off her glasses, and swiped her forehead with her arm. "She is — well, I'm not sure I'd call her a prodigy. But she is very talented. Very." She put her glasses back on and looked at me. "In fact, I have never met a child as talented as she is, and I don't know enough to teach her. I mean, I know enough about the instrument — it's not that. I don't quite know how to make the best of her talent. And Dr. Trevor does. She's spent her whole career working with gifted children."

Very talented. Gifted. "Wait a minute," I said. "You're telling me that this little girl . . ." I frowned. "That what Caitie is doing with that violin is different from what other kids do?"

Brenda looked at me, frowning a little. "Very different. Can't you tell?"

"Well, no, I can't," I said regretfully. "To tell the truth, I have a tin ear. I know when Caitie makes a mistake and plays something over, and I know I love to listen to her. But I don't know the first thing about music." I was beginning to feel very foolish. I must have a tin ear when it came to being a mother, too. I didn't even know enough to catch the signs of talent that Brenda had so easily spotted.

Brenda chuckled. "Well, unless I miss my guess, Caitie is going to show us all a thing or two. I'm looking forward to seeing what she makes of herself over the next few years." She got to her feet. "Dr. Trevor wants you to call her. She'd like to discuss some options."

173

"Options?" I got up, too, still trying to process this entirely unexpected news. "For lessons, you mean?"

"For lessons, and for a recital. And for the youth orchestra program here at CTSU." Her smile transformed her pudgy face, as she held out her hand. "I think she's planning to keep your little girl busy this summer."

Your little girl. The words echoed after Brenda had gone, and I heard them again as I picked up Caitlin's violin case and went down the slope to the river, where she was feeding the ducks, carefully tearing the last piece of bread into tiny pieces.

"I wish I'd brought more," she said. "I don't have enough for him." She pointed to a black duck swimming all by itself. "The others get all the bread before he does."

"You can bring more next time," I said, and hesitated. "Brenda told you that you'll be having lessons with Dr. Trevor from now on?"

"Mmm," Caitlin said, nodding. She threw her last crust of bread as hard as she could. It landed in front of the black duck. He gobbled it instantly.

"Is that okay with you? Changing teachers?"

"Did you see that, Aunt China?" Caitlin

demanded excitedly. "He got it before they did! Finally!" She turned back to me. "Sure, it's okay. I'll miss Brenda, but she says I'll move along faster if I change to Dr. Trevor."

I regarded her. "Is that what you want to do? Move along faster?"

"Uh-huh." She took her violin case from me. "Brenda says I might even get to have a recital this summer. If I do, she'll come to hear me play." She took my hand. "You and Uncle Mike will come, too, won't you?"

"Of course," I replied, as we started up the hill toward the car. "Wouldn't miss it for the world."

As I said, life is full of surprises. I had barely gotten used to being a mother to a teenaged boy when Caitie joined the family and I had to get used to being a mom to a little girl.

And now I had to get used to being a mom to a little girl who was also a talented violinist. I wasn't sure I was ready.

But Caitlin apparently was, and that was all that mattered.

Jessica was very much on my mind for the next twenty-four hours, although I heard nothing from her. I thought of calling Hark to ask how the story was coming along, but postponed it. And anyway, there wasn't time. On Tuesday, I was busy nonstop at the shop, and a dozen members of the library's Senior Book Club came in for their monthly lunch in the tearoom, which meant a hectic couple of hours at midday. I also had to finish my article for the *Enterprise,* which I somehow managed to do, between customers.

It was nearly four when I glanced at the clock and realized I hadn't heard from Donna Fletcher, either, not since the morning of the day before. I phoned and caught her just coming in from the gardens.

She sounded dispirited as she answered my questions. No, Terry hadn't come home. And no, the police hadn't turned up any sign of her. "She's probably hanging out somewhere in Mexico," she added bleakly. "With my truck." The fact of the trailer fire ballooned between us, but she didn't mention it, and I didn't, either. There was nothing we could say that would change what had happened. Either Terry had been in that trailer or she hadn't.

"About the truck," I said, finally. "We're not using McQuaid's pickup right now. Would you like to borrow it until you get yours back?" I was sure that McQuaid would make the same offer, if he were here right now. "It's older than anything else on the road, but it runs."

Her breath whooshed out. "Oh, thank you!" she said, sounding overjoyed at the prospect of having wheels again. "Margie Laughton is here right now. Maybe she could drive me to your place to pick up the truck. What time will you be home?"

I looked at the clock again, thinking that I probably owed it to Hark to talk to him about Jessica. "I have to stop at the *Enterprise* for a few minutes, then pick up Caitlin at Amy's house." That morning, Caitie had come in with me and helped out in the shop. She was spending the afternoon playing with Baby Grace. "Maybe six? Is that too late for you?"

Donna consulted with Margie and came back to the phone. "Margie says six will work." She took a breath and managed a small laugh. "Thanks, China. I don't know which is worse — worrying about my sister or worrying about my truck."

I knew she didn't mean that. But it felt good to help her solve at least one of her problems.

Pecan Springs was established in the late 1840s by German immigrants who settled on the Fisher-Miller Land Grant, under the auspices of a German emigration company called the Adelsverein. The company hoped to establish a German colony in the Republic of Texas, which had won its independence from Mexico in 1836 but had not yet been annexed by the United States. For safety, the colonists were dispatched in groups, a smart strategy, considering that the local Indians were not absolutely thrilled at the thought of new people moving into the neighborhood. They arrived by ship on the Gulf Coast and trekked overland by horse and wagon to the gently rolling hills of the Edwards Plateau, where they settled the towns of Pecan Springs, New Braunfels, and Fredericksburg.

The Indians were definitely a problem for a year or two, but they were soon outnumbered and persuaded to retire from the field. The Germans proved to be an extraordinarily industrious lot and all three settlements prospered. Before long, Pecan Springs was the trading center of the local agricultural commerce, with grist mills, sawmills, and manufacturing shops that supplied pioneer families with farm implements, leather goods, furniture, clothing, and wagons. Settlers built their first houses out of cypress logs, but as time went on, the German stonemasons began building more permanently, with stone. A great many of the buildings in town date from that period, and they all share a distinctive look.

The *Enterprise* building, for instance. It's two stories high, three times longer than it is wide, and constructed of square-cut blocks of light-colored native limestone. Last year, Hark moved the newspaper's production plant to a more modern facility on the outskirts of town, brought the archives downstairs, and leased the remodeled second floor to an architect. But the editorial offices remain on the first floor, and — for better or worse — Ethel Fritz is still the first person you see when you open the front door.

Ethel is the office manager. A largish, busty, fiftysomething woman, she loomed even larger today in a purple-striped dress, her bleached hair newly done up in a towering bouffant that made her look as if she were balancing a golden beehive on her head. Ethel has never won prizes for her people skills, and she greeted me with her usual frown.

"It's late," she said, glancing pointedly at the clock on the wall opposite her desk. I knew that "it" was my "Home and Garden" page, which had been due today at three o'clock. It was now five fifteen. Ethel doesn't go home until five thirty.

"Actually, it isn't late," I returned, with a barely hidden note of triumph in my voice. "I emailed it to Hark's computer at two forty-five."

"Huh." Ethel's frown deepened. She resists learning to use the computer. She says that people are losing their memories because they trust everything to the computer and then can't remember a "durn thang," as she puts it. (I have the sneaking feeling that she might be right.) Hark inherited Ethel — as well as a reporter named Gene, of the same vintage — when he bought the paper from the previous owners. He has threatened several times to replace both of them, but Gene is earnest and dogged and knows Pecan Springs inside and out, and Ethel is similarly valuable. She has worked for the *Enterprise* since she graduated high school and is acquainted with all the native Springers. She knows their family trees and all their in-laws and outlaws. She knows their sins, too, ancient and modern. She jots them all down in her mental black book.

"Actually," I added, "I'm here to see the boss. Is he in the office?"

"Can't say he's in the best o' moods." She pushed her long yellow Number 2 pencil into the back of her beehive, where it stuck

180

out like a chopstick. Ethel has a habit of sticking pencils into her hair and forgetting about them. I counted a half-dozen once. "You know what's good for you," she added darkly, "you better tippy-toe."

"Tippy-toe? Why? What's wrong?"

She gave me a stern look. "Might wanta ask your friend Ruby 'bout that." Ethel has the idea that Ruby has been toying with Hark's affections, which puts Ruby in Ethel's black book. In fact, Ruby probably has a page all to herself. Maybe two pages.

"You know she was seein' Mr. Hibler when that Colin fella came along," she added, with barely concealed bitterness. "Threw him for a loop. Looks to be happenin' all over again, I'm sorry to say." She picked up another pencil and stuck it in her hair. "Some cowboy this time, is what I heard."

"That Colin fella" was Colin Fowler. And yes, it is true that Ruby lost her heart to Colin, and that Hark took it hard when it happened. But Colin is dead now, and I was hoping that this episode had been forgotten. It had not, obviously, by Ethel. And if she had already heard about "some cowboy," she had probably been listening in on a phone conversation between Hark and Ruby.

There was nothing I could say except, "Thanks for the warning, Ethel." I was already on my way down the narrow hallway, on tippy-toes.

The door was open and Hark was hunched at his desk, his chin on his hand, staring into his computer monitor. His tie was loose and the sleeves of his rumpled white shirt were rolled up. A large electric fan on the filing cabinet riffled the papers at his elbow. There was a mug of black tea on his desk. Hark drinks it by the gallon, unsweetened, always blistering hot, always strong as barbed wire. Says he can't take the caffeine in coffee, but caffeine in tea is different. Says it keeps him going without making his heart jump like a hoppy-toad.

He looked up at me when I appeared in the door. "Got your file," he said grumpily. "Thanks. Looks like your page is good to go."

"Ethel says I'd better tippy-toe."

"Ethel's right."

I frowned at him. "Well, maybe if you'd danced with the one you brung, Ruby wouldn't be rodeoin' with that cowboy."

"I was playing pool," Hark replied defensively.

"So I heard. *C'est la guerre.*"

"It was an important game. Bailey was up

from San Antonio. We've been rivals for years. I had to do it."

"Must've been. An important game, that is. I hope you beat the pants off Bailey, whoever he is."

"I didn't. And Bailey is a she. Which makes it worse." He sighed.

"Lost the game to a dame and now you've lost your girl," I said remorselessly. "How much worse can it get?"

"I don't know." He gave me a pleading look. "How can I make it up to her?"

"I guess you'll have to ask her."

He picked up his mug and hunched down with it in his chair, shoulders sloping with discouragement. "And on top of everything else, today's lead story has evaporated. The trailer fire."

"Evaporated?" I was surprised. "I had lunch with Jessica yesterday, and she was hot on the trail. She had a list of places to go, people to talk to, things to see. Including the crime scene photos. She was super excited about getting a byline. In fact, I was worried that . . ." I bit my tongue. If Jessica had missed her deadline, now might not be the time to share my worries with her boss.

"Well, if our Girl Reporter is hot on the trail, she hasn't bothered to let me in on the secret," Hark growled. "I'm holding two columns above the fold, page one." He looked up at the clock. "It's getting late. And all I've got to lead with is the county commissioners' meeting tonight. Or the rodeo. Whoopee. Maybe I can get Ruby to do a story on bull riding. She tells me she has a date with one of the bull riders." His sigh was laced with sarcasm. "She's always loved cowboys. Likes to live dangerously, I guess."

I frowned. "Jessica hasn't phoned?"

"Nope."

"Then where is she?"

"How the hell should I know? Keeping track of delinquent interns isn't in my job description."

"I am not your enemy, Hark," I said succinctly. I leaned my shoulder against the door jamb. "I am your friend. And I am worried about Jessica."

"What's to worry about?" He put up his feet, tilted his chair back, and clasped his hands behind his head. His shirt showed circles of perspiration under his armpits. "It's true that I expected more from her, yeah. It's also true that I expected her to be professional enough to meet her deadlines." He was being sarcastic. "But hell, she's only a kid, China. Kids don't take their responsibilities seriously."

"This one does." I stepped into his office and stood in front of his desk. "Do you know what she's up to?"

"Up to? Yeah. She's covering the trailer fire. I probably shouldn't have assigned it to her, but she's been after me to give her something she could get her teeth into, and I thought she was woman enough to handle it." He glanced across the room at a whiteboard on the wall, where assignments and story lineups were posted. "Looks like she's also got the ribbon cutting at the high school tomorrow and the rodeo this weekend. After that —"

"She's not just covering the trailer fire, she's involved in it. Her mom and dad and twin sister died in a house fire. She wasn't home that night, so she escaped. This story is intensely personal to her, especially after she learned that the victim was alive when the fire got to her. She wants to find out everything she can about the girl. She wants to get acquainted with the killer. She —"

Hark's frown had been getting darker and darker. Now he dropped his feet and his chair came forward, hard. "She *what?*"

"You heard me. She has read *In Cold Blood* and taken it to heart. She wants to be Truman Capote when she grows up. The investigative journalist, getting to the heart of the crime — and the criminal."

"Aw, hell," Hark growled disgustedly. "What do they teach them up there at the college? I tell these interns, over and over. Stay objective. Don't get involved. But do they listen? Hell, no. She's probably hoping to win a Pulitzer."

"Have you tried calling her place?"

Instead of replying, he flipped through his Rolodex, found a number, and punched it in. When the answering machine began to pick up, he cut it off. "No answer," he said unnecessarily. "Nobody's there."

"I think she said her roommate had gone camping for the week." I put my hands on my hips. "So what are we going to do?"

"Do?" Now he was snarling. "I am going to bang out a two-column story about a girl who burned to death in a trailer on Limekiln Road on Saturday night, that's what I'm going to do. I am going to call the sheriff's office and get the latest on the investigation. I am going to send Gene and his camera out to take a photo of what's left of the trailer — since the reporter I assigned to the job hasn't met her deadline." He narrowed his eyes and poked a finger at me. "And *you* are going home. You are going to do whatever you had planned for the evening. Cook dinner for McQuaid and the

186

kids. Go bowling. Weed your parsley. What-ever."

I bit my lip. "But don't you think we ought to —"

"Ought to what?" He was shouting now. "Jessica is over twenty-one, damn it. She doesn't need anybody holding her hand. All she needs is to file her story, whatever the hell it is. All she needs is to meet her responsibilities."

I looked up at the clock. My daughter was waiting for me. My friend would be over soon to pick up my husband's truck. I had responsibilities, too. I sighed. "Okay, go ahead and write the friggin' story. But give me her address and home phone number. I've got her cell."

He almost threw the Rolodex at me. I copied the phone number and address (on Santa Fe Street, north of the campus) and left before our friendship could be ir-revocably damaged.

"I told you so," Ethel said darkly, as I hur-ried past her desk. She stuck another pencil into her beehive. "Didn't I tell you so? Didn't I say to tippy-toe back there?"

"Yes, Ethel," I gritted, "you did." I am ashamed to say that I slammed the door, hard, on my way out.

As a Valentine's present, McQuaid had

fitted my car with one of those hands-free cell phone devices. I used it now, trying Jessica's cell as I drove to Amy's house to pick up Caitlin. No luck. I tried the house phone as Caitie and I headed for home, and got the answering machine. Tried the cell phone again. Still nothing.

When we got home, Donna was waiting on our back porch.

"I have some good news," she said, as I handed over the keys to McQuaid's truck. "Margie Laughton and I are going into partnership together. We signed the papers today, so it's official. We're putting it in the farm's newsletter this week." She let a smile creep across her mouth. "Really good news, for a change."

"Wow — that's exciting, Donna. How's it going to work?" My impulsive question sounded nosy. "If you don't mind my asking," I added apologetically.

But Donna didn't seem to mind. "Margie is buying fifty percent of the business. She's going to be responsible for marketing and sales, while I manage production." She chuckled ironically. "Production. That's a fancy word for planting and harvesting, of course, same as always. Hard labor."

Fifty percent? That made Margie a full partner in the farm. "But what about —"

"What about Terry?" she interjected. Her mouth hardened. "Terry and I thrashed this all out before she . . . went away. She wasn't in favor — mostly because she doesn't like Margie. Or maybe it's Stu she doesn't like."

I was nonplussed. "Stu? Why?"

"Who knows? Terry gets strange ideas sometimes. I had no idea the two of them had even met." She straightened her shoulders and looked me full in the eye. "My sister is totally out of the farm, China. Totally. After she was released from prison, she said she needed money and she wanted me to buy her out. I didn't ask why, because I was sure it had something to do with drugs and I didn't want to know." She made a face. "I didn't have the cash, but Aunt Velda loaned it to me. The whole amount, bless her heart. So I paid Terry a fair market price for her share. She and I are square."

You didn't have to be an accountant to see that this was painfully unfair. Terry had contributed neither labor nor cash to the business during the years she'd spent in jail, and any success the farm now enjoyed was entirely due to Donna's hard work.

"Sounds to me like Terry took advantage," I said, beginning to understand Donna's attitude toward her sister — and glimpse a possible explanation for Terry's sudden disappearance. I was guessing that the two women had a big fight.

"I've been trying awfully hard not to let it get me down," Donna replied with a little shrug. "But I don't mind telling you I've been pretty crazy about it. You can imagine how relieved I was when Margie Laughton offered to buy in, out of the blue, really. I jumped at the chance. I'll trade Margie for Terry any day. And now that she's officially on board, I can use her funds to pay Auntie back for Terry's buyout." She grinned ruefully. "I don't mind telling you that I'm glad to have the help, especially with marketing and sales. Margie has a knack for that. And with the new book, she and Stu will be making a name for themselves. That should be good for business, too."

"It should," I agreed — enthusiastically, because I like Margie Laughton. She's not as charismatic as her husband, maybe, but she's a hard worker with plenty of common sense.

Donna turned toward the door, then hesitated. "About Terry," she said. "I know you think I'm avoiding the obvious, but I somehow don't think it was her in that trailer, China. Terry is tough and powerful and as strong as most men, you know. She doesn't let anybody mess with her. I can't

190

believe she'd get into a situation where somebody else could get the upper hand."

I nodded. I hadn't seen Terry for quite a while, but my experience with her had given me that impression, too. However, if you're unarmed and somebody pulls a gun on you, it doesn't matter how tough or how strong you are. Which brought up another question.

"Does Terry have a gun?" I asked.

Donna shifted uncomfortably. "She's . . . she's not supposed to, you know."

"Yes, I know," I said. As a felon, she is banned by federal law from ever possessing any firearm or ammunition, anywhere, inside or outside her home. If she was caught, she could get up to ten years in prison. "But . . ." I let my voice trail off. But plenty of felons possess guns. Sometimes they use them.

Donna tightened her jaw. "Yes, Terry has a gun. One of those ugly little Saturday night specials. I made her hide it out in the barn. I didn't want it in the house."

Great. That was just great. I didn't suppose Donna had thought to mention this when she filed the missing-person report. "She took it with her when she left?"

Donna sighed. "I wish you wouldn't ask me all these questions, China. And please,

please don't tell anybody about the gun. But yes, she took it. It was gone, anyway, when I checked. Good riddance, too."

And then another thought came into my mind. "You don't suppose," I said, and stopped.

No. Donna had enough on her plate. I wasn't going to burden her with a wildly speculative guess. But was it so wild? Terry was strong, powerful, tough. Tough enough to tie up a woman, shoot her, light a fire, and walk away?

I shuddered. Yes. Tough enough.

"Suppose what?" Donna asked, frowning.

"Nothing," I said. "Just . . . nothing."

She nodded and held up the keys. "Well, thanks again, China. I appreciate this more than I can say. If there's anything I can do for you, let me know."

Caitie fed Howard while I reheated some leftover bean soup, sliced cold meatloaf for sandwiches, and poured two glasses of milk. We were just sitting down to our impromptu supper when Howard padded to the kitchen door and stood there, whining. Like most bassets, he is remarkably vocal, with a repertoire of sonorous barks, gruff growls, complaining mutters, pleading whines, and beseeching whimpers. Now, he was offering the low, murmuring whine that he uses to let us know that something unusual is happening on the other side of his back door — might be a blue jay on the porch or an audacious squirrel on the roof or even a thunderstorm brewing.

"I'll go see," Caitie said, getting out of her chair. "What's up, Howard?"

Howard wagged his tail earnestly, shifting from one big paw to the other in that little "Let's get moving here" dance of his.

Caitie opened the door. "It's a cat!" she cried. "Look, Aunt China, it's a lost kitty!"

Definitely a cat, although I didn't think he qualified as a "kitty." An alley cat was more like it. A gaunt, scruffy-looking orange tabby with slanted amber eyes and one torn ear. He sat on his haunches and meowed piteously. He was wearing a dirty red collar but no tag — probably somebody's lost pet, but out here in the country, it was impossible to say whose. From the looks of him, he had been on the road for quite a while. A hard road. With a great many bumps and brambles and ambushes and not much in the way of provisions.

Caitie bent over and gathered the cat into her arms. Without hesitation, he pushed his head under her chin, flexed his paw on her shoulder, and cranked up a gritty purr loud enough to be heard across the room. This was an opportunistic cat. He knew his way to a little girl's heart.

"He's starving, Aunt China! Let's give him some milk."

This was one of those crossroad moments that occur in every family's life. You've probably been there yourself, maybe more than once. Pour a dish of milk for a hungry cat and he's yours forever. Tell a little girl that she can't give him milk, and she'll remember it forever, too. Which will it be?

I looked at Caitie, cradling the cat, and passed the buck. "Let's ask Howard Cosell. Maybe he doesn't like cats."

This wasn't exactly fair, because I know from personal experience that Howard doesn't like cats. He despised Khat from the moment they were introduced, and none of us got any peace until Khat went to live at the shop. It was more than likely that he would detest this scruffy, obviously low-class interloper and make it plain that he was not going to tolerate the intolerable presence for a single instant.

But Howard double-crossed me. Caitie put the cat on the floor in front of him, and I braced myself for the inevitable flying fur. One inquiring sniff, two. The cat sat still, chin up, eyes slitted, managing to look entirely at home, completely in charge, and totally bored, all at the same time. Howard circled around the cat and sniffed at his backside. Then he sat down beside the beast, thumped his tail on the floor, and smiled.

I frowned.

"You see, Aunt China?" Caitie crowed triumphantly. "Howard *loves* him! Does that mean he can stay?"

"Love" was still an open question, it seemed to me, but Howard didn't object when Caitie poured some of her milk into a saucer and set it on the floor in front of the cat. The tabby put his head down and began to lap hungrily. While Caitie sat on the floor and watched, encouraging him, he emptied the saucer. Howard gave it an extra lick just to make sure there wasn't anything left for him.

I tried not to show my dismay. "You'd better eat, too, Caitie," I said after a minute.

Coming back to the table, she asked again, wistfully now, "Oh, *please,* can we keep him?" The cat crouched by her chair, folded his front paws under his orange bib, and closed his eyes. His purr was loud enough to rattle the windows.

I looked down at the cat and thought wistfully of Alice's cute little white kitty. "You're sure you wouldn't rather look for a kitten,

Caitie? This one has used up five or six of his nine lives already." I was being charitable. He looked like he might have spent seven or eight of them — recklessly — and was well into the ninth.

"But that's why I want this one," she said, and picked up her sandwich in both hands. She wasn't looking at me. "He's like me when I came to live here. He doesn't have any family. He doesn't have a home. He's lonesome. He needs somebody to take care of him. He needs *me*."

There was no disputing this observation. I sighed. "We need to ask Uncle Mike when he calls tonight."

She nodded vigorously. "I'm going to name him Pumpkin. Because that's what he looks like." She gave me a sideways look. "And if he's a girl, her name can be Pumpkin, too."

"Good thinking," I said. "But let's see what Uncle Mike says. And the vet will have to take a look at him. Or her, as the case may be. If he's sick, we'll have to look for another kitty. I'm sure the vet could help us find a little baby who needs you, too. Okay?"

She nodded, unconvinced. Howard gave the cat another sniff. I could see how the voting was likely to turn out. It was already two in favor.

After we ate, Caitie took Pumpkin upstairs to practice her violin and I called Sandra Trevor to make arrangements for lessons and find out about the summer youth orchestra program at CTSU and the recital. As I dialed, I noticed that the light was blinking on the answering machine, and felt a stab of irritation at myself. When was the last time I checked the machine? Another thing: we'd had a power outage a few days ago — had I reset the clock to get a valid time-date stamp?

But Sandra was on the line. "Let's keep the lessons at the same time, same place," she said. "The orchestra meets on Thursday afternoons. And I'll know more about the recital after I've worked with Caitie for a few weeks." There was a deep warmth in her voice. "I'm delighted to have her, China. Brenda says she shows surprising promise for a first-year student."

"She's certainly dedicated," I said, as the strains of the Canon wafted down the stairs. "Actually, Sandra, I'm feeling a little guilty. I keep thinking I should have paid more attention to her progress. Been more on top of the situation." Aren't mothers supposed to be advocates for their children?

"Nonsense," Sandra replied briskly. "Cait-lin's opportunities will broaden out a bit now — it'll be up to her to figure out how to handle them responsibly." She paused. "You know, I often think that the real challenge for these talented youngsters isn't the talent itself. It's the discipline they need in order to develop the talent. You can't give them that. They have to find it in themselves. And for parents, the challenge is finding the right level of involvement. There's a difference between nurturing and pushing." She chuckled. "To tell the truth, I'm glad you're not one of the pushers."

"Thanks, Sandra," I said. "That makes me feel better — a little, anyway. We'll see you on Monday." I hung up and started to clear the table, thinking I'd call Leatha and let her know about the change in teachers, and why. She'd be interested — and delighted, especially since I had dashed her dreams when I showed no interest in the family violin. Then I remembered the blinking light on the answering machine, and hit the PLAY button. The voice indicator claimed that the message had come in at 12 a.m., which meant that I hadn't reset the machine after the last power outage. Drat. Maybe it was time for a new machine — one that could tell the time all by itself.

Then I heard the message. "China?" The whisper was low, furtive, surreptitious.

"China, it's me. Jessica. Listen, I'm in trouble. Really, I mean it. I need help. I —"

There was the sound of a scuffle, a stifled cry. And then the connection was broken.

Chapter Eight

Because of the powerful volatile oils emitted by some plants, their aromas are capable of altering our moods — calming us down, perking us up, making us more alert, stimulating our appetites, or encouraging sleep. The scent of lavender, for instance, helps to soothe headaches, relieve depression, and ease us into sleep. The scent of eucalyptus seems to enliven us and give us energy. The scent of peppermint can relieve anxiety, as well as stimulating the appetite — so much so that the poet Homer wrote of rubbing the dining table with mint before food was served. And of course we all know that the fragrance of coffee is itself a powerful wake-up call.

China Bayles
"Mood-Altering Plants"
Pecan Springs Enterprise

I stood staring at the receiver in my hand, trying to think. Jessica needed help. But where was she? Why was she whispering? Why had the call been broken off so abruptly? A scuffle, a cry — and then nothing.

I took a deep breath. I didn't like this situation, not at all. Wherever she was, Jessica needed help. So what could I do? Of course, if Kinsey Millhone had gotten a call like this, she would have jumped into her car and raced off to do . . . well, something. I might have raced off to do something, too, at an earlier time in my life. In fact, I was sure I had.

But I had no idea when this call had come in. What's more, I was a mom now, and my daughter was upstairs practicing her violin. Even if I had known where to look for Jessica tonight, I had responsibilities. I couldn't leave Caitie and race off into the dark, especially when it might be dangerous.

But maybe I could do something else. I picked up the phone and punched in Blackie's number. I caught him at a meeting of the county commissioners. He told me to hang on while he went out into the hallway to take my call. A moment later he was back.

"What's up, China?" That deep, comforting voice of his — I relaxed immediately. Whatever was going on with Jessica, I could turn it over to Blackie. He'd take care of it.

"Did you happen to meet Jessica Nelson from the *Enterprise* yesterday afternoon?" I asked. "She said she was stopping by your office to see the photos of the trailer fire. She was going to interview you."

"Yeah. I showed her the photos myself, and gave her a few things she could use in her story. An intern, she said, but she seemed to be really on top of it." He chuckled. "Cute kid. Passionate. Involved." You bet, I thought. Very involved. "The photos really got to her, though," he added. "Afterward, I thought I probably shouldn't have let her see the victim."

I nodded. "I'm asking because she was supposed to turn in her story this afternoon. I saw Hark a little after five, and he hadn't heard from her. Then I got this call —"

"Hang on a minute, China." I could hear voices in the background. "Sorry, but I've got to go," Blackie said hurriedly. "I'm up next, and the commissioners are ready for me."

"But I need to tell you about Jessica, Blackie! She didn't turn in her story, and Hark hasn't heard anything from her. Nobody answers at her house. And I just picked up a phone call —"

"Sorry, China," Blackie interrupted. "I've really got to go, but Sheila's here with me. You can tell her whatever it is, and she can relay the message."

I frowned. Sheila was at the county commissioners' meeting? That was a little unusual, wasn't it? She reported to the Pecan Springs city council.

But Sheila was already on the line, asking, "What's this about, China?"

I went through my story again, ending with, "And I just picked up a phone call from her that came in sometime in the last day or so on my machine. She was whispering. And then it sounded like the phone was taken away from her, and the connection was broken."

"Well," Sheila said, "I can think of —"

I broke in. "I have a bad feeling about this, Smart Cookie. I had lunch with this girl yesterday. She was really excited about writing a feature story on the trailer fire on Limekiln Road, where the woman was killed. Shot and then burned to death. Turns out that Jessica's family — her sister and her parents — also burned to death, so she has a strong personal connection to the story. To make things worse, she's been reading *In Cold Blood*. She admires the way

203

Truman Capote got close to his story — to the victims, and to the killers."

"Damn," Sheila muttered. "Lord deliver us from investigative reporters — especially the young ones. You're not thinking that she's tracked down the killer?"

I thought of the excitement on Jessica's face when she talked about the story, and about Blackie's remark that she was passionate and involved. "I think it's possible. She's bright and determined — and personally engaged. She might've been able to dig up some leads that the investigating officers missed." I had seen this kind of thing before. The cops interviewed people, and they clammed up. They told the officer only as much as they felt they had to, and they didn't volunteer anything that might develop into a lead. But Jessica was young and personable and nonthreatening. She might be able to tease out information that would never be given to an official investigator.

"Any idea where she might've been phoning from?" Sheila asked.

"No. That's why I was calling Blackie. The trailer fire is his investigation. I was hoping that he could . . ." I hesitated. What was it I had wanted him to do? "Put a deputy on it, I guess," I finished lamely.

Yes, that was part of it. But the truth was

that I wanted to be able to turn the problem over to somebody else. To reliable, dependable Sheriff Blackwell. Tell him, and he'd take care of it. He'd fix it. He always fixed everything. That's what he was good at.

Sheila sighed. "I don't want to sound like a bureaucrat, China, but if this intern is really missing, the best thing to do is file a missing-person report. You could do this, or Hark, or her roommate. Or her parents or . . ." She stopped, remembering what I had told her. "Where's her family?"

"I don't think she has any. Her grandmother died a year ago. She has a roommate." I paused. "But what about that phone call?"

"Did you pick up the number from Caller ID?"

"We don't have Caller ID on our land line. We're rural out here. We don't get all the services available in Pecan Springs."

Sheila was patient. "Well, I can think of a couple of legitimate reasons for that phone call, and none of them have anything to do with the story this girl is working on. Car trouble, for instance. Or a boyfriend problem. Is she seeing anybody?"

Car trouble. A boyfriend. Why hadn't I thought of that? "I . . . I don't know," I muttered. "I guess I really don't know her very well." Actually, I didn't know anything about Jessica, other than what she had told me about her family and a few other little bits she'd shared in our conversations. I was beginning to feel foolish. Talk about jumping to conclusions. Here I was, making a big scene, and there was probably nothing to it at all.

Sheila's voice was sympathetic. "I understand that you're anxious, China, but there's nothing anybody can do tonight."

Now I really felt foolish. I know very well that there are things the cops can do and things they can't. I had reached out to the sheriff for help, but all I had really wanted to do was turn the problem over to him and be done with it.

Sheila was going on. "Tell you what. If she calls you back and you can pin down a location, let me know. If not, and if she still hasn't been heard from by midday tomorrow, come in and —"

"I know, I know." I sighed. "File the report."

"You got it. File the report." She paused for a moment, then lowered her voice. "Maybe you were wondering why I'm here? At the county commissioners' meeting, that is."

"Well, yes, I was wondering, sorta. But I

thought maybe you and Blackie were going out somewhere afterward." I chuckled wryly. "Like maybe dancing. Or a late dinner. Or whatever a pair of law enforcement officers do when they're off duty."

"I'm here for moral support," Sheila said. "Blackie's turning in his badge tonight. Well, not tonight, exactly," she amended quickly. "Tonight, he's telling the commissioners that he's decided not to run again."

"Not running . . ." I sucked in my breath. "You . . . you're kidding, Sheila!"

"Uh-uh." She was all business. "There'll be a press release tomorrow. I thought you and Mike would like a little advance warning."

"Not running? I can't believe it. I really can't. I mean . . ." I was nearly speechless. "What made him . . ."

And then I understood. "It's the wedding, isn't it?"

Blackie had always said that two cops in one family are one cop too many, so he was quitting. I was astonished at the thought. If anybody left the profession, I would have expected it to be Sheila, when she got pregnant — *if* she got pregnant. But Blackie? Law enforcement had been in his family for decades. It was in his blood.

"Yes, it's the wedding." Sheila's laugh was

deep and rich. "We decided that the only way we could get married was for one of us to quit."

"But . . . but how did you . . ." I broke off. It wasn't any of my business how they decided.

But Sheila understood what I wasn't quite able to ask. "How? I'll tell you if you promise never to tell a soul — except Mike, of course. Blackie wants to have a talk with him when he gets back from his trip. He has some ideas for what he'd like to do after he leaves office."

"Okay, I promise, Smart Cookie," I said weakly. "Tell me how you decided."

There was a silence. At last, Sheila said, "We tossed for it."

"You tossed for it?" I repeated incredulously. "No. No way." Blackie and Sheila are the most rational people I know. The idea that they would submit their futures to the toss of a coin —

"Honest, China. That's what happened. We discussed the issue from all sides, but we couldn't come up with a logical way to decide. We figured the best thing to do was to flip for it. Heads he quit, tails I quit. It came up heads."

"I can't believe it."

"Believe it," Sheila said. "It's true." There

was a buzz of crowd noises in the background. "The commissioners are finished, China. Blackie's coming out. I have to go. Good night."

Shaking my head, I hung up the phone. Blackie Blackwell leaving office? That's something I would never in the world have predicted. Well, at least I knew one thing for sure. Hark would have a great headline for the next edition of the *Enterprise:* "County Sheriff Turns In Badge, Will Wed Pecan Springs Police Chief." Even without the coin toss, it was a great story.

But none of this took me any closer to a decision about Jessica. I put on the kettle and spooned some dried mint leaves into a tea ball. A cup of mint tea was what I needed. Might help me think a little more clearly.

While I was waiting for my tea to brew, I sat down and replayed Jessica's call, listening carefully.

"China, it's me. Jessica. Listen, I'm in trouble. Really, I mean it. I need help. I —"

Car trouble? Well, maybe. A boyfriend problem? I suppose, although it didn't quite sound like that. And why had the call been cut off? Jessica had been so determined to get her byline on the story. Surely she wouldn't let something minor get in the way of making her deadline.

I picked up the phone again and called Hark's cell. He answered on the third ring. His voice sounded blurry and I could hear music in the background, and the sharp crack of a pool cue. I tried to tell him about the phone call, but he wasn't listening. He was at Beans', he said. He had tried calling Jessica several times, both her cell and her home phone. He had even driven over to her house on Santa Fe, in the hills above the campus. She wasn't there.

"Place is locked up tight as a drum," he growled. "No lights in the house. No cars in the drive. No story, either. Next time you see that kid, you can tell her from me that she's fired." There was a clink and a rattle of glasses, and he shouted, "Hey, Bob — another round over here." To me, he said, "You got that, China? You see her, you tell her she's fired. F-I-R-D, fired." He cut off the call.

I rolled my eyes. Even good guys can occasionally have one beer too many.

I put the phone on the table and picked up my cup, frowning as I sipped my peppermint tea. I was beginning to get the idea that nobody cared about Jessica but me — and that made me feel . . . well, responsible, damn it. She was young and energetic and passionate and impulsive — a combination that had gotten me into trouble more times than I cared to remember. What if Jessica was in some kind of trouble right now?

I picked up a pencil and paper and tried to remember the conversation I'd had with her in the car. Where had she said she was going when she dropped me off after our lunch? After a few moments of frowning concentration, I came up with a list. She was going back to the burned-out trailer, where she planned to take a few more pictures. After that, she was going to stop at the auto parts place and talk to Scott Sheridan. Then the sheriff's office, to interview him and get a look at the crime scene photos. And then she wanted to talk to . . . who?

Oh, yes, the girl who used to live in the trailer. The one with a name like a B-movie actress. LaFarge. Lucy LaFarge, who had an apartment on North Brazos: 101 North Brazos, Jessica had said, which put it at the corner of Brazos and Matagorda.

I couldn't do anything about the situation tonight. But tomorrow was another day, and I now had a list of the stops Jessica had planned to make: the burned trailer, A-Plus Auto Parts, the sheriff's office, Lucy LaFarge. And then home.

And in addition to the list, I had a new determination. Looking for Jessica wasn't something I could turn over to the police. I needed to follow her trail — the trail she'd given me. I looked at the list and added one more item, off to one side, because I wasn't sure how it was connected. Terry Fletcher, who hadn't been seen since before the trailer fire. I put a question mark after her name. Was Terry involved with this, or was her absence just a coincidence? If she was connected, how? Could it have been Terry who burned to death, or Terry who —

My questions were interrupted by a small voice. "Have you asked him yet, Aunt China?"

I turned to see Caitie standing at the door to the kitchen. She was wearing her pink pajamas and her fuzzy pink slippers with the floppy rabbit ears and a black nose on each toe, a gift from McQuaid's mother.

"Who?" I replied blankly, still puzzling over my questions. "Asked him what?" The orange tabby cat pushed past her legs and came into the kitchen, and I remembered, guiltily.

"Oh. Okay. Let's call him right now, and you can ask him yourself." I picked up the cell phone again, and when McQuaid came on the line, I said, "Caitie's got a question for you, Uncle Mike, and then I have some breaking news. About Blackie."

Caitie reached for the phone. "We have a new kitty, Uncle Mike!"

It took her less than five minutes to negotiate the terms of Pumpkin's admission to the family (she had to feed him, clean his kitty litter tray, make sure he didn't snack on Brian's lizards, and so on). Meanwhile I located a can of Khat's food that hadn't found its way from our cupboard to the shop. I opened it and Pumpkin demonstrated that the saucer of milk had barely taken the edge off. He was hungry for the real thing, and lots of it, if you don't mind.

"So Pumpkin is a keeper?" I asked McQuaid, when Caitie handed me the phone, her eyes shining, her smile a joy to see. Carrying the phone, I went to the cookie jar and took out two for her. "Pour yourself a glass of milk, honey," I added, and she went to the fridge.

"I've already got a beer," McQuaid said with a chuckle. "But yeah, I'm okay with the cat if you're okay. What does Howard say? If I remember right, cats are on his do-not-call list."

"Howard votes yes," I said, "the dirty double-crosser." The cat had finished his cat food and was climbing, with purposeful deliberation, into Howard Cosell's basset basket beside the kitchen stove, where Howard was already curled up. "You'd never believe what I'm looking at," I added. "Howard just allowed the cat to get into his basket with him. Looks to me like they've adopted each other." Which was nice, I supposed. Now that Brian is growing up, Howard often seems lonely. Lizards are not very good company.

"Will wonders never cease," McQuaid said. "So what's Blackie's breaking news?"

"He turned in his resignation tonight. Effective at the end of his term. July."

McQuaid sucked in his breath. "He *what?*"

It took a few minutes to tell the story. When I got to the part about the coin toss, he whistled incredulously.

"I never would've believed it," he said. "Flipping a coin for his job? Blackie Blackwell? He actually did *that?*"

"Yep. Smart Cookie told me herself. But we're not supposed to tell anybody else how they decided." I paused and added significantly, "My guess is that he won't be retired long. You know Blackie. He can't stand having nothing to do."

Caitie finished her milk and gave me a hug. "Bedtime for you, sweetie," I said. "I'll be up to kiss you good night in a little bit."

She smiled and went toward the door. "Come on, Pumpkin."

Pumpkin, obviously aware that he owed his happy home to this girl-child in pink pajamas and rabbit ear slippers, jumped out of Howard's bed and pattered after her. Howard, not wanting to be left out, clambered to his feet and followed.

"You're right about Blackie needing something to do," McQuaid said thoughtfully. "I'm finished here, China. I'll be home tomorrow afternoon. Let's talk about it tomorrow night."

"You're wondering whether he might want to go into the P.I. business with you?" I asked.

"Yeah. What would you think about that?"

"If it works for you, it works for me," I said. In fact, it sounded to me like a good idea. McQuaid was still teaching, which meant that he had turned down a couple of cases. If he and Blackie teamed up, the firm could take on more work, in a wider range.

"Good. If you see him, tell him I'd like to talk to him."

"Sure thing." I hesitated, thinking again about Jessica and wondering how much I should tell him about her phone call. I decided against telling him anything, because I knew exactly what he would say. He would tell me (as he always did) to let somebody else handle it, and not get involved. And anyway, Smart Cookie was probably right. Jessica was having car trouble, or a boyfriend problem. Nothing to worry about. Probably.

But after McQuaid and I did our ritual kissy-over-the-phone thing and said good night, I called Ruby and asked her if she'd mind opening the shop for me in the morning.

"No problem," she said. "What's up?"

"It's Jessica Nelson," I said, and told her what had happened.

"Gosh," she breathed. "That sounds serious. Do you think she might really be in danger?"

"I don't know," I said honestly. "All I know is that if I don't try to check up on her and it turns out that something is wrong, I'm going to feel pretty awful."

"Do what you need to do," Ruby said in a comforting tone. "Cass and I will hold down the fort tomorrow."

I said a grateful, "Hey, thanks," and headed upstairs to kiss Caitie good night. I paused at the door of her room. She was already in bed, with Pumpkin curled up beside her and Howard sprawled across her feet.

And for the first time in recorded history, Howard didn't claim his half of my empty bed.

CHAPTER NINE
JESSICA

Jessie opened her eyes and tried to look around — without turning her head, which hurt abominably. But even if she could have moved, there wasn't anything to see. Wherever she was, it was absolutely pitch-black. Or maybe she couldn't see anything because she'd been cracked hard on the head with something pretty solid, and the blow had blinded her. That was a definite possibility, considering the thudding, pounding pain in her head, which seemed to worsen if she moved it even an inch.

In which case . . .

In which case she might as well close her eyes.

She did.

CHAPTER TEN

Two of the most powerful mood-altering plants — tobacco and marijuana — are smoked in order to achieve their effect. But while marijuana smoke is often considered by its users to be less harmful (and less addictive) than tobacco smoke, recent research suggests that smoke produced by both plants has serious long-term effects on the structure of lung cells.

Like tobacco, marijuana has been associated with chronic respiratory problems. Unlike tobacco, neither marijuana plant extracts nor THC (delta-9-tetrahydrocannabinol, the main psychoactive component of marijuana) have been definitively linked to lung cancer. The researchers found, however, that marijuana smoke was more likely to kill cells in the lungs, while tobacco smoke was more likely to cause mutations that can result in cancer.

China Bayles
"Mood-Altering Plants"
Pecan Springs Enterprise

I was up early the next morning, putting on khakis, a sleeveless red-and-brown-plaid blouse, tucked in, and leather sandals. While I was warming up breakfast tacos in the microwave and pouring orange juice and getting out bananas for Caitie and me, I made a call to Jessica's cell phone and another to her house, thinking — hoping, really — that she had showed up at home overnight.

But there was no answer on her cell phone and the answering machine picked up at her house. I followed up with a call to Hark, catching him in his car on his way to the Nueces Street Diner for breakfast. He sounded hungover. He hadn't heard from Jessica either, he growled, and asked why I was bothering him about it.

"Because I think somebody ought to be bothered about it," I said, nettled. "After all, she was on a story and —"

"Yeah, well, that somebody ain't her editor. I checked out her house, and that's all I'm going to do. Period. Paragraph. She's

220

fired. You find her, you tell her so. And damn it, China, I mean it."

Maybe Hark wasn't really one of the good guys after all. Then I thought of something. I had leverage.

"Trade you," I said.

A wary silence. "Trade me what. For what?"

"Trade you a breaking news story for Jessica's job."

"Breaking news?" Eager, not so wary. "What's up? Another trailer fire? We've got a serial arsonist?"

"Jessica's job," I reminded him. "Trade."

"Okay." He sighed heavily. "Trade. But it better be good."

"Sheriff Blackwell's not running again. He's hanging up his star at the end of this term."

"Damn!" It was the howl of a wounded editor. "Gene was supposed to be covering that meeting! He should've let me know!" He clicked off abruptly. I had not made his day. But I had saved Jessica's job. Maybe.

Caitie said she'd rather stay home to help Pumpkin get acquainted with his new place and practice her violin. That was okay with me, since McQuaid would be back in the early afternoon and Caitie wouldn't be alone all day. Also, Tom Banner, our up-the-lane neighbor, works from home and is usually around in case he's needed. But I thought again that living in the country might be difficult for a young girl, especially in the summer. All her friends lived in town. Would she be lonely? But she didn't seem to mind, especially now that she had Pumpkin, and I didn't push it.

I had told Ruby that I would be late getting in, so the shop was covered. My first stop, on my way into town, was the burned-out trailer. I drove up to what was left of the place, parked, and got out. I didn't know what I was looking for — evidence that Jessica had been here, maybe?

If so, I was disappointed. There was plenty to see, all of it ugly. The scarred hulk with its remains of burned furnishings. The blackened foliage of the trees in front and on the hillside where the firefighters had subdued the flames. The tire tracks left by the trucks and the drag marks of the hoses. The crime scene tape was gone, which suggested that the fire marshal's and the sheriff's investigations were concluded. There was no sign that Jessica Nelson had been here on Monday with her camera. And if something had happened to her here, there wasn't a trace. None, at least, that I could see.

I was about to get back in the car and be on my way when a battered black Dodge Ram pickup, the tires and door panels plastered with splashes of Texas mud, pulled up the drive and stopped beside my Toyota. There were four bales of hay and three dogs in the back of the truck, two blue heelers and a short-legged beagle, all barking their heads off. The driver — a young woman, tall, wearing jeans, a red Western shirt, scuffed cowboy boots, and a blond ponytail — got out and shushed them, then came around the truck.

"Hi," she said, putting out her hand. "I'm Becky Sanders. I live in the double-wide up the road a mile or so. The place with the blue roof and the dog kennels out back? Sanders' Animal Services." Her speech was fast and clipped, Yankee-style.

"Oh, sure," I said. "I'm China Bayles. I live a few miles past you." I had noticed the sign, which offered dog training, grooming, and baths. When I saw it, I wondered briefly if this was something Howard Cosell might like — the grooming and bath, that is, not the training. Howard is confident that he is already perfectly trained and knows everything a dog should know.

Becky looked at the charred wreckage, wrinkling her freckled nose at the smell of burned wood and wet carpet that still hung over the place. "I was driving by on Saturday night and saw the fire — the fire trucks and the ambulance, too. I didn't want to stop, though, with all the emergency vehicles around. Do you know what happened?"

"The police say it was arson," I replied.

"Arson?" She frowned. "The insurance, maybe? But that's pretty silly — not that much insurance money involved here, I would think."

"A woman was killed," I added. I thought it might be a good idea to leave out the details until the sheriff's office released them.

"Oh, good lord, no!" Her eyes widened in alarm. "It wouldn't be . . ." She corrected herself. "No, of course not. Not Lucy. She and Larry moved out several weeks ago. But there was somebody else living here? I didn't know the place had been rented again."

"It wasn't," I said. "It was supposed to be empty, according to the owner." I eyed her curiously. "So you knew the people who rented this place?"

She scuffed the dirt with the toe of her cowboy boot. "I didn't know Larry except to wave at — he was gone a lot. Classes and stuff like that. But I met Lucy one afternoon when I was out walking with the dogs." She waved her hand toward the hill. "There's a trail back there — I like it because I can let the dogs run. We got to talking, and after that, we got together sometimes. You know, we'd sit down and talk over coffee, here or at my place. She's a student at the university."

"Lucy LaFarge," I said helpfully.

"Yes, that's her. Lucy. You know her? She's okay? You're sure she's not the woman who . . ." She shivered, frowning. "Really? Somebody died here?"

"That's what I heard. But so far as I know, it wasn't Lucy." By this time, I was feeling more comfortable about telling this woman more of what I knew. "She was wearing a bracelet, engraved with the initials G.G. Does that ring a bell?"

"G.G.?" She squinted thoughtfully. "Sorry. Don't know anybody with those initials."

I nodded, and took it a little further. "My husband heard that the renters might've been doing drugs. Did you ever see any sign of it?"

She gave me a sideways glance. "Well . . . how come you're asking?"

"Oh, just out of curiosity, I guess." I

shrugged. "Not that I care. Maybe I'm just nosy."

"Yeah, that's me, too. Nosy. But not in a bad way. I just like to know what's going on in the neighborhood." She paused. "I never noticed that Lucy was actually stoned, but you could certainly smell pot when you went in the trailer. And she mentioned that Larry was doing some sort of research on plants." She grinned. "I figured maybe he was studying marijuana, with the idea of growing some. In fact, I kinda wondered if he was cultivating a pot plot back in the woods somewhere. People do, you know. But I didn't ask."

I returned her grin. "She probably wouldn't have told you, anyway. Did you ever notice anybody hanging around here? After Lucy and Larry moved out, I mean."

She tilted her head. "Well, I saw the A-Plus Auto Parts truck a couple of times. That's the guy who bought the place, Lucy told me. He was planning to do some repairs, plumbing and stuff like that. In fact, a week or so ago, when I saw the truck, I stopped and asked him when it was going to be for rent again. My sister is looking right now, and since this is pretty close to where I live, I was hoping the place would be available before the end of June. That's when Sybil has to move. I gave the guy my phone number and asked him to call me as soon as he was ready to rent. It would be great if Sis and I could be within walking distance." She looked around regretfully. "I guess that's not going to happen. Not after this."

"I'm afraid you're right," I said. "Aside from the auto parts truck, did you see anybody else?"

She tucked her hands into her jeans' pockets and thought about that for a moment. "You know, I did. But that was before I talked to the owner. I remember feeling disappointed, like maybe it had already been rented before I could find out for Sybil whether it was available."

"A car?" I asked. "A truck?"

"A red Mustang convertible. New, too. Parked over there, behind those trees." She nodded toward the far end of the trailer. "I probably wouldn't have noticed it unless I'd been kinda keeping my eye on the place. With Sybil in mind, I mean."

"A new Mustang convertible?" I chuckled. "Come on, now. Really?"

"That was my reaction, too." She grinned and her eyes glinted. "I kinda wondered, you know." She glanced around. "I mean, there's nothing wrong with living in a trailer, and this one was really pretty nice, before it got incinerated. Furnished and all, and the carpet and furniture was decent. But most people who drive new cars would probably live in a condo or something. I just thought it was curious."

"I do, too," I said. "You didn't stop to find out who it was?"

She shrugged. "None of my business. For all I know, it belonged to the new owner, or somebody who was helping him. Anyway, it was late one evening, almost dark." The dogs were barking again. "Listen, I've got to get going, Ms. Bayles. This guy is coming to talk about training a boxer. Nice to meet you." She looked at the trailer and shuddered. "Hate to think of somebody dying in there. It must've been just awful."

"Yes, awful," I said, and waved as she got into her truck, the dogs barking wildly now, happy to be back on the road.

A-Plus Auto Parts opened at eight. When I pulled into the parking lot, I saw that the front glass window was plastered with signs. An announcement of a gun show, notice of a rifle club meeting, decals of the Texas state flag and the U.S. flag, and a big red, white, and blue We Support Our Troops banner.

It was eight ten when I opened the door

and went in, but I was already third in line, behind two guys. One of them — a hulk the size of two Dallas Cowboys linebackers — wanted a fan belt for a '98 Honda Civic. (If the Civic belonged to him, how did he fit into it?) The hulk got what he asked for. The other guy didn't. He needed a radiator hose for a '95 Saab, but the man behind the counter told him he'd have to get it from the dealer. The customer was disappointed, and not a very good sport about it, either. He muttered something under his breath and slammed the door on his way out. The slam roused an elderly black Lab with a grizzled muzzle, snoozing peacefully under a display rack. He opened his eyes to check for issues he needed to confront. Seeing none, he closed them again and went back to sleep.

It was my turn and there was nobody standing in line behind me, for which I was grateful. Maybe I could find out what I needed to know without being rushed.

"Help you?" Scott Sheridan (the name on the embroidered badge over his pocket) was short and thickset, strands of black hair crisscrossing his bald scalp like carefully laid thatch. The hair might have migrated south from his head, for his Groucho Marx eyebrows were black and heavy, he sported a bottle-brush black moustache, and a mat of dark chest fur showed at the open collar of his work shirt.

I had my answer ready. "I'll take a can of that oil additive," I said, pointing to a rack of yellow and blue cans behind the counter. The sign on the rack promised that the stuff would clean my engine, which struck me as a good thing, generally. In a friendly tone, I lied, "My Toyota's running a little rough, and Mike McQuaid — he's my husband — suggested I get some of that stuff."

"Oh, yeah. Sure. Miz McQuaid. Nice to meetcha. Always a pleasure to do business with Mike. Nice that he's keepin' that old truck runnin'." He grinned as he rang up the sale. "Say, how's that alternator holding up? He have any trouble installin' it?"

"Not so far as I know." Alternators are a mystery to me, but this one must be working, since the truck was running. At least, I hoped it was running, for Donna's sake. She didn't need any more problems.

"Great. So what else can I get you today?"

"That's it, thanks." Sheridan dropped the can into a plastic bag, pushed it across the counter, and took my ten-dollar bill.

As he counted out the change, I said, in a casual tone, "I wonder — did Jessica Nelson from the *Enterprise* drop in to see you on

Monday afternoon?"

"The reporter?" He shut the cash drawer. "Yeah, she was here. Cute girl. Hark sure knows how to pick 'em." He leaned an elbow on the counter. "She was asking about my trailer. The one out on Limekiln Road. It burned last weekend. Maybe you saw it when you were driving into town this morning, huh?"

"Actually, I'm the one who turned in the alarm. I happened to be heading home on Saturday evening and saw it burning. I was standing in front of it when it exploded."

"No kidding." He squinted at me. "Jeez. So that's where you left your eyebrows."

"Yeah," I said ruefully. "Got a little scorched. But not as bad as the woman who was in there. She burned to death." I shuddered, remembering. "Did you know her?"

"Don't think so." He turned away to pick up a parts catalog and add it to a stack beside the register. "Nobody's told me who she was. Don't guess the cops have identified her yet. Hell of a thing," he added gloomily, shaking his head. "Hadn't had that place more'n sixty days, and now it's gone. Burned to the ground — nothing left to salvage, even."

"Insured, I guess," I said, taking the paper bag.

"Yeah, it was insured. Won't get near enough to replace it, of course. Now I gotta figure out what to do with that property. Maybe I'll see if I can find a cheap used trailer to turn into a rental. A repo, maybe." He put his head on one side. "Why're you asking about that reporter?"

Was there a suspicious edge to his question? "Because she was going to get in touch with me after she talked to you," I said. "She didn't turn in her story, and nobody's heard from her. Since I was going to stop here anyway this morning, I thought I'd ask. I believe she was trying to get a line on the people who were living there when you bought it?" I put a question mark at the end of my statement, suggesting that I wasn't too sure about any of this.

My tentativeness seemed to reassure him, and he relaxed a little. "Yeah. Well, she stopped in here twice." There were some business cards in a bowl by the cash register and he fished through them. "Here it is. Her card." He pulled it out and handed it to me. "Her number's on it, in case you don't have it," he added.

I took the card. "Twice, huh?"

He put the bowl back. "Yup. When she talked to me the first time, she was asking how long I'd had the trailer and who was renting it when I bought it, stuff like that. I gave her the girl's name, but I couldn't remember the guy. Told her I'd have to hunt it up. So she came by on Monday afternoon to see if I'd found it."

"And you did?"

"Yep. Larry Wolff. Two *f*s. I didn't get a forwarding address for either of the kids, the boy or the girl, though I guess maybe I should've." His grin was crooked. "Didn't figure I needed addresses. Didn't reckon anybody'd ever ask. The cops didn't."

"The police asked you about the trailer?"

He straightened up. "Yeah, sure. But not about the renters."

That struck me as a bit sloppy on the part of the investigators, since it might've been a good idea to check out anybody who had recently been involved with that place. But I didn't say anything, and Sheridan was going on.

"Deputy just told me it looked like arson and wanted to know if it was rented when it burned, and if it was, who was living there. I said the place was empty, so whoever it was got burned up in there, wasn't somebody I'd rented to. Fact was, I was gonna rent right away as soon as I got the kids out. But after they was gone, I found a plumbin' problem. Figured I'd get it fixed and do a few other repairs while the place was still empty." He frowned. "Guess that turned out to be a good thing, huh? Might've been my renter in there when it burned. That would've been really bad. Might've got my ass sued."

I could see his point, although it seemed to me that it was pretty bad as it was, at least for the person who had died. "Was she a student?" I asked, remembering what Bob Godwin had said.

"Somebody at Beans' said maybe she was," he replied vaguely, "but you couldn't prove it by me."

I nodded, thinking that there probably wasn't any way to track down that bit of information — or misinformation. Could've been somebody speculating. "My husband mentioned that you evicted the former renters."

"I sure did," he said emphatically. "Dopers, both of 'em. I've got a couple more rental properties, y'know, students mostly, and I don't stand for that kind of shit. I make it clear up front. You wanna use, you can live someplace else."

"I don't blame you," I said. "How did you figure out what the renters were up to?"

"How?" He snorted. "How'd you think? I could smell the stuff. Pot, and lots of it.

High-grade, too, from the smell of it." He paused, casting his eyes upward in a gesture of humility. "I ain't no saint, mind you. Done my share of foolin' around. I just don't aim to have it happenin' on my property, that's all."

"Just pot?" I persisted. "No needles or anything like that?" I was trying to get a fix on what kind of dope they were doing. If what had happened in that trailer was a drug deal gone wrong, it might be useful to know what might've been involved.

"Well, yeah. I didn't happen to notice, but the deputy said they found some stuff like that. Which made me glad I'd kicked 'em out." He frowned defensively. "I was perfectly within my rights. They didn't have no lease."

I nodded. "I suppose you changed the locks after you evicted them?"

He looked chagrined. "Guess I should've done that, too, but I didn't think it was necessary. They was students. I figgered they'd be gone — and anyway, the place was empty, except for furniture and appliances. I didn't think they'd come back and steal that. I was meanin' to rekey it after I fixed it up. Makes people feel better, hand 'em a new set of keys." He eyed me. "I told all this to that reporter girl, and she wrote it down in that skinny little notebook of hers. You say you're lookin' for her?"

I nodded. "She was going to interview me again for her story. Human-interest angle, you know. I haven't heard from her."

"Yeah, well, she was here, all right." He turned to a pot keeping warm on a hot plate, picked it up, and poured coffee into a crockery mug. "If you don't mind me sayin' so, Miz McQuaid, I'm glad it was you that came along and saw the place burnin', rather'n me. The deputy said that woman was still alive in there when you showed up."

I shuddered, the image suddenly clear in my mind again. "Yes, she was," I said softly. "I wish I could've helped her." The door opened and another customer came in. "Oh, by the way — I was wondering. Do you drive a Mustang convertible? A red one? New?"

He hooted a laugh. "Do I look like the type to own a Mustang convertible?" he asked sarcastically. "I got me an F-150. Why're you askin'?"

"Because one of the neighbors noticed it parked at the trailer recently," I said. "Just thought I'd mention it."

"Not mine. No idea whose, neither." He put his mug on the counter and looked over my shoulder, raising his voice. "Mornin', sir. Can I help you?"

Out in the lot, I dropped the bag with the additive behind the seat, saying a little apology to my car for bad-mouthing its engine and another for lying. But I had learned a couple of things that might turn out to be useful, including the name of the other person who had previously rented the trailer. Larry Wolff. Wolff with two *f*s. I made a note of the name on the same piece of paper on which I'd written Lucy LaFarge's name and address. I thought briefly about Scott Sheridan. He'd seemed a little edgy when I asked about Jessica, but maybe that was my imagination. He'd certainly been forthcoming enough with the other information.

And whoever the new red Mustang convertible belonged to, it wasn't Sheridan's — or at least, so he said. So who had been there? Why?

I put the key in the ignition and started the car. The sheriff's office wasn't far away. It was my next stop.

CHAPTER ELEVEN
JESSICA

It could've been a moment later when Jessica opened her eyes again, it could have been an hour, it could have been a day. She thought it must have been a pretty long time, though, because she was terribly thirsty. Her mouth was dry as cotton and her tongue felt as if it were swollen. It was hard to tell, though, because her mouth was taped shut, so tight it hurt. And there was no way to tell time because there was nothing but blackness around her, except for a faint smudge of light, somewhere off to the right, over her shoulder. She couldn't see where it was coming from, exactly. But her head hurt less, and when she risked turning it slightly toward the light, the pain wasn't any worse than it was when she held it still.

Her head was the only thing she could move, though. Her ankles were tied and her hands were bound behind her, so tightly that she couldn't feel her fingers. She was lying on her right side, her right shoulder under her, her trunk twisted and knees bent, her cheek pressed against what felt like a cement floor. Around her there was nothing but dark, heavy and smothery, with that faint smudge of light somewhere out of her range of vision, high up.

But if she couldn't see, she could smell, and as she pulled in a shuddery breath, she recognized the smell, and images flashed through her mind. The fruit cellar under her grandmother's old frame house in Louisiana, which had one of those slanting wooden doors, where she and Ginger had slid down like it was a sliding board and got splinters in their butts. To get to the cellar, you had to lift up the heavy door and go down the wooden steps that led into the shivery dark, where there were snakes and spiders and creepy things that Ginger loved to scare her with. The floor was cement, always damp and cold and smelly, and the concrete block walls were lined with boards stacked on bricks for shelves, loaded with rows of canned peaches and tomatoes and green beans. And one lightbulb hanging from the ceiling, turned on by a string pull, and one wall was bare, scraped earth. Damp earth, underground.

At the thought, Jessie's stomach muscles

clenched and she was convulsed by a shudder of fear that ran through her entire body. Underground. Underground! She was in a hole somewhere, alone in the dark, with her hands and feet tied. She struggled against her bindings, seized by a sudden panic as sharp as a lancing pain that froze her breath and numbed her brain. But she at least had the sense not to cry out, because if she did, *he* might come — the man who had put her here — and do whatever else he was planning to do with her.

He — who? Jessica stopped struggling. Who was *he?* Why couldn't she remember? She concentrated, trying to recall the exact moment when the man — she was sure it was a man, wasn't she? — had slammed something hard against her head and she'd gone down into the dark.

But she couldn't bring it back. Her brain was filled with a dense gray fog that obscured the past, and all she could think of was what might happen next. What was he going to do? Was he going to shoot her? Or torch the place and let her burn to death, like the victim in the trailer, like Ginger and her mom and dad, like the girl in her fiery nightmares?

The image, lit with flames, made her shudder almost uncontrollably, and she squeezed her eyes shut and waited until the shivering had mostly passed and she could think again. Or maybe he didn't mean to kill her outright. Maybe he'd just go away and *leave* her here, so he wouldn't have to risk a gunshot or attract attention with a fire. If he left her here long enough, she would starve to death. No, she wouldn't starve, she would die of dehydration, wouldn't she? When had she last had anything to drink? How long could a person live without water? In earthquakes, didn't they find people who had been buried for four or five days without water, longer than that, even? But not everybody, of course. A lot of people died.

She lay very still and tried to breathe slowly. There weren't any answers to those questions. Letting herself go there — letting herself imagine how he planned to kill her — would just send her into a panic, and panic would keep her from thinking. The best thing was to try not to feel, try not to be afraid. To numb herself in the same way she'd numbed herself after her family's death. Stop feeling. Feeling hurts. Turn off the feeling, turn off the pain, anesthetize herself. Breathe deep, just breathe, the way her yoga teacher said. Breathe in, breathe out, listen to her breath, focus on her breath.

After a few moments, she was calmer. She opened her eyes again, willing herself not to feel, not to be afraid. But she could think, could at least try to grope through the dense gray fog of confusion in her head. Could try to remember what had happened.

She took another breath, slow and steady. Okay, think. Remember. Start with this morning. But which morning was that? She didn't know what time it was now, or even what day it was. Well, then, go back to the last morning she could remember. Which was . . . which was . . .

Tuesday morning? She wasn't sure. Maybe it would be better to start with Monday. Ordinary Monday. She had gone to Thyme and Seasons, but China had forgotten about making lunch, so they'd driven over to Beans', where China told her that the girl had been burned alive, like Ginger, like her mom and dad, which she hadn't known until that very moment. Until then, it had been just a story, but when China had told her about the girl's screams, it had suddenly become real. It had become her nightmare.

Her stomach clenched, and she made herself leave that moment and go on. She had left China at the shop and then she drove to the trailer to take some photos, then —

The trailer. Where did she go after she'd left the trailer? Her head was hurting worse, but she took another deep breath, forcing herself to remember. The auto parts place. Yes, that was it. She'd talked to the owner again, Scott somebody, and he'd given her the name of the other renter. The guy, with the name that ended in two ƒs, which she couldn't think of at the moment. After that, where?

Oh, yes, to the sheriff's office, where she'd seen the crime scene photos — oh, God, those awful, unspeakable pictures, which made her want to throw up. She hadn't seen her family's bodies after the fire. Had they looked like that? She'd seen the bracelet with the initials, and she'd written them down in her notebook. She remembered wondering whether she should tell the sheriff about the guy, the other renter, and the girl, Lucy LaFarge, but decided not to. That was part of her exclusive human-interest story. Anyway, that stuff was before. Before the girl died. It had nothing to do with her death. It wasn't connected to the sheriff's investigation.

At the thought of the girl, and the gruesome photos she had seen on the computer, she began to shake again. The girl who had burned to death, all alone in that trailer, screaming for help. And suddenly she was swept by a grief so breathtakingly heavy and compelling that it seemed to press down on her chest like a physical force, and she gave in to the rush of hot tears.

Was she crying for her family? Was she mourning the girl? Was she mourning herself, still alive, still breathing, but maybe not for long? Was she mourning all of them, all the sad, forgotten dead? She didn't know. All she knew was that it was the first time she had cried since she'd made herself stop crying all those years before.

But she couldn't make herself stop now, so she cried until the pain in her head became so brutal that she couldn't cry any longer, and she fell into an exhausted sleep that was lit by the fires of nightmare.

CHAPTER TWELVE

You're probably not growing a kola nut tree in your garden, but its primary active chemicals, caffeine and theobromine (the chemical in cocoa), are likely to be an important part of your day. The kola nut (*Cola spp.*) is a genus of about 125 species of trees native to the tropical rain forests of Africa. For tens of centuries, kola nuts have been used by humans as a stimulant, a euphoric, and a medicinal, in the treatment of respiratory ailments, headaches, poor digestion, and depression. In many West African cultures the seeds are chewed, individually or in a social or ritual group, and are often ceremonially presented to tribal chiefs or guests.

In the West, kola nuts are best known as a flavoring and as the source of caffeine in Coca-Cola. In Dr. John Pemberton's original 1886 Coca-Cola formula, the two key ingredients were caffeine (from kola nuts) and cocaine (from fresh coca leaves). After the Pure Food and Drug Act was passed in 1906, the company began using decocainized leaves.

China Bayles
"Mood-Altering Plants"
Pecan Springs Enterprise

Until a few years ago, the Adams County Sheriff's Department was housed in a nineteenth-century building on one corner of the courthouse square. The old place had its problems, to be sure: small rooms, gloomy halls, antique restrooms, limited parking, even bats in the belfry — Mexican free-tailed bats whose guano created a terrific stink that made the tourists complain. But it also boasted beautifully polished wooden floors, dark oak woodwork, and tall windows with stained glass panels at the top and a view of the courthouse kitty-cornered across the street. It was a genteel place, built in a time when life was lived at a mannerly pace. When you came into the office, it was like stepping back into the old, slow days. People smiled at you. They knew your name and they said hello. They were friendly.

There's nothing friendly about the new

building on the outskirts of town. It's a two-story gray concrete bunker with few exterior windows, built to withstand almost any imaginable twenty-first-century assault — a terrorist's car bomb rammed through the front door, maybe, or a Stinger missile attack by unfriendly agents from a neighboring county. You have to show your driver's license to the grim-faced guard at the door, and once he's let you inside, you might wish he'd told you to go away. It's not a comfortable place. The hallways and rooms all have the same gray-white walls, gray tile floors, gray steel desks, gray filing cabinets, everything washed in the chilly, featureless glare of fluorescent lighting.

I flashed my driver's license at the guard and waited while he noted my name and TDL number in his big black book and gave me a Visitors badge, so I wouldn't be shot on sight. Classified and properly tagged, I made my way to Blackie's office at the far end of the corridor, passing staff offices as I went. All the people I saw were wearing dour expressions and several of them had their heads together, whispering. I guessed that they had heard the shocking news. Sheriff Blackwell was hanging up his star. It was the end of three generations of Blackwell law enforcement in Adams County, the end of an era. It was also the beginning of a political storm, and they didn't like the idea one bit.

The sheriff's door was open and I rapped with my knuckles on the jamb. He looked up from a pile of papers, a Coke can at his elbow. There was no computer on his desk. Blackie uses one when he has to, but he says he doesn't want to be chained to it.

"Mornin', China," he drawled, and leaned back in his chair. "Sheila get you fixed up last night?"

"No, but she straightened me out," I said. Before he could speak, I added, "Sheila told me, Blackie. About your quitting." I raised both eyebrows. "Imagine my surprise."

"I'll bet," he said dryly. "You're not the only one who's surprised."

"I'm sure. Anyway, I passed the word along to McQuaid on the phone last night. He'll be back today. He said he wanted to talk to you, when you have some time."

"Yeah, sure." He ran a hand through his buzz cut, looking rueful. "I told the folks here this morning. Hard to do. Really hard."

"I'll bet," I said sympathetically. Blackie has always been completely dedicated to his job and to his staff, and the people he works with know it. Leaving must feel like he's letting them down — and letting them in for months of the crazy political chaos that can happen only in Texas, with candidates tossing their Stetsons into the ring and dancing their two-party fandangos. It won't be a pretty sight.

He threw his pencil down on the desk. "The thing is, Sheila and I know we'd never make it work if both of us stayed in this business. So . . ." He lifted his shoulders and let them fall.

"So you had to make a choice. Either you quit, or she quits."

"Yeah. That was pretty much it."

I grinned. "I ain't never gonna tell how you two decided which was which, Blackie. But personally, I think flipping a coin is pretty cool. Fair, too."

"Only rational way to do it," he said, answering my grin. "So what can I do for you this morning, China?"

"You can let me see the crime scene photos that you showed to the intern from the newspaper on Monday. And tell me about your interview with her."

He tilted his head, his eyes curious. "Oh, yeah? Why?"

"Because nobody knows where she is. I wondered if there was something in those photos or the interview that might have . . ." I shrugged, not wanting to finish the sentence. "I guess maybe I'm clutching at straws. Did Sheila tell you why I called you last night?"

"Yeah. There was a phone call on your answering machine. Got you worried. The girl still hasn't turned up?"

"No. Her roommate's out of town. Hark went by her house and it was locked up tight. I phoned there again this morning and got no answer — no answer on her cell, either."

"And you think this has something to do with this arson-homicide?"

"Your guess is as good as mine. All I know is that nobody's heard from her. Okay if I see the photos?"

He gave me a dubious squint. "You sure you want to?"

"No. But I figure if anybody has the right to see them, I do. I was the one who made the 9-1-1 call. I have the scorched eyebrows to prove it."

"Yeah. But these photos are . . ." He broke off and pushed his chair back. "Well, come on, then. Down the hall."

The computer was on a table in a small library. He pulled out a chair for me, booted the machine, and brought up a photo of the victim in gruesome color. "I told you so," he said softly, and stepped back.

Until now, the dead woman had been only a compelling voice, an awful idea. But the photograph gave her an inescapable reality, although the body was so grotesquely burned that I couldn't have told that it was a woman. The charred corpse lay on a charred sofa in the rubble of a charred room, hands and feet bound, writhing in the throes of an awful death. I looked, looked away, and looked back, forcing myself to confront the almost incomprehensible fact of her pain.

"There's more," Blackie said. "Click on the arrow at the bottom."

I clicked through a series of two dozen photographs of the victim and more of the blistered area around the trailer, most of the photos taken at the eastern end and around back, where the accelerant had apparently been applied. By the time I'd looked at all of them, I was feeling sick.

"Ugly," Blackie said flatly. "That was the reporter's word for it. Ugly."

"Yes," I said. I'd seen dead bodies before and I had been there when this happened. I had been at least halfway prepared for the awfulness, but still it was hard. It must have been harder still for Jessica, whose sister and parents had died by fire.

I navigated back to the photo of the area

where the accelerant had been applied and studied it for a minute. "What did the arsonist use?"

"Coleman camp stove fuel, we think. We found three empty gallon cans not far from the trailer." He clicked the mouse a couple of times and an image of three cans came up on the screen.

"Camp stove fuel," I exclaimed. "That's what I thought I smelled, Blackie, the night of the fire! I think I told the dispatcher. You can probably hear that on the 9-1-1 tape." I frowned. "Three cans? That would be an unusual purchase, wouldn't it? I mean, three gallons would keep a Boy Scout camp in business all year. Somebody might remember selling that much."

"Yeah, but the brand is commonly available. Walmart, Academy, sporting goods stores. Probably not all bought at the same place or the same time, either. A gallon here, a gallon there. We're checking, but I'm not betting on turning up a lead."

"Fingerprints on the cans?"

"Several, smudged, nothing usable." He pointed to a burned patch of ground in the photo. "The arsonist piled up some trash and branches next to the trailer skirting, right here. Then doused the whole place with it and hauled ass. Must've finished up just before you got there. Took a risk of being seen. The place isn't that far off the road."

"But there's not that much traffic out that way," I said. "And the fire could've smoldered for a while, until it got going good." I clicked forward a couple of photos to a print of a shoe, fairly sharp. "Where'd this come from?"

"The area where the accelerant was applied. Looks like the arsonist spilled some, softening the ground, then stepped in it. Lucky for us. Unlucky, though, because while this square-and-diamond pattern is unique to the brand — Converse — the brand is ubiquitous. The shoes have been sold for decades, every shoe with the same pattern. This one looks like a size ten."

"A man," I said thoughtfully. "Or a woman with big feet." I leaned forward, studying the photo. "Did you see this?" I pointed to a barely visible scar that slashed diagonally across the four bars in the heel pattern.

"Yeah. Here's another view." He clicked again, and the scar was magnified several times. "The slash is about an eighth of an inch deep. Looks like the wearer stepped on a blade of some sort." He clicked again, to a higher magnification. "It happened a while ago, too. The edges are worn. See here?" He took a pencil out of his pocket and pointed. "And here."

"I see." I looked up at him. "What kinds of questions did Jessica ask you?"

"The standard stuff. Identification of the victim, leads we're following, that kind of thing. I gave her what we'd already released, more or less, and a couple of quotes. She made some notes and asked to take a photo of me for her story, to which I said no. She said Hark would probably run her article with the photos she'd taken at the scene. And that was that."

I hadn't expected much, so I wasn't disappointed. "Anything new on the victim's identification?"

He shook his head. "Not yet. Did Donna Fletcher tell you that she brought in her sister's hairbrush for a possible match?" When I nodded, he said, "The DNA will take a while, and the dental's lost somewhere in the prison system. I didn't mention that to the reporter. So keep it close, please."

"How about the gun?" At his inquiring look, I added, "I heard about that from Donna, too. Small-caliber handgun, she said."

He nodded. "There's nothing new on the gun, but the coroner recovered the bullet from the victim's body."

"Donna also said she was shown a bracelet with initials on it. G.G.?"

"Right." He clicked to another enlargement, the engraved letters faintly visible through a sooty black film. "Of course, there's no way of knowing whether the initials are the victim's. Here's the bracelet. Those initials mean anything to you?"

"No, sorry," I said regretfully.

"Well, then, that's the lot. That's all we've got." He bent over and logged out.

"Thanks." I got up from the chair. "Oh, there is something," I said. "I stopped at the trailer earlier this morning to have a look around. While I was there, somebody else stopped. A neighbor, Becky Sanders. She mentioned that she noticed a red Mustang convertible — new — parked at one end of the trailer sometime recently, behind the trees."

"Oh, yeah?" Blackie frowned. "Sanders? I sent a deputy out there to canvass the neighborhood, but I didn't see that name in his report."

"She lives about a mile up the road. Sanders' Animal Services. It might be worthwhile sending somebody back out there to talk to her. Turns out that she was keeping an eye on the trailer because she was thinking her sister might want to rent it. She said she even talked to Scott Sheridan about its availability. Anyway, she noticed the Mustang because it looked out of place. She might come up with a few more details when she's had some time to think about it."

His frown had deepened. Blackie does not like it when his deputies screw up. The guy — or gal — he had assigned to talk to the neighbors had missed Sanders' Animal Services and would hear about it. Shortly.

"Thanks. I'll get on it this morning." He paused. "This reporter, Jessica Nelson — you think something serious has happened to her?"

"I wish I knew, Blackie. Sheila suggested car trouble or a boyfriend problem. I suppose that's possible, but I somehow don't think so. Jessica was really hyped about this story — in fact, a little too hyped, it seemed to me. She wants her own byline, and she wants to do a good job, but it goes deeper than that. She's not just covering the trailer fire, she's involved in it."

"Involved?"

"Her twin sister and her parents died in a house fire ten years ago this month. This story has taken on some sort of symbolic significance for her. She wants to find out all she can about the victim. She wants to understand the killer's motives."

"Oh, hell," Blackie said eloquently.

"She had a plan for interviews, for writing the story, but she didn't make her deadline. And there was that phone call on my answering machine."

"And you're thinking her disappearance might be connected to the trailer fire?" He was taking me seriously now.

"It's possible. I'm going to check out her house, and then I have one more person to talk to — somebody I know she intended to see." I shrugged. "After that, I guess I'll file a missing-person report."

"Well, keep in touch." He opened the door for me and we left the room.

"You bet." We walked back down the hall to his office, past open doors where people were working. One or two of them glanced up, then away. Nobody looked very happy. "Are you going to miss this?" I asked, gesturing.

"Some of it," he said. We were passing a vending machine and he stopped to fish in his pockets for change. "Not the paperwork, that's for sure. And dickering with the commissioners over the budget — I won't miss that. I'll damn sure miss the people, though." He fed quarters into the machine, punched a button, and waited for the can to rattle down the slot. "The county's come a long way from the days when my mother used to cook meals for the jail inmates. But the department still runs on people. Whoever gets this job next is going to inherit a great bunch of folks."

"Any idea who that's going to be?" It wasn't an idle question. In rural areas, we depend on the county mounties. I'd hate to see Blackie's job fall into purely political hands — somebody with friends in high places but little law enforcement experience. And that could happen.

He popped the top of the can. "I've got some ideas — not sure I want to think about it, though, since there's not a helluva lot I can do to affect the outcome."

"You might be surprised. Plenty of folks respect your opinion. Isn't there anybody you'd like to see get the job?"

"Not hardly." His grin was tight. "Anyway, I just announced last night. The names won't start popping up for a couple more days, I reckon." He gave me a sideways glance. "So what does McQuaid want to talk to me about?"

"What do you think?" I countered archly.

He regarded me, head to one side. "You'd be okay with that? If McQuaid and I went into business together?" He paused. "Sheila and I have talked about it some. With both of us in enforcement, the big problem is the hours. McQuaid's business looks pretty flexible, far as the time commitment is concerned." He grinned briefly. "And nobody's shot at him yet, so far as I've heard."

"I'd be okay with it," I said, and stood on my tiptoes to give him a kiss on the cheek. "Whatever you guys can work out is great with me. I'm just glad that you and Smart Cookie were able to come to terms. Better marry the girl quick — before she changes her mind again."

"Yeah," he said. "My thoughts exactly." He lifted his soda can in salute. "I'm optimistic, though. She's wearing that ring, and we've even got an appointment with a photographer for an engagement photo."

But as I went out to the car, I couldn't help wondering. Blackie had been in law enforcement his whole life. Being the sheriff of Adams County was his reason for being. It created a structure for his daily activities, gave him a reason for getting up in the morning.

I had to wonder how he was going to manage without it, especially when Sheila was the one who was bringing home all the latest law enforcement news.

I sighed. Maybe there wasn't a lot of room for optimism, after all.

CHAPTER THIRTEEN

The Christmas vine, *Turbina corymbosa* or *Rivea corymbosa,* is a species of morning glory that grows wild from Mexico to Peru. It is a perennial climbing vine with white flowers, often grown as an ornamental. Its flowers produce a great deal of nectar, and the honey the bees make from it is clear and aromatic. Known to natives of Mexico as ololiuqui, its seeds have been used ritually as a psychoactive drug. In 1960, Dr. Albert Hofmann (the creator of LSD, d-lysergic acid diethylamide) described the chemical component of the seeds as ergine (LSA, d-lysergic acid amide), an alkaloid similar in structure to the LSD that came into use during the counterculture decade.

China Bayles
"Mood-Altering Plants"
Pecan Springs Enterprise

Back in the car, I picked up my list and checked off "Get a look at the crime scene photos and talk to Blackie." I paused for a moment, thinking. What had I learned? That the accelerant the arsonist used was naptha — Coleman camp stove fuel — and that he or she was wearing size ten Converse shoes with a slash across the heel tread. And that the bullet had been recovered from the victim's body. It wasn't much, but it was something. With luck, the cops might find the gun and match it to the bullet.

I looked down at the list again. Jessica's house was next, on Santa Fe Street, and after that, Lucy LaFarge, who lived not far away, on the north side of the campus. I started the car and drove off.

Santa Fe is a street of frame and stucco houses, most of them built in the 1950s and early '60s, when Pecan Springs was creeping up onto the hills and away from the flat-land development along the highway between Austin and San Antonio. It wasn't yet an Interstate in those days, but it was already beginning to spawn real estate developments and strip centers along its route. This is the kind of neighborhood I like, with shaded streets and wide yards and modest houses that fit comfortably into the landscape, rather than towering over it, like

262

baronial castles. A neighborhood of kids and bikes and vegetable gardens in the front yard and clotheslines and swings in the back.

The address I'd gotten from Hark's Rolodex was at the end of the street, with another small house on one side and a dense cedar brake on the other. Across the street, more cedars and a large clump of live oaks. For a city neighborhood, this had a country feel.

I turned around at the end of the street, pulled up at the curb, and got out. There were no other vehicles at this end of the street, except for a mean-looking red Harley chained to the porch rail of the house next to Jessica's. I thought of what she'd said about the neighbor being a jerk and wondered if it was that motorcycle that had bothered her.

As I was thinking this, the front door opened and a man came out, a heavyset, long-haired guy wearing boots, black jeans, and a blue work shirt with the sleeves cut off at the shoulders, showing off muscular, hairy arms, heavily tattooed. He looked like one of those wrestlers you see on TV. He slammed the door behind him, locked it, then stood on the porch for a moment, staring at me.

"What'd'ya want?" he demanded.

"I'm looking for Jessica Nelson. Any idea where I can find her?"

"Nah." He turned away with a sly, half-furtive sideways glance. "Ain't seen her in a week." He bent over to unlock his bike. "Both of 'em gone. Ain't nobody home."

A week? But on Monday, when Jessica was telling me about this jerk, she'd started to say something about "last night," as if she'd had a recent run-in with him.

"You're sure you haven't seen her in a full week?" I asked. "What about Sunday night? She said —"

"Buzz off, sister," he said contemptuously. "I ain't got time. Gotta get to work."

He was ignoring me now, muscling the Harley down the porch steps, kicking it into raucous life, then roaring off with an earsplitting bellow. He jumped the four-inch concrete curb in a show of Evel Knievel bravado and stood on the pegs as he rode down the street. I stared after him, thinking that the word *jerk* didn't exactly do justice to this particular jerk. He definitely wasn't somebody I'd like to have for a next-door neighbor.

But he was gone, and I focused my attention on what I had come for. I checked the front door, which was securely locked, and rapped and called until I was sure that if someone was home, she wasn't going to answer. Then I made a quick tour around the perimeter, checking the windows and noticing that the blinds were all drawn tightly, as if to keep out prying eyes. The back door was locked, too, but there was no blind and I could see into a small kitchen. It was empty and tidy, with a tea towel draped across a rack, a geranium on the kitchen windowsill, a pair of copper-bottomed pans hung over the stove. I repeated my knocking and calling, but the place had a hollow sound and nobody answered.

I turned and looked out across the backyard. There was a white-painted lawn swing under a large cedar elm, and a narrow border of zinnias and marigolds blooming bravely against the ratty-looking hedge that grew between Jessica's house and the jerk's backyard. In a small, square vegetable garden set into the grassy turf, carrots, green beans, and peas were flourishing. A pair of cardinals, male and female, were sharing a splashy bath in a birdbath beside a pink-blooming rosebush. A lovely, peaceful scene.

I went to the hedge and peered over. The jerk's place looked like a wrecking yard, with shoals of beer cans, mounds of rusted vehicle parts, an abandoned camper top, a pile of used tires, and a heap of junky detritus piled up against a small, tin-roofed shed. The house was of the same design and vintage as the one Jessica lived in, but not nearly as well kept up. The screens were torn or missing, the door to the fruit cellar under the house was boarded up, and the back door looked as if it had been kicked in once or twice. The house could do with a fresh coat of paint, too.

But now that the jerk had driven off, the neighborhood was very quiet, only the warbling, melodic chatter of a talkative mockingbird breaking the silence. I turned and contemplated Jessica's back door for a moment, weighing possibilities and options, then went up the steps. Criminal trespass in a habitation is a Class A misdemeanor in Texas, punishable by as much as a year in the county hoosegow and a fine of up to four thousand dollars in cold, hard cash — probably a fair price to pay for breaking into somebody's house and getting caught at it.

But I could argue that I had reason to believe that one of the occupants might be in that house, sick, injured, or worse. It was a standard defense against trespass, but in this case it would probably work, since I had explicitly stated my concern to the chief of police, the county sheriff, and the editor of the local newspaper. My worry was on the record, which would definitely count for something.

The back door was securely locked, but the window beside it wasn't. *Naughty-naughty,* I thought as I raised the old-fashioned wooden sash and climbed into the kitchen. Naughty of me to come in this way, naughty of Jessica and her roommate to make it so easy. Good thing I wasn't a burglar or a rapist or somebody equally nasty.

The house was small, and a couple of minutes inside were enough for me to see all there was to see. Kitchen, living-dining, one bath, two bedrooms. One bed neatly made, the other not. The neatly made bed was in what I assumed was Jessica's bedroom, judging from the books (agriculture and journalism texts) on the bookshelves. I was surprised to feel the relief that flooded through me — I must've been expecting to find a battered body or an ugly bloodstain on the floor. I hadn't. Whatever had happened to Jessica, it didn't look as if it had happened here.

There was an answering machine on the kitchen counter, and the message light was blinking. Being thorough, I checked it. The first message was from Jessica's roommate.

"Hey, Jessie, it's me, Amanda. Just to let you know that Steve and I are staying an extra few days. Weather's good, sex is better." A giggle. "Listen, I've lost my cell phone. If you need me, here's Steve's number." She rattled it off. "Hope you're having a good time all by yourself."

I jotted down Steve's cell number, although there was nothing in the call that would help me track down Jessica, and checked the time stamp on the message. It had been left on Monday at 2 p.m. and was still a "new" message, which meant that Jessica hadn't picked it up. Which suggested that she hadn't come back here on Monday. Whatever had happened to her happened before she got home. I thought of the jerk next door. Or before she'd had a chance to listen to her messages.

The second call, Monday at 5 p.m., was more intriguing. A male voice, thin, strained. "I just don't get why you're avoiding me, Jessie. You know I'd never hurt you, not for the world, and we both know it's over. We ought to try to get some closure. We'll feel better if we do. I will, anyway. Trust me, you will, too. Let's get together. Real soon." The last two words seemed almost ominous, as if they held a threat.

My skin was prickling. The voice was familiar, but I couldn't quite place it. I played the message again. Same prickle, same puzzle. I knew this man — who was he? It sounded as if he was pleading for a final meeting to tie up the ends of a broken relationship. And then I happened to glance at the little screen on the phone. A number appeared there — the caller's phone number, a local number. I copied it down, and went on with the playback. There were several hang-up calls — Hark, maybe? — and a third message from me, this morning. That was it. I looked around, thinking that there was nothing more to be learned here. I locked the kitchen window and was preparing to go out the ordinary way, through the back door, when the phone rang.

One, twice, three times. I hesitated, waiting for the answering machine to pick up. Jessica, maybe? Calling to see if Amanda had come home?

Jessica's voice gave the usual "leave a number" instruction and a bright female voice chirped, "Hey, Jessica, it's Zoe Morris. You know that girl we were talking about when you stopped by the Hort Center on Monday? The one Larry Wolff gave the key to? Well, I found out her last name — Graham — and her address. She lives in Hill Country Villa, Unit 1, Apartment 204." She gave the street address, then repeated it more slowly, and said good-bye.

File it under "Small World," I thought. As it happens, I know Zoe Morris. She had worked for Donna at Mistletoe Farm the previous summer and had become an occasional customer at the shop. I wasn't sure what her phone message had to do with anything, but I went to the machine and replayed it, copying the information on a scrap of paper. Hill Country Villa was a new, exclusive apartment complex on Sam Houston Drive, on the east side of campus, an upscale place for young singles with plenty of money. If Jessica was looking for a new apartment, the Villa didn't seem like the kind of place she could afford.

I let myself out, locking the door behind me, and went to the car, where I sat for a few moments, staring at the house next door and wondering if the Harley jerk whose property looked like a wrecking yard had anything to do with Jessica's disappearance. After a few moments, I pulled my attention away. I wasn't going to get anywhere guessing about the neighbor.

I glanced at the list I had made the night before. The trailer, A-Plus Auto Parts, the sheriff's office, Jessica's house.

Next, I needed to see Lucy LaFarge, who had lived in the trailer until Scott Sheridan kicked her and her roommate out.

I didn't phone ahead, because my experience as a lawyer had taught me that certain questions are better asked face-to-face and that I'm more likely to get true answers when the person I'm asking doesn't have time to think up lies. I put the car in gear and headed down the hill.

North Brazos is a short side street west of the campus near the Horticulture Center. It's an older residential area with a hodge-podge of apartment buildings and houses built shoulder to shoulder on a narrow street lined with pecan trees and live oaks that lean protectively over the sidewalks. This side of campus is almost entirely rental, with the constant stream of the traffic you see in student areas: skateboards, in-lines, scooters, bicycles, motorbikes, people, and dogs, some leashed, some loose.

Around the corner on Matagorda are a pizza parlor, a video rental shop, and a Wi-Fi coffee shop, where the customers stare into their laptops or play games on their iPhones while they sip their coffee. Most are young, dressed in unisex shorts and T-shirts, both male and female sporting ponytails and various earrings and nose rings, almost all outfitted with earbuds. Some of the students are as old as I am or older, though. That's the thing about college campuses these days: the student body is made up of people from their late teens into late middle age and beyond. McQuaid had a sixty-eight-year-old retired cop in one of his classes last term, and a ninety-year-old great-grandmother recently lined up with the twentysomethings to get her diploma.

The apartment building at 101 North Brazos turned out to be an older two-story unit, flamingo pink stucco with a tile roof and pseudo-Spanish wrought iron gates, flanked by spiky yuccas that had snagged McDonald's discards, newspapers, beer cans, and a pair of pink panties. The building was constructed in a U around a center square that had at some point contained a swimming pool, now filled in and featuring waves of tired-looking grass and a cresting surf of litter. This was not a high-class place.

A row of key-lock mailboxes was displayed on the entryway wall. I cruised along it, looking, until I hit pay dirt. The words *LaFarge/Wolff, 210* were handprinted on a card taped to the box. Well, well, lucky me.

The two former renters of Scott Sheridan's trailer were still sufficiently together to share a mailbox.

Two-ten was located on a narrow balcony that ran in front of all the second-story apartments, motel-style. The dirty purple door had at some point in its life been yellow, and the flaking paint gave it a pocked look. The wide window to the right of the door was covered by a dark green drape, and a girl's battered bicycle was padlocked to the balcony railing. The doorbell was crisscrossed with tape, so I lifted the tarnished knocker and rapped, waited a brief moment, and rapped again. A moment later, the door opened on a chain.

"Yeah?" The girl wasn't much over twenty, with dark curly hair, a perky, freckled nose, and wide-spaced brown eyes.

"Hi. My name is China Bayles. Are you Lucy?"

"That's me. Lucy." Her voice was perky, too. "What's up?"

I hadn't been sure just how I was going to handle this. I still wasn't. But she seemed friendly enough, and I might get more information if I told the truth. "I'm looking for a friend," I said. "Jessica Nelson. Did she stop by to talk to you?"

"The reporter from the *Enterprise?*" The

door opened a little wider. The girl was wearing cutoffs and a clingy V-necked red top that displayed an attractive cleavage. Her legs were long and tanned, her feet bare. "Yeah, sure. She was here. She's writing a story about a place I used to live. It burned down last weekend."

"She was here on Monday, maybe?" I hazarded.

"Right. Monday afternoon. She caught me after my hort class."

"Great," I said. "Listen, Lucy, I think you might be able to help me. Mind if I come in and visit for a few minutes? I won't take up much of your time."

"I guess," she said with a shrug. "If you want to." If I'd been her, I might've been a little more careful who I let into my apartment, but she unhooked the chain and opened the door.

The air in the small living room was heavy with tobacco smoke, a couple of overflowing ashtrays scattered here and there, but beneath the tobacco I caught a whiff of marijuana. Scott Sheridan had been right about that, anyway. The room was furnished with a sagging sofa and chair, a battered coffee table, a television, a couple of brick-and-board bookcases, and a desk and chair. On the desk was a laptop computer, and above it, on the wall, were several large photos of plants. The computer was on, the monitor displaying a word processing program and a document. It looked like I'd caught her working on a class paper.

Lucy went to the window and opened the drape. "Have to close this when I'm on the laptop," she said. "The light glares in the monitor." She nodded at the sofa. "Wanna sit down?"

"Thanks." I sat. There was a full ashtray on the table in front of me. Mixed with the cigarette butts, I saw what was left of one joint. At least.

Lucy folded herself into a chair, bare legs pulled up beneath her. "So what was it you wanted to know about this reporter?" She frowned. "She was on the up-and-up, wasn't she?"

"Oh, definitely," I said. "She's working on an assignment for her editor." I started with something simple, just to get her talking. "What time on Monday was she here?"

"After my hort class." She wrinkled her nose, nodding in the direction of the computer. "Research paper's due tomorrow, and I'm just getting started." She followed my glance at the photos. "Those are the plants I'm writing about."

The plant photo nearest me pictured a

275

remarkably vigorous specimen of *Cannabis*. The photo next to it was a full-throated blue morning glory. The one above that was wormwood; next to it, salvia. "Let me guess," I said. "Your paper is on psychoactive plants. Marijuana, artemisia, *Ipomoea violacea, Salvia divinorum.*"

She straightened, surprised. "Hey," she said admiringly. "You're good. How'd you know those Latin names? I mean, *I* don't even know them, and I'm writing this paper."

I didn't want to tell her that I was giving a talk to the Pecan Springs Garden Club on the topic — that would probably have made her laugh. Instead, I said, in a careless tone, "It's just one of my areas of interest, you might say."

She looked down at my Thyme and Seasons tote bag and the light dawned. "Oh, my gosh — you're China Bayles! You own that herb shop over on Crockett, across from the Farmers' Market." With a knowing grin and a glance at the wall, she added, "That's why psychoactive plants are in your 'area of interest,' I suppose. I'll bet you have most of these plants in your shop."

"Not all of them." I grinned back. "My interest in psychoactives is purely academic." Pointedly, I looked down at the ashtray. I didn't want to have to say no to a joint offered in the spirit of friendly camaraderie, or tell her that I wasn't dealing in something she might want to buy.

" 'Purely academic,' " she repeated with a chuckle. She pushed a pile of magazines off an ottoman onto the floor and stretched out her legs. The soles of her feet were dirty, but her pretty toenails were painted bright red. "That's what Dr. Laughton always says at the beginning of a class. All this shit is purely academic. Of course," she added confidingly, "that's his *story*." Her attitude toward me seemed to have changed subtly. I had the feeling that she thought that the herb business — and particularly our shared interest in psychoactive plants — made us sisters under the skin.

"You're in one of Dr. Laughton's classes?" I asked.

"I was. Last spring. Directed study." She eyed me. "You know him, huh?"

I nodded, leaning forward. We were getting pretty far off-topic here, and I needed to bring us back. "Look, Lucy. Here's the problem. Jessica Nelson — the reporter who came to see you — has disappeared. Nobody knows where she is, and I'm trying to track her down. I came here because I knew she wanted to ask you some questions about the fire in the trailer where you used to live."

"Disappeared?" Lucy asked, puzzled. "You mean, like, you don't know where she is? Like, nobody's seen her?"

I nodded. "That's right. So far as I've been able to figure out, you might be the last person she talked to." I paused. "She did interview you, didn't she?"

A pair of hairy, half-naked boy-men, running and shouting, thudded past the apartment window, followed by a barking dog. The balcony rumbled with their heavy footfalls.

Lucy got up and closed the curtain again, and the room fell into a green-tinted dimness. "God, I hate that noise," she muttered. "Drives me crazy. One of the things I liked about the trailer was that it was quiet." She sat down again. "Yeah, sure, she was here. She interviewed me about the place that burned. She wasn't the first, though. The cops were here on Sunday."

"Sheriff Blackwell?"

"No, some deputy. Clyde somebody-or-other. Really cute. He asked me if I knew of anybody who might've got into the trailer after we moved out. Maybe somebody I'd loaned a key to."

"What did you tell him?"

"That I never loaned my key to anybody.

When we moved out, I gave it to the land-lord. After Larry and I got this place, I never went back to the trailer."

"Larry?" I asked, pretending not to know.

"My roommate. Larry Wolff. We rented the trailer together. That's his room, back there." She nodded in the presumed direction of a bedroom.

I smiled. "Boyfriend?"

"Sort of, sometimes." She fished through the litter on the table beside her and found a package of Salems and a lighter. "More like good friends, really, with sex when we feel like it." I would've blushed to say something like that. She didn't. "It's an open relationship," she added, lighting a cigarette and blowing out a cloud of blue smoke. "I mean, like, we have other friends." She smiled dreamily. "We aren't possessive."

I watched her smoke and thought about something I had read recently about menthol additives in cigarettes. Menthol (made synthetically or derived from peppermint or other mint oil) makes the smoker's throat feel cooler and reduces the cough reflex. People who smoke menthol cigarettes can inhale deeper and hold the smoke in longer. Makes it harder to quit, researchers say.

I went back to the subject. "So you liked being out in the country?"

"Yeah, it was kinda nice. But I don't have a car, so if Larry wasn't around, I was stuck. There's a lot more commotion here, but I'm close enough to the campus to ride my bike or walk." She hesitated, her face darkening. "It's so awful about that girl, you know? The one who burned to death in that fire, I mean." She shuddered. "Saturday night, wasn't it?"

"Yes. Saturday night. I happened to see the fire and turned in the alarm. But it was too late for the victim. She died before anybody could get to her."

She squinted at me through a cloud of tobacco smoke. "Is that how you lost your eyebrows?"

"Yeah. I was standing too close when the place blew up."

She bit her lip. "Was the dead girl a student? The deputy didn't know. The reporter didn't know, either."

"I don't think anybody knows for sure. She hasn't been identified yet." I paused, wondering where to go next. I opted to fish. "Did Jessica spend much time with you?"

"She was here maybe a half hour, something like that." Lucy pulled on her cigarette, appearing to be subdued by the idea of someone dying in a place where she had lived. "She said she was writing a human-interest feature, so she was interested in all kinds of stuff. Like how long Larry and I lived in the trailer, what it was like to live that far out in the country, that sort of thing. Oh, and she wanted to know whether we ever had any problem with the wiring or the electrical. Anything that would cause a big fire."

I guessed that neither the deputy nor Jessica had told Lucy that the fire had been set by an arsonist, so I didn't enlighten her. "What did you tell her?"

Lucy pressed her lips together. "Well, I said there wasn't anything like that wrong with the place, not that I knew about, anyway. Once a skunk made a nest underneath and had some babies, and there was some sort of problem with the plumbing. But the rent was right, and . . ." She paused, frowning. "I wonder how come that girl couldn't get out when the place caught on fire."

"Smoke inhalation, maybe," I said. "Why did you want to live out in the country?"

She gave me a quick glance, then looked away. "Mostly to get away from neighbors," she said evasively. "Although we had some nice neighbors out there. They just weren't right under our noses, like they are in this place." She put out her cigarette in the overflowing beanbag ashtray in front of her and clasped her hands around her arms, as if she were cold. "Gosh, just thinking about that girl gives me the shivers. If I had stayed there, I could've ended up dead. Like her, poor thing. So I guess the new owner did me a favor, kicking Larry and me out the way he did."

"He kicked you out?" I asked experimentally.

"Yeah." She didn't take the bait. "Which is why we got this place."

I tried another tack. "Was your roommate here on Sunday, when the deputy came?"

"Uh-uh." She shook her head. "I've got the place all to myself for a month or so. Larry left early Sunday morning to drive down to San Antonio, where his folks live. After that, he's going to Mexico. A field trip. For his research."

"Does he know about the fire?"

"I'm sure he doesn't — and definitely not from me. I haven't talked to him since he left." She nodded toward the photos on the wall. "He's the one who's really into stuff like that. Plants, I mean. This year, he's working on some sort of native corn, that's why he's going to Mexico. But last year, he did a big paper on the psychoactives that are used in native cultures. Like, in rituals

and that kind of stuff. The way they do it —
it's not like recreational drugs, the way it is
in this country. They're not doing it for fun,
or just to get high. The plants are part of
their religious celebrations."

I nodded sympathetically. "That's sometimes hard for people to understand."

She unclasped her hands and sat back
against the sofa cushions. She was silent for
a moment, then: "You know, I said I never
loaned my key out. But Larry might've —
at least, that's what I heard. I didn't tell the
deputy because I didn't know it until after
he was here, but . . ." She stopped, frowning. "I don't want to get Larry in trouble,
though."

I smiled in what I thought was a sisterly
way. "Oh, you won't." I paused. "So?" I
asked invitingly.

"Well, I was over at the Hort Center for a
class on Monday morning and I ran into
this girl — Zoe — who was a teaching assistant during the spring. In a class Larry
and I had with Dr. Laughton."

"Zoe Morris?" I hazarded. The person
who had left a message on Jessica's answering machine.

"Oh, you know her?" She brightened, as if
my knowing Zoe forged another link in our
sisterly friendship. "Small world, isn't it?

Anyway, I happened to run into Zoe and I was telling her about the fire and the questions the deputy asked and all that, and she said she thought Larry might have loaned a key to the trailer to somebody else. Some girl."

I was beginning to connect the dots. "And you told Jessica Nelson about this?"

She took out another Salem and lit it. "Yeah, and it turned out that she knew Zoe, too." She flicked the lighter flame. "Jessica and I, we talked about a lot of different stuff. This feature she's writing — well, it's really in-depth. She's trying to put herself inside that trailer."

"I know," I said ruefully. "She wants to get close to the story."

"Absolutely," Lucy said. "And I wanted to help her. Anyway, I told her what she wanted to know. She asked if she could get in touch with Larry, so I gave her his parents' phone number in San Antonio." She tilted her head to one side, gazing at the curling smoke. She was frowning slightly. "You say she's disappeared? Like, nobody's heard from her?"

I nodded. "Did she say where she was going when she left here?"

Lucy thought about this. "Well, not exactly. But she seemed really interested in finding out about that key — you know, whether Larry had actually given it to somebody, and if so, who that was. So I sorta have the idea that she might've been headed to the Hort Center to talk to Zoe."

Given what I'd heard on the answering machine, I thought that was a pretty good guess. But I had another question. "Do you know anybody who drives a new red Mustang convertible? Maybe somebody who visited you when you were living at the trailer?"

"A new Mustang?" She blew out smoke, giggling. "A convertible? We had friends out there sometimes, but nobody like *that.*"

I nodded. "Thanks. Oh, there's one more thing, Lucy. Would you mind giving me the number for Larry's parents? If I can't locate Jessica, I might try there. It's possible that she got in touch with them." And if Larry was still in San Antonio, she might have driven down there to talk to him. Even in traffic, the city is no more than a forty-minute drive from Pecan Springs — an easy trip.

Lucy got out of her chair, carrying her cigarette. "Sure, I can do that. I'll get it." As she passed the wall of plant photos, she glanced up, then back to me. "Oh, by the way," she said, in an offhanded tone. "Morning glory seeds really do work. Since you're into herbs, you oughtta give 'em a try. I mean, it's just another aspect of plant culture, like the way some plants taste and smell. Something you ought to experience. And it's legal. Completely and totally legal."

I stood, too, regarding her thoughtfully. "Maybe I'll do that. How many seeds should I take?"

"It would be better if you take them in capsules. That way, you'd know how much you're getting. You don't want to use seeds you get from a seed store. Those are treated with all kinds of poisonous stuff. You need to get them from . . ." She gave me a glance. "From somebody who knows not to use treated seeds."

I frowned curiously. "Capsules? You mean, you process the stuff?"

"Sure. It's so simple, even a kid can do it." She was candid, showing off, bragging a little, telling me something I didn't know and she did. "You grind up the seeds, see, and soak them in naptha and then in alcohol. Everclear is good, or vodka or gin. You want hundred proof."

"Naptha," I mused aloud. "That's a solvent, isn't it? Could you use lighter fluid, maybe? Or camp stove fuel?"

"Yeah, people do use lighter fluid. And

camp stove fuel is really good, because it's easy to get. You can buy Coleman's at lots of places around town." She paused at the door to the other room. "Anyway, after you've soaked the seeds in alcohol, you strain out the seed mash and throw it away and then you evaporate off the alcohol you've soaked it in. What you get is a yellow gummy stuff on the bottom of your pan. Scrape it up and put it into capsules. It's good. Really good. Not as potent as LSD, of course, but close. LSA, they call it." She paused, eyeing me, and got cautious. "Of course, we're speaking academically here, as Dr. Laughton says."

I became enthusiastic. "Really? The effect is like LSD? Gosh, I had no idea. That could be really interesting!"

She pursed her lips. "Lysergic acid amide, is what it is. An all-natural high. Nothing synthetic about it. Heavenly Blues are the best. Pearly Gates and Flying Saucers are also good." She grinned. "Speaking academically."

Naptha was natural? "These untreated seeds — where did you say I should get them?"

Whatever she had been about to tell me, she suddenly thought better of it. "Oh, off the Internet," she said, with a vague wave of her hand. "Google it. You'll find them. Or maybe . . ." She paused.

"Maybe locally?" I hazarded.

She shrugged. "Mine come direct from Mexico. My friend Matt brings them back a couple of times a year."

I filed the information. "The process sounds like a lot of work," I said, as if I were having second thoughts. "Have to get the seeds, then there's all that grinding and soaking and evaporating."

"Yeah." She gave me a sly grin. "If you're doing it just for yourself, probably it is. Too much work, that is. Of course," she added, in a meaningful tone, "you could just buy the capsules. I might have a few to spare."

I nodded. I was beginning to get the picture. And it wasn't a pretty one.

Chapter Fourteen
Jessica

When Jessica woke up again, her eyes felt gritty and swollen and her nose was dripping and she wondered if she'd been crying in her sleep. She lay very still, pretending for a precious few moments that this whole thing had been just a very bad dream and she would be waking up in her bed, safe at home, with the early-morning sun coming through a crack in the blind and the wonderful fragrance of coffee wafting from the kitchen. Coffee, that was what she needed. She would swing her legs out of bed, grab her wrap, and pad barefooted to the kitchen, where she would pour herself a mug of rich, dark coffee. With that in her hands, she could face the world. She could face Amanda. She could — probably — even face Butch, next door.

But she could pretend for only a moment, for it wasn't her bed she was lying on. It was rough, cold cement, and she couldn't get up because her wrists and ankles were bound so tightly that she couldn't feel her hands and her feet. Her mouth was taped shut. There was no coffee, no kitchen, no Amanda.

She stirred, shifting her head, which didn't seem to hurt as much as it had before, and strained to listen to the silence, trying to hear any sounds, any sounds at all. Nothing, as still as the grave, and dark as the grave, too, a heavy, smothery dark that was so thick she could almost eat it. She turned her head to look over her shoulder, imagining that the smudge of light was a little brighter than the last time she had looked. Was it sunlight? A lightbulb somewhere in the distance? No way to tell. Maybe there was no smudge at all, just a trick of her imagination.

Feeling helpless, hopeless, she fought back another threatening flood of tears. No. No, no, no. She wasn't going to cry again, and she wasn't going to let herself *feel.* Feeling led to crying and crying drowned out thinking, and she had to think. Think. She'd go back where she was before, to the business of remembering her movements, what she had been doing before whatever happened that had brought her to this place.

Okay, Jessica, she told herself, back to

remembering, one step at a time, pushing through the gray fuzziness that filled her brain. Lunch with China, and that awful tortilla soup with too much something in it. Cinnamon? She couldn't remember what China called it. Too much something. Anyway, after lunch and after their talk (China didn't think she ought to get involved, just write a straight story), she had gone to the trailer to take more pictures, and then to the auto parts place, where she'd gotten the name of that guy. She couldn't remember it right now, except that it had two *f*s in it. Or maybe it had been the other way around, the auto parts place first, then the trailer. But that didn't matter. Somewhere along the way, she had gone to the sheriff's office, where she'd seen the photos of the charred body, those awful, horrible photos. She pushed the memory away. She needed to stay with something safe. The silver bracelet with the initials G.G. The footprint, which the sheriff had said was made by a Converse shoe.

She squeezed her eyes shut to think better, although it was so dark it didn't matter whether her eyes were open or closed. After the sheriff's office, she'd gone to see the girl with the B-movie name, Lucy LaFarge, who lived in that cruddy little apartment with the purple door on North Brazos. She remembered the door very clearly because the paint had been flaking off, and there were ugly green drapes at the window. Lucy's face was a little foggy, but she remembered going inside and talking, and the way the place smelled of tobacco smoke and marijuana, and the photos of plants taped to the wall over the computer. Lucy had already known about the fire, because a deputy had been there the day before, but there was something else, something —

She pressed her lips together, pushing herself to remember.

Oh, yes. Yes, there it was. The key, which the guy who lived in the trailer with her, the guy with two *f*s in his name — Cliff, maybe? Or was it Jeff? She couldn't remember — had loaned to a girl in one of his classes.

Yes, that was it! She pressed her lips together harder. Zoe Morris, at the Hort Center, had told Lucy about the key, and Lucy had told her. So she'd gone to the Center to see Zoe, and Zoe had said that the girl's name was Gloria and that she had been in one of Dr. Laughton's classes. And Zoe had also known the guy's name — Wolff, Larry Wolff, with two *f*s. Yes, that was it, not Cliff or Jeff, but Wolff, and he was the one who had given the key to Gloria.

That was all Zoe could tell her, although she'd promised to do some checking and call with anything she found out. But on her way out of the building, Jessica had had the bright idea of checking the bulletin board beside Stu Laughton's door — although she was crossing her fingers that Stu had already gone home for the day because he was the very last person on earth she wanted to see. She had been ducking him for weeks, ever since she'd broken off their relationship. It was one thing to be involved with a man who was separated from his wife. It was another thing entirely if he and his wife were still trying to keep it together, even if it was only for the kids. And the kids were twins, for pete's sake, twin girls, like her and Ginger.

She sucked in a breath. Stop, she told herself sternly. Don't go there. Don't think of Ginger. It hurts. Go back to the bulletin board, where she'd hit pay dirt, because she'd found a typed list of students' lab assignments. There was Larry Wolff's name, along with two other guys, Matt Simmons and Brian Lafferty. And Gloria. Gloria Graham.

She had stared at it for a moment, clutching her notebook. There it was! Gloria Graham. G.G. The initials engraved on the

293

bracelet in the photo. Which meant that the dead girl was probably the one to whom — according to Zoe, anyway — Larry Wolff had given the trailer key. Gloria Graham. She had felt a surge of triumph. If she was right, she was way out front of everybody else, ahead of the police, even!

She had a name, what she needed now was an address. So instead of going home, the way she had intended, she had driven over to the newspaper office, where she could log on to all the up-to-date address and phone directories. From there on, it was a bit of good luck, bad luck.

The good luck was that she had found an address for Gloria Graham, in a rundown, neglected-looking apartment building at the west side of campus, not far from Lucy's place on Brazos. When she got there, though, it turned out that Gloria had moved. This bad luck was canceled out by some good luck when the girl who was living in the apartment — Vickie Vickers — turned out to be Gloria's former roommate. Vickie confirmed that the Gloria she was tracking was the same Gloria who was taking classes in horticulture and gave her a new address on the east side of campus.

So that was her next stop. No, next was Taco Bell, because it had been hours since she had eaten (just the salad, not that awful soup) and she was hungry. Then she had driven to Gloria's apartment complex, which was very different, new and upscale and obviously much more expensive than the other place, with a clubhouse and a great-looking pool and a parking garage for tenants. She had parked in the lot and —

She stopped. The thick, shadowy silence around her had been broken by a sound. A thud, maybe, like the slam of a heavy door.

Instinctively, Jessica closed her eyes against the dark. Better pretend to be asleep or unconscious. Better not let on that she was awake and thinking. And remembering.

CHAPTER FIFTEEN

Archaeological evidence tells us that for native peoples of the Andes, coca (*Erythroxylon coca*) has been an important medicinal plant for at least five thousand years. Chewed as a stimulant, it enhanced physical strength and energy, enabling the body to make better use of the limited oxygen at the high altitudes. As a tea, coca was used for digestive problems. As a poultice, the leaves were used to treat headaches and were chewed to relieve toothaches and sore throats. As a salve, coca soothed arthritis pain and muscle aches.

The plant was also considered to have spiritual properties, and tribal shamans still use it to induce a trance-like state. Coca enables the shaman to cross "the bridge of smoke" and enter the world of spirits.

Cocaine (a crystalline tropane alkaloid obtained from the leaves of the coca plant) is second only to marijuana in its use as a recreational drug in the United States. The drug is responsible for street crime, organized crime, and government corruption in both North and South America.

China Bayles
"Mood-Altering Plants"
Pecan Springs Enterprise

The Curry Horticulture Center was only about six blocks away from Lucy's apartment, but the morning was already hot and I wasn't going to hoof it. On my way to the car, I phoned Caitie, making sure that everything was okay at home. She asked if she could make lemon icebox cookies, which was fine with me — she could chill the dough in the fridge and we'd bake the cookies when I got home. They'd be a nice welcome-home treat for Uncle Mike. I suggested adding some lemon balm and lemon verbena out of the garden, an idea she liked. I also suggested taking Pumpkin out to the catnip patch to see if he was one of the lucky cats that got turned on by the scent of catnip. That made her giggle. I loved hearing the lightness in her voice and imagining the answering light in her eyes.

Then I called Ruby, to check on things at the shop. It was a slow morning, she said, only a couple of customers so far. But there had been a small problem — small, as in about the size of Baby Grace. Kate was in Austin at an all-day professional meeting, and Amy had left Grace with her Tuesday morning sitter and gone to work at the vet clinic. But the sitter had a family emergency and needed somebody to come and get Grace. Guess who? Ruby had gone to get her granddaughter, and Grace was now happily coloring at a table in the tearoom.

Uh-oh, I thought, but all I said was, "I hope things will be okay." Ruby had kept Grace at the shop ever since she was a small baby, so that was nothing new. But now that Grace is beginning to walk, it's more of a challenge. She's not crazy about staying in her playpen. She loves to get into things.

"We'll be fine," Ruby said reassuringly. "Cass is already in the kitchen, getting ready for the lunch bunch, and Lisa is due in before long, to help out in the tearoom. There are plenty of hands on board." She paused, adding worriedly, "Any sign of Jessica?"

"I wish," I said. "I've been to her house and nobody's there. But it looks like I may have a line on someone who can give me some more information. With luck, I should be back at the shop in twenty or thirty minutes."

"No, Grace!" Ruby exclaimed. "Don't pull on —"

There was a splintering crash and a loud wail.

"Later," Ruby said, and clicked off.

I pocketed the phone, wishing I'd hung up at the point when Ruby had said they'd be fine. But there wasn't a thing I could do about whatever small catastrophes were happening at the shop. I had plenty of other things to think about as I made my way through the west campus traffic.

The drugs, for instance. Scott Sheridan had known about the marijuana, but there had been something going on at the trailer that he hadn't known about. From what Lucy had said, I was pretty sure that she had been cooking LSA — and not for her own personal consumption, either. She was doing it for the street trade.

And she was wrong about the legality of her operation. Morning glory seeds themselves are not prohibited, and there's nothing illegal about growing all you want and saving the seeds for next year's garden. There's nothing illegal about selling them or giving them away to family, friends, or the members of your garden club, either.

But turn those seeds into a drug, and

you're in deep trouble. LSA is federally scheduled as a Class III controlled substance. In Texas, the penalty for manufacturing, delivering, or possessing with intent to deliver can be anything from a state jail felony to a first-degree felony, depending on how much they catch you with. This translates to a sentence that can be as little as 180 days to as much as 99 years, with a fine of somewhere between ten thousand and fifty thousand dollars. Plus, you will get a visit from the IRS, who will want you to tell them why you haven't paid taxes on whatever you've earned from your morning glory cottage kitchen. They won't take "duh" for an answer, either.

Of course, this was all academic, right? Hypothetical? I didn't think so, and the thought gave me a deep concern. Jessica Nelson had been down this trail before me, and it was beginning to seem very likely that she had stumbled into something seriously illegal. What was it, exactly? Who was involved? Where had her investigation taken her?

And most urgently, where *was* she?

CTSU's Horticulture Center is housed in a new building, only a couple of years old. But the program itself was established more than a half-century ago as a complement to the agriculture program, which focuses on large-scale ranching and farming — still a huge industry in Texas, of course. Horticulture has to do with plant science, irrigation technology, greenhouse culture, and the commercial development and management of garden plants, landscaping, greenscaping, and xeriscaping. It is fast becoming one of the biggest, greenest businesses in Texas.

The Hort Center is definitely the greenest building on campus. It features a rainwater recycling system, energy-saving natural ventilation and solar panels, and recycled and renewable products throughout, such as recycled flooring and wall materials and furniture hand-crafted from salvaged urban trees. I attended the opening of the new building when it was dedicated. I was impressed then, and am still impressed. Usually when I go there, I browse through the native plant garden on the hill behind the building, picking up ideas for plantings and landscaping at the shop. But the morning was moving along — it was already nearly ten o'clock, so I went looking for Zoe Morris.

After asking directions, I found the hallway where the teaching assistants' cubicles were located. Halfway down the hall, I found the room. It was one of those big bull-pen arrangements, with low partitions separating a dozen small carrels. Several of them were occupied by people reading, writing, one with her head down, taking a nap.

A row away, surrounded by stacks of books and student papers, I found Zoe Morris, hunched over her laptop, scrolling through a chart that took up the whole screen. The fact that she had a window in her cubicle designated her as one of the senior TAs. Through it, I could glimpse the outline of the hills behind the campus.

"Got a minute, Zoe?" I asked.

She looked up from the computer blankly, and then her eyes focused and she smiled. "Oh, hey, China. Nice to see you!" Zoe and I had met when I went out to Mistletoe Creek Farm to pick up my subscription baskets of fresh vegetables, and I saw her occasionally at the shop.

"Nice to see you, too. Are you working with Donna this summer?" I came into the carrel and took the straight chair, the one reserved for students. The low partition was papered with charts, photos of plants, and snapshots of people in gardens — friends of Zoe's, I guessed, or fellow students.

"I'm out there some, but not as much as last year," Zoe said regretfully. She was petite and wiry, dressed in jeans and a green T-shirt that said "Plant a Garden" on the front. "I'm working on my thesis. With any luck, I'll finish it by the end of the summer term." She sat back in her chair, rolling her eyes. "If it doesn't finish me first. That's a strong possibility."

"Who's your director?"

"Dr. Laughton. I've got a good topic — developing markets for sustainable local food production in Texas." She wrinkled her nose ruefully. "I'm pretty strong where the research is concerned, but I'm not the world's best writer."

"You'll be fine," I said in a comforting tone. "Listen, I need to ask you about Jessica Nelson. I'm sure you know her from Donna's farm — she worked there when you did, last summer. She's also an intern at the *Enterprise.* Has she talked to you in the past couple of days?" I didn't think it was a good idea to let Zoe know that I had been standing in Jessica's kitchen when she called that morning, and that I already knew they had connected.

"Jessica? Sure. She stopped in to get some information for a story she was writing." She paused curiously. "Why are you asking?"

"Because nobody's heard from her in a while."

"Really? Like . . . how long? I just saw her on Monday afternoon. She said she was on deadline with the story, so maybe she's holed up, writing. Have you checked her house? I left a message there this morning."

"I've checked — looks like she hasn't been home since she saw you. She missed her deadline, and there was a weird message on my answering machine that suggested that she was in some kind of trouble. I'm worried." I leaned forward. "Look, Zoe. Here's what I know. Jessica was working on a feature article about the girl who died in the trailer fire on Limekiln Road on Saturday night. I was the one who turned in the alarm, and —"

She broke in. "So that's how your eyebrows got scorched."

"Right." I was beginning to wonder if I shouldn't hang a sign around my neck, announcing the fact. "On Monday, Jessica paid a visit to the girl who used to live in the trailer — Lucy LaFarge. I talked to Lucy a little while ago, and she told me that you had an idea that Larry Wolff — he used to live in the trailer, too — might have loaned his key to somebody. I thought maybe Jessica dropped in to see if you could tell her who."

"You're right," Zoe said. "Jessica told me about the trailer fire. She said she had talked to Lucy, and she asked about the key."

"Did you tell her what she wanted to know?"

"Well, sure. I mean, it's not like it was a huge secret." She paused. "But I don't think Larry loaned that key."

"No? Well, then —"

"From what I could gather, he just . . . well, he gave it to her."

Ah. Well, okay. "To —"

"To Gloria. Gloria Graham. He told her that his roommate had already turned in two sets of keys to the new landlord. His was extra and Gloria could have it."

Gloria Graham. I pulled in my breath, catching the significance. G.G. The initials on the bracelet the victim was wearing.

"Why?" I frowned. "I mean, why was he doing this? And why would she want a key to an empty trailer?"

"Well, I didn't tune into that part of the conversation. But I got the idea that Gloria wanted to use it for some extracurricular activity." She arched her eyebrows. "If you know what I mean."

305

"Involving Larry Wolff, or somebody else?"

"Could've been Larry, I guess. I know that he's still living with this other girl — Lucy, I mean. But I'm not sure it's a closed relationship. In fact, I think it isn't. You know how these things are. But maybe Gloria was hot for somebody else — or she had something else in mind altogether. Anyway, the place was going to be empty for a while. That's what Larry said."

Ah, the sexual adventures of youth. Twosomes, threesomes, even foursomes. If you ask me, monogamy definitely has its advantages. At least you know that you're going to be in the same bed every night, and that he's going to be there with you, instead of somewhere else, with someone else.

"And that was when?" I asked. "This business with the key, I mean."

She shrugged. "A couple of weeks ago, maybe? The week before finals, I think." She began fishing around among the litter of papers on her desk. "Jessica said she wanted to get in touch with Gloria, but at the time, I couldn't remember her last name. That's why I phoned her this morning — I remembered it. Graham. I found an address, too. Do you want it?"

I had heard it before, on the answering

machine in Jessica's kitchen, but I wrote it down anyway. I was still scribbling when Zoe added, "But if Jessica is still looking for Gloria, she'd better hurry. She'll only be here through the middle of next week. I meant to say that on the phone, but I forgot — didn't remember it until I happened to look at the field trip list again. When you locate Jessica, will you tell her?"

"Sure," I said. And then, "Where's Gloria going?"

"On a field trip to Mexico."

I frowned. "Lucy mentioned that Larry Wolff was going on a field trip to Mexico. I wonder if it's the same one."

"Could be," Zoe said. "I don't think there's more than one trip planned for this summer." She paused, crinkling her nose. "Why are you so interested in all of this, China?"

I hesitated, then decided it was time to tell her what I knew. "Because the girl who died was bound hand and foot and shot in the chest. And then the killer set the place on fire."

"Oh, no!" Zoe exclaimed. "Jessica didn't mention anything about . . ." She gulped. "About a *murder.* I thought it must have been an accident."

"No accident. The girl wasn't dead when

307

the fire got to her. I was standing outside. I could hear her crying for help, but I couldn't get to her. There was nothing I could do."

"Dear God," she whispered, horrified. Her hand went to her mouth.

"I'm pretty sure God didn't have anything to do with this," I said grimly. "I don't think this was something He would have approved."

She dropped her hand, beginning to put the pieces together. "And Gloria Graham may have had a key to the place . . ." She hesitated. "Do you think she was the person who died in the fire?"

"The victim hasn't been identified yet." We were getting into police business now. "I know Sheriff Blackwell. This is his case. I'm going to phone him as soon as I leave here, and give him the information about Gloria and the key. I'm sure he'll want to talk with you."

"Here's my cell." She picked up a piece of paper, wrote a number on it, and handed it to me. "Tell the sheriff I'm available any time. I'll be glad to help."

"Thanks. Oh, one more thing. Do you happen to know what kind of car Gloria drives?"

"As it happens, I do. I've seen her pulling in and out of the parking lot from time to time. She drives a really hot-looking Mustang. A red convertible." She tilted her head. "Does that tell you anything?"

It told me that Gloria — or somebody driving her Mustang — had used that key at least once. Didn't nail it, but it might come close. And it was another bit of information for Blackie. "Thanks," I said.

She was frowning deeply now, still putting pieces together. "What about Jessica? You said that nobody's talked to her since Monday. You don't think she's in any danger, do you?"

"I think it's possible," I said. "Jessica is intense. She's passionate. And this particular story has a personal angle. She could be so deeply involved that she's not thinking clearly. Which could put her in a vulnerable position."

"A personal angle?"

"Yes. Her sister Ginger — her *twin* sister — died when their house burned. Her mom and dad, too. Jessica was on a school trip when it happened," I said. "Otherwise, she told me, she'd be dead, too."

"Uh-oh," Zoe said, her face sober. "Are you suggesting that she's making an emotional connection between the victim of this trailer fire and her twin?"

I nodded. "It could be her way of mourning the death of her sister and her parents." And maybe a kind of repayment, I thought, for having survived. Irrational, but that's what grief is like. You think you're finished with it, and then something comes along to reopen the old wounds.

"Her twin sister," Zoe repeated softly. "How awful for Jessica, how truly awful." She took a deep breath. "Well, I can tell you that she was really calm and collected when she talked to me — you know, crisp, professional. I got the feeling that there was something going on inside her, though, something deep. I attributed it to her desire to get a good story. But now I can see that there was more to it than that."

"She does want to get a good story," I agreed. "She's been covering the city council and the ladies' club, stuff like that. She wants this arson-murder story for her portfolio, and she wants an exclusive, which means that she's playing her cards close to the chest. Putting all that together with her phone call to me, I think it's entirely possible that she's somehow managed to connect with the killer."

And if Jessica had gotten close to the killer, or if the killer had gotten close to her, there was no guarantee that she was still alive. He — or she — had killed once. It would be easy to kill again. I had traced her steps this far, but where did I go from here?

"Did she give you any idea where she might be heading after she left you?" I asked.

"Home, was what she said. She had a taped interview to transcribe and she wanted to get started on her article." She frowned. "Hang on a minute. No, she said that she needed to do some more checking on Gloria. But that's all I —"

Zoe's telephone rang and she reached for it, spoke briefly, then covered the receiver with her hand. "Are we about done, do you think? This is a student. I'm afraid it's going to take a while."

"Just one more thing," I said. "Was there anybody else around when you and Jessica talked on Monday?"

"In this room?" She frowned. "Maybe. I didn't really notice. But the late afternoon class had just let out. There were probably a couple of TAs in their carrels, and maybe several students. I couldn't tell you who, though. I wasn't paying attention."

"Thanks." I reached into my bag and pulled out a card. "If you think of anything else, could you call me? I'd really appreciate it."

"Sure thing," she said. She twiddled her

fingers at me and turned back to the phone.

I glanced at my watch. Ten twenty. I needed to call Blackie and give him the information about Gloria Graham and the key to the trailer, as well as Zoe's name and phone number. I'd suggest to him that he talk to Lucy and find out whether she had left a stash of camp stove fuel at the trailer, where it could have been used as an accelerant. I needed to go to the PSPD office and turn in a missing-person report on Jessica. And then I had to get to the shop. It was getting late and Ruby would wonder —

As if my cell phone were hard-wired to my brain, it rang. A few weeks before, Brian had decided I needed a new ringtone, and (since I'm a Willie Nelson fan) he'd downloaded "Mamas, Don't Let Your Babies Grow Up to Be Cowboys" to my cell phone. It rang now, and I flipped it open. Ruby, calling from the shop. She sounded frazzled.

"China, Lisa just phoned. She can't make it this morning."

"Rats!" I exclaimed. "Have you tried calling Laurel?" Laurel Riley frequently helps out at the shop, and is almost always available on short notice.

"Yes, but there's no answer at her place, and I remember something about visiting her mother. What time do you think you'll be in?" She paused, adding in a pleading voice, "Grace — Grace, sweetheart, Gramma doesn't want you to play with that. Put it down, please."

"I've got one more stop," I said, going out into the hall. "I should be there in twenty or thirty minutes." That's the nice thing about small towns. You're never very far from where you need to be.

She gave a sigh of relief. "That would be wonderful, China. As soon as you can. Also, Bob Godwin is here. He's looking for more cilantro. He wants to know if you can bring some in."

I scowled. "Tell him I took all I had to the market on Saturday. I won't have any more for a couple of weeks." That wasn't strictly true, but I wasn't going to contribute my cilantro to Bob's tortilla soup. If he wants his customers to OD on cilantro, he can find it somewhere else.

"Okay," Ruby said. "Anything new on Jessica?"

"Not specifically, but I have the feeling that I might be getting a little closer."

"Good luck," Ruby said.

I had just clicked off on the call when McQuaid phoned. "I got out of Knoxville okay," he said, sounding disgruntled, "but we're stuck on the ground here in Dallas.

Mechanical problems. Looks like I'll be a couple of hours late."

"Could you call Caitlin and let her know?" I paused. "By the way, I stopped in to see Blackie this morning. I mentioned that you wanted to talk to him. He seems down about leaving office, and I think he's eager to take a look at his options. Maybe you could give him a call, too."

"I'll do it," McQuaid said, and sighed. "Haven't got anything else to do for the next hour or so. What's happening there?"

"Not much," I said evasively. "You know how it goes — same old, same old." I hadn't told him about Jessica, since I knew he'd only tell me not to get involved.

"Listen," he said, "since I've got a little time, maybe I should ask you about that cat Caitie wants to keep. Are you sure it's all right with you?"

"More or less," I said hurriedly. "Hey, I'm sorry, but I really can't talk right now. I'm kind of busy at the moment."

"Oh," he said, sounding disappointed. "Well, okay. Sorry I bothered you."

"No bother, really," I said. "Love you."

His voice was gentle. "Love you, too, babe." We clicked off.

I closed my cell phone thoughtfully. Used to be, when I was away from the house or the office, I was really *away* — completely disconnected, out of reach, out of touch. And to tell the truth, it felt good, especially since privacy and personal space have always been one of my hot-button issues.

Don't get me wrong: I very much appreciate having a gadget that saves me time, keeps me on task, allows me to check on the kids, and helps me deal with emergencies. And of course, there are those days when everything that happens, happens by phone. Without it, you'd come completely unglued.

But I sometimes wish I could go back to the time when it wasn't so easy to reach out and touch someone.

Chapter Sixteen
Jessica

Jessica's hearing had grown acute in the stillness, and she heard him coming. First the sound of a heavy door opening (an outside door, she thought), then footsteps moving across the cement floor, then the clicking of a combination lock and the opening of another door — a wooden door, maybe, with a squeaky hinge. Then light, very dim, a flashlight with some sort of dark fabric fastened over it, just enough to see that the man who held it was wearing a ski mask and carrying a paper bag.

Her sense of smell had grown acute, too, and she knew that the bag held chicken nuggets from McDonald's. He set the flashlight and the bag on the floor and, without untying her hands or her feet, pulled her upright so that her back was propped against something solid. She had peed her panties some time ago and was still uncomfortably wet. She could smell herself, too, the stale urine and fear. But being wet and smelly were small matters, compared to being hungry and thirsty.

But her hunger and thirst didn't keep her from glancing quickly around her. In the dim light of the flashlight, she could see that she was in a small room with a concrete floor, about the size of a walk-in closet. The back wall was concrete blocks, the others sheetrock partitions. One of the walls was stacked with boxes, a golf bag leaning against them. A tennis racket, a machete with a badly nicked blade, and a pile of well-read *Sports Illustrated* lay on the floor.

The man took a small gun out of his pocket, so small it looked almost like a toy, and put the muzzle against her cheek. It didn't feel like a toy. It felt heavy, cold, real.

In a low, growly voice, obviously disguised, he said, "I'm going to pull the tape off your mouth so you can drink and eat. If you so much as squeak, the tape goes back on and you can go hungry. Yell and I'll kill you. Got that?"

She wanted to ask why he hadn't killed her before now, why he was keeping her alive, why he was feeding her, what he meant to do with her. But the smell of the food was overpowering, and she nodded. Swiftly, he yanked off the tape — oh, that hurt! — and opened the bag, pulling out a drink cup with a straw. She sucked on the straw, swallowed, sucked again. Coke. It was Coke. She sucked again, hearing the straw stir the ice, feeling the blessed coolness sliding down her throat.

Then, crouching beside her, he fed her the nuggets one at a time, as if she were a dog. She gobbled them at first, almost gulping them whole, then chewed and swallowed more slowly, making them last. He thrust the drink cup toward her, and she bent her head for the straw.

Too soon, the nuggets were gone and she had slurped up the last of the Coke. He was bagging the wrappings when she heard the sound of the outer door opening, and a light female voice calling, "Hey, Joe, bring that box, will you?"

Jessica's jailor tensed, and she could sense his panic. He snatched up the tape and hastily plastered it across her mouth and shoved her down on the floor, the gun to her head. He picked up the flashlight and turned it off, as a garish overhead fluorescent flickered and came on.

"Thanks, Joe," said the girl's voice. "Just set it down. This'll just take a minute — if I can remember the combination."

The speaker was not far away, less than

ten yards, Jessica thought. The man now had his knee on her back, pressing her shoulders painfully. He put a hand over her eyes, but his fingers, smelling of nuggets and cigarettes, left a gap, and in the bright light, just a couple of inches from her nose, she could see the hem of his jeans, ragged, and his high-topped basketball shoes, striped red and white, with a blue tongue.

"There. That's it," the female voice said with satisfaction. "Let's just slide the boxes in."

"You sure there's room?" a guy's voice asked with a chuckle. "Looks pretty full to me. You've got way too much stuff, Janet."

"Yeah." The girl sighed. "I keep thinking I've got to clean this place out. But not today."

A door slammed shut. A lock clicked. Footsteps. The light went off. A heavy door closed.

The knee on Jessica's back relaxed and the hand moved away from her eyes. The shrouded flashlight came back on. The man stood looking down at her for a long moment, then bent over, picked up the McDonald's bag, and left, closing and locking the door behind him. A moment later, she heard the sound of the heavy door closing.

She lay there until she was sure he wasn't coming back, and then she got to work.

Chapter Seventeen

We may not be able to grow coffee or tea in our Texas gardens, but we can easily grow yaupon holly (*Ilex vomitoria*), a popular landscape shrub with bright red berries that are attractive to birds and wildlife.

Yaupon is the only North American plant that contains caffeine. (It also contains antioxidants and theobromine, the chemical in cocoa.) Yaupon tea was brewed by the indigenous people of the Southeast as a stimulant beverage, medicine, and ritual drink. The dried leaves and twigs were roasted and boiled into a rich, dark tea known to European explorers and colonists as "black drink." Medicinally, a stronger decoction was drunk as a laxative and purgative, while a weak tea made from the bark was used as an eyewash. During tribal ceremonies, high-status males drank a much stronger brew as an intoxicant and purgative. That's where the plant got its name. But rest easy; it won't make you throw up.

Given the environmental damage associated with other crops grown for caffeine production and the fact that our caffeine comes from distant places, it's too bad that yaupon tea has not survived into modern times. Ironically, yerba maté, a tea brewed from the leaves of its South American cousin (*Ilex paraguariensis*), has survived — and thrived, economically speaking.

China Bayles
"Mood-Altering Plants"
Pecan Springs Enterprise

I was on my way out of the building when a young woman — the girl I had seen napping a row away from Zoe's carrel — stopped me just inside the door. She was in her early twenties, tall, flat-chested, almost anorexic-looking, with stringy brown hair and a dark tan. She wore shorts and sandals and a striped purple and red knit top, with a chunky pottery amulet on a thong around her neck. One upper arm was tattooed with an art nouveau flower and the other with an intricately embellished Celtic knot. She glanced nervously over her shoulder.

"Listen," she said, in a tense, edgy voice.

322

"I was in the TA room when you and Zoc were talking about Gloria. I didn't mean to listen in, but I couldn't help overhearing. I can't believe . . ." She chewed her lower lip. "Is it really true that she's the one who died in that trailer fire Saturday night?"

"The victim hasn't been identified yet — but yes, it's possible." I paused, thinking that this girl had been too far away to "overhear." She had to have moved closer and deliberately listened in. Why? "I'm China Bayles," I added. "And your name —"

She hesitated, turning half away as if she were going to leave, then turning back. "You're not a cop, are you?"

I repressed the urge to smile. "What makes you think that?" I countered, trying to decide whether my being a cop would be a plus or a minus with this young woman.

She tossed her head. "The way you talk. You sound, like, official." She scrutinized me doubtfully. "You don't look like a cop, though."

"I'm not a cop," I said, and she relaxed a little. "I'm looking for information about Gloria Graham."

"Why?"

I gave her a steady look. "Because a reporter covering the fire for the local newspaper has disappeared. I think her disappearance is linked to her investigation. What do you know about Gloria Graham?"

It was a simple enough question, one that an innocent, unknowing person would answer with a shrug and a regretful smile. *Sorry — wish I could help but I don't have a clue.*

But this girl didn't say that. "Disappeared?" she asked. "The reporter?" She was chewing on her lip, her glance sliding to one side. She had been nervous before, and edgy. Now she seemed out-and-out scared.

"Yes." I didn't elaborate. "Are you a friend of Gloria Graham?" I paused, frowning quizzically. "Excuse me — what did you say your name was?"

She hesitated for a moment, trying to decide whether to tell me, then made up her mind. "My name is Shannon," she said. "Shannon Fisher. No, I am not a *friend* of Gloria." There was a resentful edge to her voice. "I know her, that's all." Another jittery glance over her shoulder, more lip-chewing. "Listen, classes will be out in another few minutes. I might be able to tell you something, but not here. How about the native plant garden, behind the building?"

"Sure," I said. "If that works for you." But why shouldn't we talk here? Who was she afraid of? Or maybe it wasn't fear at all. Shannon had the look of a drama queen. Maybe this encounter was one of her self-dramatization games, in which she starred as an informant in an espionage caper and I was her contact. If that was true, I wouldn't learn anything helpful. And it was getting late.

I looked pointedly at my watch. "I need to be somewhere else in just a few minutes," I said. "If you have information —"

"Do you want to hear this or not?" she demanded.

"Depends on what it is."

"Well, I guess you'll have to decide that when you hear it, won't you?" She gave one more glance, making sure that nobody was around, and then took another precaution. "Wait a couple of minutes before you come. Then take the path to your right, the Wood-land Trail. Go up the hill a ways, and you'll come to a bench. I'll meet you there." She headed off.

Well, heck. While I was waiting, I'd put the time to good use by calling Blackie. I caught him on his way to a meeting and gave him a quick outline of what I had learned from Lucy LaFarge and Zoe Morris.

"I think you need to talk to both of them," I said. "It might be better to drop in on La-Farge unannounced, but Morris is anxious to cooperate. Of the two, Morris may be able to help you identify the victim. I think we have a name: Gloria Graham."

"Initials G.G.," Black said. "That works with the bracelet."

"Plus, she drove a red Mustang — *and* she had a key to the trailer. LaFarge may be able to tell you about the accelerant," I added, "although I'm pretty sure she doesn't know anything about the fire. However, she does know quite a lot about turning morning glory seeds into a street drug. You might want to ask her about that."

"Hang on." There was a pause as Blackie noted the names and contact information. "Anything else?" he asked dryly.

"Yeah. An address for Gloria Graham. Hill Country Villa, on Sam Houston Drive." I gave him the information I had jotted down from Zoe's message on Jessica's answering machine.

"Good lord, China." Blackie sounded exasperated. "How'd you dig all this stuff up?"

"By following Jessica Nelson's trail. She

dug it up first. And more, probably. Listen, Blackie, I was on my way to the PSPD to file a missing-person on Jessica. But I've just met somebody who may have some more information, and I need to talk to her. Could you possibly —"

"Hark Hibler has already filed the report," Blackie interrupted. "We just got the notice here."

"Hark?" I was surprised — and relieved. One less thing I'd have to do. "That's great." He was a good guy after all.

"Yeah. I don't know the details. But there's an APB on Nelson's car. Hopefully, we'll turn something up. Where are you?"

"On the campus — at the Hort Center." I pushed through the doors and began following the sidewalk that leads to the back of the building. "I have to go and talk to this person. I'll keep you posted."

"Do that," Blackie said. I could hear the grin in his voice. "And any time you get tired of fooling around with plants, you might apply here, as an investigator. I'll be glad to put in a good word for you with the next sheriff."

The next sheriff — a reminder that Blackie's days were numbered. I chuckled. "Maybe you could put in a good word with a certain P.I. we both know," I said. "I could pick up a few dollars in my spare time."

He chuckled, too, and we clicked off.

I reached the stone gateway that leads to the garden, hoping that this wasn't a colossal waste of time. What were the chances that Shannon could add anything significant to the information I'd already managed to collect? More likely, she was just satisfying a need to put herself in the middle of the picture. Meanwhile, Ruby was going crazy at the shop, having to keep tabs on Baby Grace every minute. That was where I needed to be. I picked up my pace. Much as I might like to loiter in the garden, this wasn't the morning for it.

The Curry Center Native Plant Garden is a not as extensive as the Lady Bird Johnson Wildflower Center in Austin, but it features a similar range of plants and has a similar look, with stone paths and a few stone picnic shelters. There's a large central space where flowers and native plants are grown in beds so they can be observed and studied. Beyond that, there are twenty acres or so of wild gardens designed to introduce visitors to the plants found in different ecoregions of the Hill Country: the Balcones Canyonland; savannah-like meadows studded with mesquite and wildflowers; and a riparian environment along a small creek. In the spring and fall, when it's not so hot, the gardens are crowded with visitors and students. Today's bright sun would soon be daunting, though, and I saw only a few people — a girl sketching a clump of native blackfoot daisies; a young man weeding a flower bed; a pregnant mom with a toddler clutching a pink balloon.

The Woodland Trail is marked with a signpost just past the gate. I followed it off to the right, across a sunny meadow filled with yucca and blooming prickly pear, bright yellow coreopsis, orange and red and brown firewheels, and yellow bitterweed, with pink pavonia spilling across the limestone rocks and purple coneflower beginning to bloom. The trail was bordered by yaupon hollies, their leaves shiny in the morning sunlight. Yaupon is the only North American native that contains caffeine — likely evolved, like nicotine and quinine, as the plant's defense against browsing animals. Makes an interesting tea that Native Americans called "black drink."

But I didn't have time to stop and admire all this lush beauty. I was on a mission. On the other side of the meadow, the trail zigzagged up the steep hill and into the coolness of the woods, where pecans, oaks, and hackberry grow together, with a wild, dense understory of Lindheimer's silk tassel and elbow bush. The campus is a noisy place — cars honking, people shouting, music blaring — but this hillside was quiet and restful. Somewhere deep among the trees a woodpecker rattled away at a tree; nearer by, a cicada sounded its resonant buzz. A moment later, I heard the crisp territorial declaration of a cardinal: *cheer-cheer-cheer.* Almost pretty enough to make me forget why I was here, and why I was in such a hurry.

Halfway up the hill, I found the bench — a thick wooden slab perched on rock supports, under a large live oak tree — and sat down. There was another bench at right angles to it. A few moments later, Shannon appeared like a silent wraith out of the woods.

"There's nobody else around," she said in a low voice. "I've checked." She sat down, shivering. "It pays to be careful," she added, and I could hear the apprehension in her voice.

"Gloria Graham," I said in a business-like tone. "You said you know her. Right?"

She gave me a sideways look. "Yes, I knew her back in grade school. High school, too. We grew up in Seguin. You know where that is?"

I nodded. As it happens, that's where McQuaid grew up. His parents still live there.

"Right. Well, it's not that big of a town. You can't help knowing the kids you go to school with." She put her hands on either side of her on the bench, stretching out her bare, tanned legs and crossing her ankles. "You know their families, too. My mom and GiGi's mom used to see one another all the time."

I leaned forward, thinking of the bracelet with its engraved initials. "That's Gloria's nickname?"

"Yeah. When she was a kid, she hated her name. Gloria was too old-fashioned, not sexy enough. So she called herself GiGi. You know, like in that old Leslie Caron movie? Or sometimes she just wrote it G period G period." With a finger, she traced the letter's shape in the air. "You know, like with the initials. Either way, it had to have two capital Gs in it." She gave me a hard, fierce look. "One of anything was never enough for Gloria. She was greedy, pure and simple. She just reached out and took whatever she wanted, didn't matter who it belonged to."

I heard the bitterness and wondered what or who Gloria had taken from Shannon —

and when. When they were kids in grade school? High school? More recently? Some people have long memories — and carry long grudges. Sometimes, long grudges end in dark doings. Still, if this girl had anything to do with Gloria's death, she wouldn't be sitting here talking to me right now. At least, I didn't think so.

"What can you tell me about her?" I asked, resisting the urge to look at my watch.

Not meeting my eyes, she gave an evasive shrug. "Like, what do you want to know?"

I was suddenly impatient. I was here because of Jessica, and for all I knew, time might be running out for her. "I want to know why somebody would tie Gloria up, shoot her, and leave her — alive — to burn to death," I said bluntly. *Sorry, Blackie,* I thought. *I'm giving too much away.* But I was being intentionally brutal. I wanted to shock this young woman. I wanted to jar loose whatever information she had.

"Shoot her . . ." This was clearly news to her. "Burn her to death?" She closed her eyes, sucked in her breath, opened her eyes again. "Oh, God," she whispered. I could hear the fear trembling in her voice — no dramatics now, nothing contrived. It was real fear. "Is that what happened?"

"That's what happened. Now, what can

you tell me?"

She tried again. "You're sure it was Gloria and not somebody else?"

"There's evidence, but I can't tell you what it is." I gave her a straight, hard look. "Why are you so afraid, Shannon? What's *your* involvement in this? Do you know who might have killed her?"

She crossed her arms over her narrow chest, holding herself tightly, as if she might come apart if she didn't. She didn't want to answer that question, so she went back to my earlier one. "You wanted to know about Gloria. Well, I can tell you about her." She paused, thinking where to begin. "She is . . . was a good-time girl, if you know what I mean."

"No, I don't know, exactly. What's a good-time girl?"

She gave me a look that said I was ignorant, or old, or both. "She liked to party, have fun. And she liked to be on top." She paused, and became more deliberate. "She was a user, in every sense of that word."

Now we were getting somewhere. Maybe. I risked another look. "User? As in —"

"As in using people, using her body, using drugs, using her father, using every opportunity she stumbled over. A manipulator."

Her body I got. "Her father?"

"She made him feel guilty for leaving her mother. He paid off. He was always giving her money."

I went for something else. "What kind of drugs?"

"Whatever she could get." She looked off to one side. "She didn't specialize." She got off the bench, threw up her arms in a dramatic gesture, and began to pace. "Ah, hell. Telling you isn't gonna change anything." She was brash and hard, but underneath, she was scared. "I don't even know who you are."

I could see the problem. Shannon wanted to tell what she knew, but she was frightened. Maybe she was afraid that somebody would come after her. Maybe she was afraid of incriminating herself. But whatever it was, I had to have something more to go on. And the only leverage I had was her fear.

"Sit down," I growled. When she didn't, I reached for a voice I don't use very often these days, but which is still in my repertoire when I need it. My lawyer's voice, hard, flat, authoritative. "Sit down and listen to me."

Startled, she sat.

I stood, looking down at her. "We're talking serious stuff here, Shannon. Arson-homicide in the case of Gloria Graham. A possible kidnapping, maybe worse, with regard to Jessica Nelson. If you know anything — anything at all — about what happened to either of these women, you can be charged as an accessory, before or after the fact." I paused. "Understand what that means?"

She whimpered. "I thought you said you weren't a cop."

"I'm not. I'm a lawyer."

"What kind of a lawyer?" She sat up straight, eyes opening wide. "Like, do you do crimes?"

"If you mean, do I handle criminal defense cases, the answer is I used to. Not now."

"Criminal defense." She chewed on that for a moment, then: "Would you . . . would you defend me? If the cops came after me, I mean?"

"I might recommend someone. *If* I thought you were shooting straight."

She hesitated. "You said 'accessory.' What's that, exactly?"

I switched into explanation mode. "If you know about a crime before it was committed, you can be charged as an accessory before the fact. If you find out about it after it was committed and help the criminal conceal it, or aid the criminal in escaping, or even simply fail to report what you know, you can be charged as an accessory after the fact." I paused, giving her time to think about this. "And then there's obstruction of justice. The police like to use that charge when they think you know something that would help them and you're refusing to cough it up."

"But I . . . I really don't . . ." She stopped, biting her lip. I could see her measuring whatever she knew against what I had told her.

I went on, evenly, quietly. "And then there's the other side of the equation. The danger to you. The physical danger."

She hadn't finished adding and subtracting yet, but this stopped her. "To me?" Her voice trembled, and she tried again. "Danger?"

"Where's your head, Shannon? This is a game you're playing? Like a video game? A reality show? One woman is dead, another missing." I had no firm evidence connecting Jessica's disappearance with the death of the girl in the trailer. But the more I learned, the more sure I was that the two were related. Whatever Shannon knew about the murder might help me to locate Jessica. And whatever Shannon knew about the murder could put her in serious jeopardy. She could turn out to be Number Three. At least, that's what I wanted her to think.

I went on. "Here's my advice to you. If you have any information about either of these women, say it out loud and say it now, and I'll consider how best to help you. Otherwise . . ." I shrugged.

She took a breath. "Well, I don't know anything about the reporter. But I can maybe tell you why . . . why Gloria got killed. Would that — would that help?"

"Depends."

Her mouth tightened. "Well, there's that trailer, for instance."

"What about the trailer?"

"You know what I was saying about her being a user?" She took a deep breath and launched into it. "Well, she was moving out of her apartment and it was going to be a couple of days before she could get into her new place. She had plenty of money. She could have afforded a motel, or she could have stayed at her mom's house. But she was putting on some sort of stupid act, the kind of thing she did a lot, whining about being broke and having to sleep in her car." She rolled her eyes. "Yeah, right. Like somebody who could afford a Mustang had to friggin' sleep in it? But Larry — Larry Wolff, he's one of Laughton's students — felt sorry for her."

"That was when he gave her the key? When was that?"

"A few weeks ago. He said he and his roommate had just moved out of a trailer out on Limekiln Road. They had another week on the rent, and the utilities were still on. There was no reason she couldn't sleep there for a night or two. He said the place was private, behind a bunch of trees."

"Was Gloria involved with Larry Wolff?"

"Involved? You mean, was she sleeping with him?" She laughed at that, a hard, flat laugh. "Well, maybe not before this happened. But when he gave her the key, he offered to meet her out there that night and make sure everything was okay. She gave him one of those calculating looks of hers, so I figured . . ." She paused. "Well, wouldn't you?"

"Maybe," I allowed. Yes, if I'd seen that transaction, I probably would've guessed that sex was involved.

Another laugh, harsh, bitter. "That's the way Gloria was, you know. She used people to get what she wanted. But it wasn't Larry she was after, if that's what you're thinking. She might sleep with him for fun, or to show that she could do it, or just because she felt like it at the moment. But she had bigger fish to fry."

"Bigger fish?"

"Dr. Laughton took his graduate seminar to Oaxaca over the Thanksgiving vacation last year. Gloria went along with us." She eyed me, as if she thought she was giving me a piece of important information, something that ought to get my attention.

Oaxaca. Oaxaca. I frowned. The only connection I could make was something about morning glory seeds in an article I had read when I was doing research for the garden club program. The Mazatec shamans in the Oaxaca region of Mexico used morning glory seeds as part of their spiritual ritual — used them for healing, too. I frowned. Morning glory seeds — the same stuff that Lucy LaFarge was processing for the street trade. Lucy LaFarge. Larry Wolff's roommate.

"Did Wolff go along on this field trip?"

She nodded.

"What was the seminar topic?"

"It was a directed studies seminar, cross-listed with Ethnobotany, in the Biology Department. Everybody designed a different research project, but all the projects had something to do with the place where we went — this little village in the mountains."

"And the projects were . . ."

She spoke impatiently, as if we had slid

away from the point she wanted to make. "Mine was collecting stories from the native people about a psychoactive plant they call *Shka Pastora — Salvia divinorum.* Larry was doing research on the native corn the local farmers grow — something about genetically modified seed contaminating their seed sources. Matt was studying ololiuqui, a psychoactive used in some of the local Mazatec rituals. Roger was doing flora surveys. We all stayed in one village. Dr. Laughton made the arrangements, even lined up translators to help us out. He takes his seminars to Oaxaca a couple of times a year, so he's familiar with the area. He did his own graduate work there."

Ololiuqui. Morning glory seeds. Lucy La-Farge had gotten morning glory seeds from somebody named Matt.

"Matt who?"

"Why do you care about that?" She shook her head impatiently, showing me that we were way off topic now. "It's not important."

"Matt who?" I repeated.

She rolled her eyes. "Matt Simmons."

I processed the information and went on. "Okay, let's talk about Gloria. What kind of research was she doing?"

"Gloria?" A sarcastic laugh. But now we were back on topic, as far as Shannon was concerned. "She wasn't enrolled in the seminar. She was doing research in . . ." She tilted her head, smiling thinly. "Connections, you might say."

Connections? I'd come back to that. "If she wasn't enrolled, how could she go on a university-sponsored field trip to Mexico?"

"A very good question, especially in this case." She eyed me again, to see if I had caught that, then went on. "But it happens sometimes, you know, if there's room in the van, and if the person pays. It helps to keep everybody's costs down. Split the gas and lodging. So you want the van to be filled. We had six, counting Stu."

Stu, not Dr. Laughton. But graduate students often call their professors by their first names, especially when they're away from the classroom. "Counting Gloria, too?"

"That's right. Counting Gloria." There was that bitter note again. Sour, jealous. She paused. "Aren't you going to ask why she went?"

I was feeling a little impatient. All this was about Shannon being jealous of somebody who got to ride along on a field trip? "Okay — why?"

She took a deep breath, as if she were steeling herself. "Because Stu was the bigger fish."

That stopped me. Cold. "Dr. Laughton?"

"You got it." She looked directly at me. "It had been going on for a few months, I guess. It was supposed to be a secret, but you know how these things are. Word gets around. People talk."

Well, no, I didn't know, actually. That is, not from my own personal experience. Of course, when I was in law school, the occasional rumor went around that some professor was sleeping with this or that student. Faculty members are no different from anyone else. Attraction happens, even when it's not in the best interests of the people involved, and there were probably other cases that didn't call enough attention to themselves to rise to the level of departmental gossip. But that was in the days before universities began formulating regulations prohibiting sexual relations between teacher and student. And there's been enough open discussion among the faculty to raise awareness of the hazards of affairs like these. A spurned student lover who is inclined toward retribution is doubly dangerous. He or she can spin a broken relationship into a sexual harassment suit in a jiffy, and blackmail is a distinct possibility.

But Stuart Laughton? I mean, he's such

an ordinary guy. Flirtatious, yes, sometimes outrageously so — although I'd never taken him seriously. But maybe he just wasn't my type, so I'd been annoyed when he called me sweetie, not attracted to him. Maybe, if I'd been a young student in one of his classes and he came on to me in that way, I might have felt differently.

And then I remembered that Margie had taken the kids and gone to stay with her mother. Had she done that because her husband was sleeping with a student?

"Gloria was a user," Shannon repeated darkly. "The affair was her idea. Stu had something she wanted, and she seduced him to get it. When she had what she wanted, she was finished with him. It was all over by Christmas."

By Christmas? But Margie had left Stu just a few weeks ago. So there had to be another reason for her leaving. Another affair, maybe?

Shannon turned away from my glance, and I wondered if this was the source of her jealousy, if she herself was recently or currently involved with Stuart Laughton and resented Gloria for throwing him over or breaking his heart or whatever. Which didn't make a lot of sense, I had to admit — but it probably wasn't important. There were other things I needed to know.

"You mentioned Gloria's connections," I said. "What kind of connections are we talking about?"

There it was again, that fear, on her face, in her eyes. She hesitated for so long that I thought she had decided to stop talking. I glanced pointedly at my watch. "If that's all you've got to tell me —"

"What kind do you think?" she blurted out. "Dealer connections. Cartel connections. This was Mexico, wasn't it?"

I blinked. *Cartel?* "You're kidding!"

She gave me a bleak look. "I wish. Why do you think we're out here in the woods, where nobody can hear us? This is the scariest thing that's ever happened to me. Gloria's dead — if that was her in the trailer — and you're telling me that some newspaper reporter has disappeared, and you think I'm kidding?" She flung out her arms. "I don't know why I'm talking to you," she cried dramatically. "You could be one of *them.* You could be about to kill me!"

I ignored her histrionics. "How do you know about the cartel connections?"

She swallowed. "Because Gloria told me. Because I saw the stuff." She threw me a quickly defensive look. "And don't go thinking I was involved in what she was doing. I had nothing to do with it. And Stu didn't either, if that's what's on your mind. He doesn't have a clue."

That might be true from one point of view, I thought. But if Shannon had known what was going on, she was involved — or somebody, several somebodies, in fact, might think she was. That's why she was afraid.

"Involved in what?" I asked, although I thought I was beginning to understand. "What was it you didn't have anything to do with?"

"Smuggling. Like, you know." She waved her hand. "The stuff Gloria brought back in the van."

I frowned. Smuggling marijuana over the Mexican border is a big business in Texas, but I wouldn't have thought that Gloria — or anybody else — would have attempted to bring it across in a university van. Most of it is hidden in legitimate shipments of agricultural or manufactured products. But it might have been —

"You're not going to tell me it was morning glory seeds, are you?" I asked. "Surely there isn't much of a market in that."

Her eyebrows went up. "You don't know much about this stuff, do you? Of course there's a market. Kids'll buy as much as they can get their hands on."

I frowned, thinking of Lucy LaFarge, industriously cooking up morning glory seeds in her kitchen. The activity criminalized her and every kid she sold it to, but it was an amateur operation, not something that would interest the big-time drug dealer — or so it seemed to me. Was I missing something?

Shannon was going on. "But we're not talking morning glories, or marijuana, either — if that's what you're thinking. It was pottery. Six pieces, with a primitive look. Tourist pottery, according to Gloria. Cheap. But it wasn't tourist pottery, and it wasn't cheap, either. It was worth a fortune."

I leaned forward, frowning. "You're not saying she was smuggling antique pots into the country, are you? I can't believe that Stuart Laughton would allow one of his students —"

She thrust out her chin. "Gloria wasn't his student. I already told you that."

I shook my head. "I can't believe he would allow *anybody* to smuggle cultural antiques out of Mexico. That would be just plain stupid. Anyway, she couldn't have gotten artifacts through customs. Officials are always on the lookout for that."

Shannon threw back her head and

laughed. "Are you kidding? If you know the right people, you can get anything through customs. Gloria could, anyway. I told you she had connections. She knew people who paid people, and the stuff came through." She sobered and her mouth tightened. "But who said anything about cultural antiques? It was cocaine."

I stared at her. *Cocaine!* Of course — and the picture suddenly shifted. We were talking big money here. Big money, dangerous money. And dangerous people. I took a breath. "Made of plaster of Paris and cocaine?"

She nodded. "You've heard about this, then?"

As a matter of fact, I had. I had read about somebody — a Chilean, as I remembered it — who was arrested at the Barcelona airport when a drug-sniffing German shepherd alerted police that the plaster cast on his "broken" leg was made with cocaine. And a statue sculpted of plaster and cocaine worth forty thousand dollars had been seized at the El Paso border crossing the year before — I had seen a photograph of it on television. Smugglers were getting creative.

"So she brought the pottery across the border," I said. "In the van, I guess?"

"Yeah." She smiled slightly. "The van was

kind of a mess, actually. Six of us had been more or less camping in it for a couple of weeks. But the customs people basically just waved us on through, which I thought at the time was a little odd. I figured they'd give us a more serious look, since we were college kids. We fit the profile."

"No sniffer dogs?"

"Nope."

"Bribery?"

She nodded. "Gloria's cartel connection did his job."

"You know that for certain?"

"That's what Gloria told me. She bragged about it." She thought about that for a second, then paled. "That makes me . . . an accessory?"

I nodded curtly. "Did everybody in the van know? What about the other students?" But I was really thinking about Stuart Laughton. How much of this was he involved with?

"I don't know," she said slowly. "Maybe, maybe not. I kinda think maybe Matt knew it. Anyway, when Gloria told me about the bribe, we were in some cruddy restroom on the U.S. side of the border. None of the others heard it." Bitterly, she added, "She always loved it when she could put something over on somebody. On everybody. She loved making people look like fools."

"So what happened after she got the pottery across the border?"

"We stopped at a hamburger joint called Smoky's, not far from Pearsall. Some of us were lined up to get our food orders, and this Hispanic guy came up to Gloria and whispered something. She dropped out of line and the two of them went out to the van. When she came back, Larry asked her what was going on, and she laughed. Said she'd just sold the tourist pottery she had brought into the country."

"As easy as that?" It wasn't a question, really. I knew the answer. I've lived a quiet life since I came to Pecan Springs, but I saw plenty of trafficking in my earlier incarnation as a defense attorney. Then, though, it was mostly criminals, experienced smugglers. Now, young people — college kids, even high school students living in border towns — were being recruited as carriers, as mules. The cartel was looking for people who didn't fit the profile, young women who needed money for their children, teenage girls looking for excitement and dollars. They could get the stuff across — sometimes in their bellies, sometimes in their vaginas — when somebody who fit the profile couldn't. Of course, when corrupt customs officials were added to the mix, all bets were off.

"As easy as that," Shannon said.

I thought about it. "You said that *some* of you were lined up, getting your orders. Not all of you?"

"Like, I'm supposed to remember something like that?" she scoffed.

"I thought you might," I said steadily. "You've mentioned Larry. What about the other two guys?"

She frowned. "Roger was there, I know, because he and Stu were arguing about whether tulip bulbs are edible. But I don't think . . ." Her frown deepened. "Matt wasn't there. He came in with Gloria, when she got back in line."

"Gloria," I repeated thoughtfully. "Did she tell you who her connections were? Did she say when she was going to make another trip?"

She shivered. "I didn't ask about her connections. I didn't want to know. But I heard her tell somebody else — Larry or Matt — that she was going to Mexico again this summer. I guess that's not going to happen now." She closed her eyes briefly. "You don't . . . you don't really think I'm in danger, do you?"

"I think the safest thing for you to do is to

tell the police what you know. Once you've done that, you've pulled the plug on whoever wants to harm you." I gave her a hard look. "Do you understand? They might try to keep you from talking to the cops, but once you've told the authorities what you know, you're no longer a target."

She nodded uncertainly. "Do I . . . do I need a lawyer?"

"Let me put it this way," I said. "If you've told me all you know — that's *if*," I repeated sternly. "If you've told me everything, I doubt that there'll be any charge. If it looks like that's going to happen, I'll see that you get the right kind of help."

She wrapped her arms around herself, rocking back and forth. "Who do I — who do I talk to?"

"The county sheriff is handling the investigation into the trailer homicide. I know him — he's easy to work with."

She considered. "You really think it will make me safer?"

"Without a doubt." I thought of Jessica, and wished I could have given her the same advice. If she had shared what she learned as she went along, she might be in a better place right now. I didn't want to think about where she might really be.

"Okay," she said in a small, thin voice. "I

guess I'd better talk to him."

I didn't trust her to do this on her own — she might change her mind before she got there. I phoned Blackie to say that I had found someone I thought he should talk to, and that I was bringing her in for an interview.

On the way to the parking lot with Shannon in tow (and needing a booster shot of encouragement at every other step), I thought of something that might take me off the hook at the shop — and get Ruby the help she needed. I pulled out my phone and punched in Gina Mondello's number. Gina gave us a hand in the shop during the Christmas rush and helped to organize a team of volunteers to work in the display gardens earlier in the spring. She's an accountant who works with Kate during tax season, and an herb gardener who has come up with a popular salt-free seasoning blend that includes rosemary and sage, her two favorite herbs, which I have a hard time keeping in stock. She has also taught several dried-flower card-crafting classes for us, so she knows her way around our shops. And best of all, she lives in the neighborhood.

I breathed a thankful sigh when she picked up. "Gina? It's China. Listen, Ruby and Cass are in a bind at the shop. Lisa didn't show up this morning and I can't get there for a little while. It would be a huge help if you could come in for a couple of hours. Are you available?"

"Sure thing, China," she said. "Oh, and I've made another dozen bottles of that salt-free blend. Want me to bring those?"

"Absolutely. I'll be there as soon as I can." I clicked off, feeling enormously relieved. Gina is a capable person and a calm presence in a crisis. She'd be a big help this morning. I phoned the shop to let Ruby know that she was on her way, and that I'd be there shortly.

"Thank God," Ruby said in a taut, thin voice. "Things are a little hectic. Do you happen to know if you have any more of that rosemary-mint soap? There's a customer asking about it. And somebody else wants to know whether you have any fennel." There was a brief off-line flurry of conversation, and Ruby was back. "Florence fennel, she says."

"All the rosemary soap I have is what's on the shelf," I said. "If we're out, tell her I'll reorder and ask her to check back next week. About the fennel, I don't have any Florence — that's the one with the fat leaf base. But I might have a couple of bronze fennels. They're on the second shelf from the top on the outdoor plant rack, behind the basil. Tell her to look there."

But Ruby didn't answer. In the background, I heard the tinkle of the bell over the door in my shop — and Ruby's frantic cry, "No, Grace, no! You can't go outside! You have to stay here, with Gramma!" The line went dead.

Caitlin, happily, was having no such troubles. She had finished mixing the icebox cookies and put the dough logs into the fridge to cool. Excitedly, she told me that Dr. Trevor, her new violin teacher, had called to say that she was invited to play in the young people's orchestra, and wanted me to phone her when I had time. Uncle Mike had called, too, and Caitie had given him an update on Pumpkin's get-acquainted activities. The cat had already encountered one of Brian's free-range lizards, on the loose in the upstairs hall. But apparently Pumpkin had sampled enough lizards to know that they are a leathery and not particularly appetizing snack; the lizard, instinctively cat-savvy, had headed for the nearest heating vent, where he was still holed up. Howard Cosell, on the other hand, had had a close encounter with a skunk in the woodpile beside the pecan tree. Was there anything she could spray on him to make him smell better? Or maybe she should just leave him in his outdoor kennel until Uncle Mike got home, because he really was too stinky to come back into the house. I voted for the kennel.

Things might be going to hell at the shop, but at our house, at least, life seemed pretty normal.

Chapter Eighteen

In very simple terms, aromatherapy is the therapeutic use of pure essential oils to improve the health and balance of the skin, the body, the mind, and the soul. Squeeze a lavender head or a sage leaf and smell your fingers. That aroma is the result of volatile oils, released by the bursting of tiny glands in the plant material. . . . Essential oils have the power to relax the nervous system, stimulate the circulation, lift depression, reduce inflammation, and ease aches and pains. The aroma of an essential oil is sensed by the olfactory nerve located in the back of the nose and carried to the brain, where it has its effect — perhaps stimulating or calming, perhaps imparting feelings of well-being and harmony to the whole self.

Victoria H. Edwards
The Aromatherapy Companion

Fifteen minutes later, I was walking Shannon into the sheriff's office. By now, she had abandoned every bit of her earlier bravado. I didn't blame her. If she had come forward with what she knew a week or two earlier, Gloria Graham might be alive today. She'd be in serious trouble, yes — but she would be alive.

"You'll stay, won't you?" Shannon asked imploringly, when I had introduced her to Blackie and was turning to go. "Please! I need your support."

"Not a good idea." I fished in my bag and took out one of the business cards. "But if you need anything, call, and I'll see if I can find someone to help you." I nodded in Blackie's direction. "Just tell him what you know, and you'll be okay."

"Thanks," she said glumly, and slumped into a chair beside the desk. She was obviously not looking forward to the interview.

Blackie followed me into the hall. "Think she'll give me a straight story?"

"If she seems to be holding back," I said, "you might show her the photo of the bracelet and the burned trailer. If that doesn't work, show her a photo of the victim. I've told her that her own safety could be at stake."

"That was smart," he said, adding, "I've

sent a couple of deputies to talk to Zoe Morris and Lucy LaFarge. Thanks for the leads. It's looking promising. Maybe we'll have a positive ID on the victim before too long." He went back into the office.

My cell phone began buzzing just as I was getting into the car. It was Ruby, sounding breathless. "China? I'm glad I caught you."

I'd only been away for a few minutes and the car was already as hot as an oven. I flicked the key and lowered the windows. "Did you manage to catch Baby Grace before she got away?" I asked, trying to make a little joke.

"That time, I did," Ruby said tersely. "Listen, China, Gina's not here yet, and Cass and I are going crazy. I need to call Gina and make sure she's coming. Do you have her number?"

"Hang on." I began flipping through the numbers on my phone, but just as I began giving it to Ruby, she interrupted, "Never mind, China. Gina's here. She just walked in."

"Thank heaven," I said fervently. "You'll be okay now, do you think?"

She was cheerful, but I could tell she was trying to be brave. "Sure. But it's definitely one of those days. You know? The Ladies Guild just called. They're sending somebody for twenty-one sandwiches and eight salads — and that's in addition to the regular lunch bunch. Cass called the girl who helped out in the kitchen a couple of weeks ago. Millie. She's coming over in a few —" She broke off the sentence with a little cry. "Gina, could you catch Grace and keep her from going into the tearoom?"

"The Ladies Guild?" They're a rather snooty club that sponsors things like bridge tournaments and style shows. Not our usual clientele, which made it all the more important. "That's terrific, Ruby! If we could get them to start doing their luncheons with us —"

"I know. That's why Cass called Millie to help with the sandwiches. She wants to make a good impression." She took a deep breath. "Oh, yes, I almost forgot. Donna Fletcher called. She asked me to tell you that —"

But whatever Donna Fletcher wanted me to know was lost in a shattering crash of breaking glass. "Grace just pulled down a display," she said hurriedly. "I have to go. Good-bye."

A display? Oh, no! Which one? The jars of prickly pear jelly? Or the bottles of aloe lotion? I could only hope that Grace hadn't been hurt, and that at least some of the jars or bottles or whatever had survived. I folded the phone and rested my forehead against the steering wheel for a moment, feeling an enormous weight of guilt settle on my shoulders. Ruby and Cass needed me, and I wasn't there. I hadn't been there for Jessica, either, when she had called on Monday night. And I had left Caitie at home alone today, to cope with cookies and cats and lizards and dogs and skunks and who knows what else.

But nobody can be there for everybody, every minute of the day. Caitie is self-reliant enough to manage, and Tom Banner is on call if she needs him. Jessica was now officially a missing person, with an entire police department on the lookout for her. And I had connected Blackie with somebody who had information that might help him find the perpetrator in his arson-homicide case. So I really ought to go back to the shop and give Ruby and Cass and Gina a hand — and try to keep Baby Grace from wrecking the place.

And then suddenly I had an idea. I wasn't far from home. I could zip out there, pick up Caitie, and take her back to the shop with me. She could watch Grace this afternoon, earn a little extra baby-sitting money, and let the rest of us do our work. I phoned her to ask if that would be okay, and got an ecstatic yes. I told her I'd pick her up shortly and phoned Ruby to let her know that her baby-sitting help was on the way.

There were a few loose ends I needed to tie up, but I could do that on the road, with my cell phone. I took out the scrap of paper on which I had jotted down the three items from Jessica's answering machine. Her roommate's boyfriend's cell number. The Caller ID for the man who wanted to see her — the man whose voice had seemed so eerily familiar. And the address Zoe had left. It hadn't meant anything to me at the time, but now I knew it was the address of Gloria Graham.

I started the car, turned on the air conditioner to high, then put in the Caller ID number. It didn't seem likely that Jessica's disappearance had anything to do with boyfriend trouble, but it might be worth checking out. It was, definitely — but not in the way I expected.

"Hello," a chipper male voice said, as I drove out of the lot and swung out onto the main road, heading in the direction of home. "Stuart Laughton here."

I was jolted. Stuart Laughton? And then, with a snap, it came together. My feeling that I knew the voice on the answering machine. The odd interaction I had witnessed at the Local Food meeting on Sunday night. The glance that had seemed to have a mysterious significance. Jessica and Stu had been involved in some sort of relationship, maybe even an affair. In fact, that might even be why Margie had left and gone to her mother's. I remembered the threatening tone of the last few words on Jessica's answering machine, and my skin prickled again. Stu and Jessica. Stu and Gloria Graham. Gloria was dead. Jessica was missing. How was this man involved?

"Stuart Laughton," he repeated, impatient. "Who is this?"

I couldn't go into any of this on the phone. I'd have to think of something else — and fast.

"Hi, Stu," I managed. "Hey, this is China Bayles. Is Margie there?"

"Oh, hi, China." He chuckled. "You've reached my cell phone, not our home number."

"Sorry." I made a left onto Limekiln Road. "Hope I didn't disturb you."

"Not a problem. Margie's out at Donna Fletcher's place today. You know they're going into business together?"

"Yeah, I heard," I said. "Sounds like a great idea to me."

"Me, too. Donna needs the help. And being a farm owner will give Margie more credibility when she talks about our book." He chuckled again. "Covering all the angles."

"I'll call out there," I replied. "Sorry to have bothered you."

"Like I said, not a problem. Talk to you soon." He clicked off.

Heading west on Limekiln, I sorted through what I knew, wondering how many other angles Stuart Laughton had covered. He had taken a group of students to Mexico, including a girlfriend who had turned out to be a mule for a drug cartel — at least, according to Shannon Fisher.

But it stood to reason that Gloria Graham hadn't come up with the Mexican connection all by herself. Somebody else had to have been involved. Stuart? He knew the area, Shannon had said. He organized the trip, made all the arrangements. Had he set Gloria up to bring those pieces of pottery across the border? If he had, then what? Had she gotten cold feet, decided to go to the police?

I shivered as I thought the unthinkable. Was Stuart Laughton responsible for the murder of Gloria Graham?

And then another thought, and more

questions. Jessica had been involved with Stuart somehow or other — involved enough for him to call and try to persuade her to see him. Had they been lovers? Or maybe it wasn't a romantic relationship at all. Maybe it was a business deal. Maybe he'd been trying to set Jessica up to do what Gloria had done and she was planning to blow the whistle on him — to write a story, maybe — and he had called to try to persuade her to be quiet. When that hadn't worked, he had —

But there was no point in speculating. I needed more facts. I glanced at the scrap of paper, checking the number I had written down for Jessica's roommate. She had said that she and her boyfriend were camping — this was his cell phone number. I put it in. After a moment, a male voice answered.

"Steve here," he said brusquely. "What's up?"

"I'm trying to reach Amanda." I hoped he wouldn't ask me her last name. I hadn't a clue. "It's about her roommate, Jessica Nelson."

"Amanda? Yeah, sure. Hold on a sec. She's over by the lake, catching some sun. I'll get her."

I was rattling across the old iron bridge over Cedar Creek before Amanda finally picked up. "My name is China Bayles," I said. "I'm a friend of Jessica's. Maybe she's mentioned me?"

"Sure. You're the one who owns the herb shop, aren't you?" Amanda's voice was as soft and Southern as molasses. I had to turn up the volume on the phone. "And you write the garden column for the *Enterprise?*"

"That's me," I said. I came up behind a tractor pulling a slat-sided livestock trailer loaded with black and white goats. "Listen, Amanda, I'm calling because Jessica has disappeared."

"Disappeared?" she exclaimed, shocked. "Oh, no!"

"I'm afraid so. No one has seen her since Monday afternoon, and she missed an important deadline at the paper. The editor has filed an official missing-person report." I slowed to a crawl behind the tractor, waiting for a chance to pass. The road along here is only two lanes and there are plenty of curves, so it could take a while. "I've spent the morning checking with people who might know where she could be. I wondered if you could help me out."

"Sure, if I can. Should I maybe come home? I mean, I was planning to be gone for a few more days, but I'll come back if I'm needed." Luckily, she didn't ask me where I'd gotten her boyfriend's cell phone number.

"I don't think that's necessary," I said, without trying to clarify my exact role in this. "At least, not yet. But maybe you could tell me if she's been seeing anyone recently. Dating anybody, I mean."

There was a pause. "Well," she said slowly, "there was somebody. They saw one another pretty seriously for maybe three or four months, but then she called it off."

I swung out, made sure that the road ahead was clear, and sped up to pass the tractor. As I waved, I noticed that the driver was a woman — Becky Sanders. Sanders' Animal Services must be branching off into goats. "She called it off? Why?"

Another pause. "She thought this guy and his wife were separated, but it turned out they weren't. The wife heard he was playing around and moved out. Went back home to her mother, was what I heard. Jessica didn't want to get between them, so she broke up with him."

"How long ago was that?"

"Not long. Three or four weeks, maybe. I don't think he was very happy about it, because he kept calling her." She cleared her throat. "You're probably wondering who, but I don't know if I ought to tell you.

I mean, he's kind of an important guy around the university. I don't want to get anybody into trouble."

"You're talking about Dr. Laughton, aren't you?" I was passing the burned-out trailer now. I didn't want to look at it.

"Yes, he's the one." She seemed relieved that she didn't actually have to name him. "So you know about him?"

"Yes. You said he kept calling. Did Jessica seem concerned about his persistence?"

"Well, she wished he wouldn't, if that's what you're asking. I think she was more annoyed than concerned, though. She said he didn't seem to be able to take no for an answer."

"I see. Was she dating anyone else?"

She thought about that. "Well, there were a couple of guys before she started seeing Dr. Laughton, but they're ancient history. Last year, I mean. I don't think she's seen anybody lately." She giggled a little. "She even talked about taking a vow of chastity for a while. She said guys were too distracting — they wanted more involvement than she did."

I gave an encouraging "Uh-huh," and she went on.

"Yeah. I mean, Jessica didn't want to get seriously involved with anybody. What she

367

really wanted, more than anything else, was a break that could help her get ahead as a journalist. She was hoping she'd get a good story to work on. She kept saying that there had to be more to life in Pecan Springs than the mayor's prayer breakfasts."

I sighed. Jessica had gotten a good story, all right — more than she'd bargained for. "What about your neighbor? The one Jessica called 'the jerk.' "

"Oh, him," she said disgustedly. "That's Butch Browning. Next door."

"Any reason to think that he might know where she is?"

"I hope not," Amanda said fervently. "We've been keeping our blinds closed at night, but Butch is a creep. There are people in and out of that house at all hours, and he's not the kind of guy who has a lot of friends. We're pretty sure he's dealing. If he . . ." Her voice rose. She sounded scared. "You don't think he did anything to her, do you? If he did, I'll hate myself forever!"

"Why?"

"Because she got mad one night and wanted to report him to the cops for peeping into our windows, and I wouldn't let her. His mom owns both his house and ours, and I was afraid she might kick us out. So I told Jessica not to call the police." She paused for breath. "If Butch has done anything to her . . ."

"There's no evidence that he has," I said soothingly. "But I'll certainly pass that information along to the police. Anyone else you can think of?"

"No," she said, more quietly now. "No, really. Jessica is kind of a loner, you know? Her sister, mom, dad — they died in a fire years ago. Her grandmother died a while back."

"Right," I said. "I wonder — did she ever mention going on a trip to Mexico? Maybe with one of her classes?"

"Mexico?" She paused. "Well, yes. When she was seeing Dr. Laughton, she mentioned that he'd invited her to go along on a trip. But that was before she broke up with him. Why are you asking?"

"Just checking. If you think of anything that might help us locate her, could you call me?" I gave her my number, then added, "Is this the best way to reach you? The number I called?"

"Yeah. I dropped my cell into the lake." She paused, and I could almost see her frowning. "How'd you find —"

"Thanks very much, Amanda," I said briskly. "You've been helpful. The police will contact you if they have other questions." I clicked off.

I slowed and made the left turn onto our lane. I had just tied up one very substantial loose end — at least, that's what it felt like. The man who had called Jessica was Stuart Laughton, and Amanda had confirmed that Jessica had been seeing him. I was going to have to give the information to the police, I thought, and immediately felt sorry for his wife. The cops would no doubt question him in Jessica's disappearance, and his relationship to Gloria Graham was going to come out. If Margie had hoped to move past her husband's marital transgressions, or keep them private between the two of them, she was going to be bitterly disappointed.

And then I thought of something else. Margie and Stuart were hoping for a great deal of positive publicity about their new book. This could throw a huge monkey wrench into the works. When word got out about this scandal — and it would, whether Stuart was criminally responsible or not — their upcoming book promotion plans might be affected. And then another thought followed on the heels of that one: could Stuart Laughton have killed to keep this scandal quiet?

Or maybe there was more. It didn't seem

likely to me that Gloria Graham had made her own independent connection with the cartel. Somebody must have recruited her. Laughton? I didn't like the idea, but I had to consider it. I had seen enough in the criminal courts to know that smart, well-educated, personable people with good ideas can make bad choices and get dragged into ugly situations. Once in, they lose control. And once they've lost control, all bets are off. Like it or not, something like that could have happened to Stu Laughton.

A few minutes later, I had collected Caitlin and we were on our way again, back to town. She had brought several books to read to Baby Grace, and she was energized and bouncy. But she had also been thinking, and she had a new idea to try out on me.

"I found something really interesting in the book rack beside the sofa this morning," she said, in her most grown-up voice. "A chicken catalog."

"Sure. It's mine. I sent off for it last summer when I was thinking of maybe getting chickens. So we could have our own fresh eggs."

"How come you didn't? Get chickens, I mean. So we could have eggs."

I turned to look at her. Should I say it? I did. "Because we got you," I said lightly.

371

"For keeps. Remember? And I thought that a new kid in the family and new chickens might be a little too much. I'm a member of the one-thing-at-a-time club." Well, not exactly. But I would *like* to be.

She giggled at that, and her girl-giggle was so infectious that I had to smile, too.

"So it was me or chickens?" she asked.

"Yep." I paused, wondering what was coming next. "We decided we'd rather have you. I am happy to report that Uncle Mike and Brian and I are thrilled with the way things turned out." I gave her a sidelong glance. "So why are you asking about this catalog? There must be a reason."

"Well, there is. The baby chicks looked really cute and fluffy. So I was thinking maybe we should have some. Like maybe two that would grow up to be red chickens, and two that would be speckled, and two that would be white? That's six." She paused. "I don't know if we should have a rooster. Do you need a rooster to get eggs?"

We had arrived at a teachable moment. But what did I want to teach? Should we have a mother-daughter discussion of the birds and bees, or was the question of responsibility more important? I opted for responsibility.

"Whoa," I said, holding up my hand.

"You've just adopted a cat, haven't you? Or did I dream that?" I shook my head as if in bewilderment. "You know, I could swear you took in a cat — just a day or two ago, wasn't it? A straggly-looking, down-at-the-heels character who has obviously spent eight of his nine lives looking for a home. And now it's *chickens?* Heaven help us."

Another giggle.

I sighed heavily. "Well, you know, Caitlin, chickens have to be taken care of. And since I have a shop, gardens all over the place, a husband, a son, *and* a daughter — not to mention a dog, a shop cat, a house cat, and a collection of loose lizards — I am not about to volunteer for chicken duty. Uncle Mike is busy, too, you know."

"I promise I'll take care of the chickens," she said earnestly. "And the cat. Anyway, he's mine. And Brian is supposed to take care of his lizards, isn't he?"

"He is. And he does, mostly, except when they get loose. But you have your violin, too, and Dr. Trevor says she would like you to be in the orchestra, and maybe in a recital. Will you have time for chickens?" I grew up in the city and chickens have not been a part of my life, so I didn't know how much time they would take. But it was something she ought to consider.

She sat back in the seat. "I'll make time," she said very seriously. "And I can pay for them myself, you know. I'll use my baby-sitting money to buy the baby chicks, and I'll sell their eggs to buy their chicken feed. I read that they need special food, that we can buy at the chicken-feed store. But I won't sell *all* their eggs. I'll keep enough so you and Uncle Mike and Brian and I can have scrambled eggs for breakfast whenever we want, and deviled eggs, too. And eggs for cakes and stuff."

She thought about that for a minute, doing some mental calculations. "I might need to start with more than just six babies, if I'm going to have enough eggs. Maybe ten?" She got very serious. "Maybe twelve? In case two of them die?"

I fell back on the tried-and-true mom tactic I had first practiced on Brian, when he was younger. "Okay," I said agreeably. "We'll think about it." I gave her a look. "We'll *think* about it," I repeated sternly. "Which means —"

"Oh, goody!" She clapped her hands. "I'll get four red ones, three speckled ones, and three white ones. And maybe a rooster."

I sighed.

"And Uncle Mike and I will build a chicken house where they can live. And

Howard Cosell can keep the skunks away, because I read that skunks like chickens' eggs every bit as much as people do."

"I'm sure that Howard will take his responsibilities very seriously," I said.

"He'd better," Caitlin said. "I don't want *anything* eating my eggs."

We walked into the shop just in time to catch Baby Grace in the act of pulling the books out of the book rack and scattering them on the floor. Caitlin, eager to start earning the money for her chicken-and-egg business, corralled Grace immediately and took her into the corner for a read-aloud time. Ruby was glad to see me, but even happier to see Caitlin.

"Thank heavens you thought of bringing her," she said, looking relieved. "I love sweet little Grace with all my heart, but she's about to drive us crazy."

"Caitie was delighted to be asked," I said. "She already has plans for the money we're going to pay her."

"Music for her violin?" Ruby asked.

"Baby chicks," I said with a sigh.

Things quieted down a little after that. Millie came in to help Cass make the extra sandwiches, Ruby seated and served customers in the tearoom, and Gina moved capably between my shop and Ruby's. By two o'clock, the Ladies Guild had picked up their sandwiches and salads, the lunch crowd was gone, Baby Grace was having a nap on her favorite blanket in the quiet cubby under the stairs, and Caitlin was reading a book about chickens she had found on my book rack and had already called the two local feed stores to see if they had any baby chicks for sale. (They didn't, but they'd be glad to order them for her.) Things were back on an even keel, and I had time to remember something that I had forgotten earlier.

I picked up the phone and punched in Donna Fletcher's number. "Ruby said you called the shop with a message for me," I said, when she came on the line. "But something came up before she could tell me what it was. I thought I'd better check and see if everything is okay."

"Glad you did," she said. "I thought you ought to know that we've heard from Terry. Well, not *from* Terry," she corrected herself, "but about her." She whooshed out a sigh of relief. "She's okay, thank God. More or less, anyway."

I felt glad for her, even though I already knew that much. What's more, from everything I had learned this morning, it didn't seem likely that Terry had had anything to do with the arson-homicide.

"More or less?" I asked. "Where is she? What's the situation?" I was expecting to hear that Terry was in jail somewhere, but that wasn't it.

Donna sighed. "In Brownsville. She's been in the hospital there, but she's out now."

"Oh, gosh," I exclaimed. "The hospital? What happened? Is she okay?"

"Not quite okay, but it's not as bad as it might have been. A broken arm, concussion, bruises. Some teenager ran a red light and smacked into her at an intersection. The truck is drivable, she says. She's getting it repaired and will drive it home, after she's released. The kid got the ticket."

"I'm glad she's okay," I said. "And that there wasn't anything more serious behind her disappearance."

"Right." Donna gave a rueful laugh. "Like getting burned up in a trailer fire." She hesitated. "Have you found out yet who it was?"

"I think so," I said. "The sheriff has a pretty good lead, anyway. We'll just have to wait and see."

"Not somebody we know, I hope," Donna said.

"I don't think so." I wasn't going to be

the one to tell her that her new partner's husband might be involved with the death. I said good-bye, feeling relieved that Terry hadn't been hurt any worse than she had. But I couldn't shake the fretful worry at the back of my mind, and the bruising question: where was Jessica?

Gina came in from the garden with Mrs. Oliver, one of our regular customers, and a tray of dill, basil, and savory transplants, all in four-inch pots.

"Did you find what you wanted?" I asked.

"I did, thank you," Mrs. Oliver said happily. "Gina knows so much about herbs, China. You should have her here more often!"

"You're right," I replied. "She's a treasure."

Gina winked at me. "Any time," she said with a chuckle, and went outside to help someone else.

I was tallying up Mrs. Oliver's tab when the shop phone rang.

"Thyme and Seasons," I said, cradling the receiver against my shoulder. "How can I help you?"

It was Sheila. "China, I just got a report from one of the patrol officers. Jessica Nelson's vehicle has been spotted in a parking lot."

"Jessica?" I nearly dropped the phone. "Where? When? Any sign of her?"

"Where, in the outside lot at the Hill Country Villa apartment complex. When, about ten minutes ago. No sign of Nelson, at least so far. But that's a busy area, lots of residential foot traffic. Hark couldn't provide a photograph of her, so we're going on a general description."

"How much is that going to be?" Mrs. Oliver asked, opening her handbag. She is a tiny white-haired woman with vivid blue eyes and a gardener's hands — that is, you can usually see a little trace of dirt under her nails.

"Eleven dollars and twelve cents," I said. I was itching to talk to Sheila, but first things first. "Including tax. How about a box?"

"Excuse me?" Sheila asked.

"A box would be wonderful," Mrs. Oliver replied. "I don't want to bruise these sweet little babies. Oh, and do you have a brochure for that other thing you do? Party Thyme, I think it's called. My little grandson is having a birthday and his mother and I would love it if Big Bird could come and bring games and food." Party Thyme is our catering service and Big Bird is Ruby, who wears her Big Bird suit when we cater a party for kids. She got a Cookie Monster suit for me, but I wear it only under duress.

"Hang on a minute," I told Sheila. I put the receiver down, made change from twelve dollars, located a cardboard tray for the plants, and found a Party Thyme brochure. "Just call if you'd like to schedule a party," I said to Mrs. Oliver. "We're available most weekends, but now that the Farmers' Market is open, we have to plan ahead."

"I will," she replied. "We'll let you know. And thanks!"

I picked up the phone. "Hill Country Villa?" I repeated breathlessly. "Is that what you said, Sheila?" It was the apartment complex where Gloria Graham had lived.

"That's right. On Sam Houston Drive. We've phoned the *Enterprise* to let Hark know, but he's in San Antonio on a story this afternoon. Since you've been worried about Nelson, I thought you'd want to know, too. There's an officer with the car."

I looked around. It was reasonably quiet, and Gina was still here. "I think I can get away for a while. And I might be able to help at the scene. I know Jessica. I can identify her." I hesitated. "Have you connected with Blackie on this?"

"Yes. He says that the apartment complex is the address of the woman he's tentatively identified as the victim in the trailer fire.

Gloria Graham. You helped with that ID?"

"I did. Got lucky this morning."

"Hang on a sec." She said something to someone else, then came back on the line. "I'm told that Blackie is getting a search warrant for Graham's apartment. He'll be there as soon as he has it."

A search warrant. That meant that the sheriff was able to persuade a magistrate that he had probable cause to believe that some part of the crime — Graham's abduction, perhaps — might have been committed in her apartment.

"Thanks for calling, Smart Cookie. I'll try to get over there." I paused, remembering that there was something I needed to tell her. "Jessica and her roommate Amanda have had trouble with their next-door neighbor. He's been peeping into their windows. I encountered him this morning, when I checked out Nelson's house." I wasn't going to tell her that I had taken the liberty of going inside. Sheila's a cop. She would quite naturally object. "He's the rough, tough type," I added, "or likes to think he is. It might be worthwhile to have a talk with him. His name is Butch Browning. When I asked Amanda about him, she mentioned lots of after-dark traffic at his place. She and Jessica thought he might be dealing." Now that I heard myself reporting these details, I thought this sounded like a promising lead. I hoped the PSPD would follow up on it.

Sheila seemed to agree. "How can I get in touch with the roommate?"

I fished up Amanda's boyfriend's number and gave it to her, then put down the phone and hurried into Ruby's shop. She was just finishing up with a customer who was buying some essential oil and a book on aromatherapy. The oil was the same one that Ruby was using in a fragrance diffuser on her counter. She used to burn incense, but the smoke (she says) can transmit harsh, even carcinogenic chemicals into the air, and it bothered some of her customers who suffered from asthma. So she turned to a diffuser instead, and creates and sells her own unique mood-altering blends. I asked her once if she could come up with a fragrance that would encourage people to pull out their checkbooks and credit cards, but she said she didn't think that was funny.

"Listen, Ruby," I said urgently. "I just found out that Jessica's car has been located. It's parked in the apartment complex where Gloria Graham lived. Hill Country Villa, on Sam Houston."

"That's good news," Ruby said. She

382

closed the cash drawer as the customer left the shop. "I think. Is it good news?" She frowned. "Who's Gloria Graham?"

Things had been so hectic that there hadn't been time to fill Ruby in on everything that had happened that morning. "She's the girl who burned to death in the trailer," I said hurriedly. "At least, that's the tentative identification. Jessica may have gone to her place because she thought she had a line on Graham's killer." I was leaping to all sorts of conclusions here, but at the moment, at least, they seemed warranted. "I need to drive over there and check things out. Is that okay with you? Gina can take over for me, and now that the lunch rush is over, the afternoon will probably be pretty quiet. I hate to leave you in the lurch, but I feel that I ought to . . ."

I stopped. Ruby was looking at me with an odd little smile. "What?" I demanded impatiently. "What's that smile supposed to mean?"

"If I told you no," she said quietly, "you would either sulk or throw a temper tantrum. Wouldn't you?"

"I would not," I said hotly. "I would just deal with it, the way I always do. I would just . . . just . . ." My voice trailed off.

"Just what?"

I sighed. "Yeah, you're probably right. I'd more likely sulk than throw a tantrum, though. I only pitch a fit when there's nobody around." I paused, remembering that Ruby had been in the room the last time I had blown up. "Mostly, anyway. With a few exceptions. I let my closest friends see who I really am."

With another smile, Ruby put out her hand and gently turned my face in the direction of the diffuser. "Breathe," she commanded.

"Why?"

"Never mind. Just breathe."

I breathed. I breathed again. Whatever she was diffusing in that diffuser, it smelled very good.

"There," she said. Her voice was soothing. "Don't you feel calmer?"

Actually, I did. I felt less jittery and jumpy, less frantic. I took another breath and began to relax. "What is it?"

"Sandalwood, with clary sage, cloves, and a few other essential oils. My customers say that they begin to feel calm the minute they walk in the door. When they feel calmer, they slow down. They're not in such a rush."

"Mmm," I said, wondering if calm customers might take more time to shop. "I guess I won't throw a tantrum this afternoon. Even for my closest friend."

"I thought so." She grinned. "So go already, China. We'll keep an eye on Caitlin."

"It's okay?" I took one last breath and straightened up. "Really? You won't be mad if I take off for an hour or so?"

"I will be *seriously* mad if you don't go find out what has happened to Jessica Nelson." Ruby reached behind her, pulled out a tissue and a small bottle, and dropped a bit of oil on the tissue. She handed it to me. "Put this on the dashboard of your car, in the sun. Now go solve a crime or two."

"What's this?" I asked, looking down at the tissue.

"Rosemary oil. It energizes the mind and stimulates the adrenal glands. Calm is wonderful, but you have a job to do this afternoon. You need to be on your game."

What did I do to deserve such a friend?

CHAPTER NINETEEN

Margaritas are traditionally made with silver tequila, which is produced from the blue agave (*Agave tequilana* Weber), a stately plant with long, stiff leaves, each defended by a row of sinister teeth and a needle-like tip. This well-armed member of the lily family thrives in an arid climate in volcanic soil. In the Tequila region of the state of Jalisco, Mexico, where much of the blue agave is commercially grown, the fields cover the slopes of two extinct volcanoes. *¡Salud!*

China Bayles
"Mood-Altering Plants"
Pecan Springs Enterprise

The Hill Country Villa rambles over a wide expanse of carefully landscaped hillsides on the east side of campus. As you drive into the complex, the first thing you see is a cluster of beautiful blue agaves — a relative of the plant that's used to make tequila — carefully mulched with white gravel. Ahead, you can see three architecturally pleasing units arranged around a swimming pool large enough to launch a Nautilus sub and a couple of tugboats. The buildings are surrounded by tennis, basketball, and volleyball courts and a soccer field — all of it designed for students who have plenty of time to play and the money to finance their leisure pursuits. There is also plenty of parking, in a residents' parking garage adjacent to the central unit and in an open visitors' lot a little distance away.

I located Jessica's green Ford easily, not only because it was the oldest car in the lot (the others were late-model sports cars, Jeeps, a Hummer, and an SUV with a rack of water skis on top and a muscle boat hitched to the rear) but because there was a Pecan Springs police car parked beside it, and a uniformed officer, making notes on a clipboard. Some Texas police departments have squad cars with onboard computers, but Sheila says it'll be a while before that happens in Pecan Springs. We're still a small town, with a small town's public safety budget. She'd rather put the money into patrol officers than computers.

The rosemary that scented my car really

did smell delicious, and I took one last deep breath before I opened the door, got out, and called to the officer. "Hey, Jerry!"

Jerry is short for Jeraldine, but if you call her that, you'd better be ready to duck. She and I met on what you might call official business, when a man with a gun broke into my shop a week or so before Christmas. Jerry was one of the officers who answered my 9-1-1 call and helped to subdue the intruder. She may be only an inch above the regulation height minimum, but she grew up on a ranch where her favorite sport was calf-wrestling, and I think she likes it when somebody is foolish enough to resist arrest. She had also liked what she'd seen of the shop that morning and had dropped in several times since.

"Hey, China," she drawled, in her flat East Texas twang. "Whatcha doin'?"

"Chief Dawson phoned me. She said Jessica Nelson's car had been spotted here. I'm a friend of Jessica's."

"She's a student?" Jerry cast a raised-eyebrow look at the car, then around at the Villa's obvious amenities. "Great little place she's got here. Must be nice."

"She doesn't live here. She and her roommate have a place north of the campus." I walked around the car. "No sign of a disturbance or a struggle?"

"Not that I can see," Jerry said, "but somebody from the investigations unit will be along in a few minutes. They'll give it a good going-over."

I understood. Jerry's job was to hang out until the investigators arrived. "Who reported it?"

"The manager noticed that the car's been sitting here for a while — at least since Tuesday morning, she said, maybe Monday night. She checked, and it wasn't registered as belonging to a tenant, so she gave it another twenty-four, then phoned for a tow truck. The towing service picked up the APB on the vehicle and called it in."

"A piece of luck," I said. That's how it's supposed to happen, but it doesn't always work that way. The car could have sat in an impound lot for weeks before it was noticed again.

A brown Adams County sheriff's car pulled up beside us, and Jerry turned. "My, my," she said in an ironic tone. "We're attracting a crowd."

"Hello, Blackie," I said, as the sheriff — wearing his brown uniform and his usual utility belt — got out of his car. He was alone.

"Why am I not surprised to see you here,

China?" He turned to Jerry. "Any sign of the car's owner, Officer?"

"No, sir," Jerry said. She aimed an inquisitive glance at the county vehicle.

"Related business," Blackie said, reading her look. "Your team is on its way."

"Sheila told me you were coming to check out Gloria Graham's apartment," I said.

"Right. Unit One, second floor." He added dryly, "I suppose you think that bringing in Fisher means that you've earned the right to tag along."

"I do." I grinned. "You got what you needed from Fisher?"

He nodded. "An interesting story. Several angles, a couple of leads." He looked at me. "I doubt if our investigation would have turned her up, China. I owe you."

He was right. There are things that cops can do and things they can't. "I need to give you a couple of other items," I said. Guiltily, I added, "I meant to call and fill you in on a phone conversation that took place after I left your office this morning, but things got hectic at the shop. If you let me tag along, I can do that now."

"Come on, then." To Jerry, he said, "Which way is the manager's office?"

The officer pointed toward the central building, which sported a fancy white-columned portico. "Inside. Hang a right. First door on the left." Her radio chirped. "Manager's name is Linda Sternfeld," she added, as she reached for it.

On the way to the office, I briefly sketched out for Blackie what Amanda had told me about Jessica's relationship with Stuart Laughton. I concluded with, "So it seems that Laughton had been seeing both Gloria Graham and Jessica Nelson. Romance, sex, or both. And maybe more," I added.

"Busy fellow," Blackie remarked. "Guy with a big heart. High-powered sex drive, too."

"I hate this," I said bleakly. "I'm acquainted with Stuart and I like him, although I've been a little uncomfortable around him sometimes. I'm sorry to hear that he's been cheating on his wife. She's a nice gal." I didn't blame Jessica, though. According to Amanda, Stuart had misrepresented his situation and Jessica had broken off their relationship when she learned the truth. I could chalk that up to a mistake. I've made a few like that in my time, and managed to extricate myself without too much damage. I could only hope that Jessica would, too.

"Uncomfortable?" Blackie asked.

"Yes. He's a little too flirtatious for my

taste. He's a hands-on guy, if you know what I mean. But more to the point, he seems to be at the center of this situation. He's a faculty member, and I like to think they're above this sort of thing. But he's made frequent trips to Mexico for his research. It's possible that he's somehow gotten involved with one of the cartels. Unlikely, but possible."

Unlikely, yes. But this kind of thing happens. Justine Wyzinski, aka the Whiz, a law school buddy of mine who practices in San Antonio and South Texas, was recently asked to take the case of a young doctor who had financed his way through medical school with a cartel affiliation. He was a paragon of respectability, according to his friends and colleagues, and couldn't possibly have done what the Feds said he was doing. But Justine took a look at the case and declined to represent him. I didn't blame her. Once you climb into bed with the drug lords, they may be reluctant to let you climb back out — especially if they like your work. If she had pled him out or gotten him off, there could have been another, and another.

"Maybe Gloria Graham wanted to make some extra money," I added, "and Laughton recruited her. It's possible that he tried to do the same thing with Jessica, too. Maybe she refused and he —"

Blackie raised a hand. "Whoa," he cautioned. "Let's not get too far ahead of ourselves. Given what Shannon Fisher reported and what I've just heard from you, I'll be talking to Laughton as soon as I'm finished here. But we don't have a positive on the trailer fire victim yet. And we don't know what's happened to Nelson. In fact, we don't know that anything has happened to her."

"Oh, right," I said, with some sarcasm. "Like maybe she parked her Ford here, then hopped a bus to Austin and forgot to let anybody know where she was going."

"Or she ran into a friend of the opposite sex, and they went off together for some fun," Blackie said. The radio on his belt chirped, and he stopped to speak into it.

Blackie was right about the identification. And as far as Jessica's disappearance was concerned, there were suspects other than Stuart Laughton. There was the jerk — the next-door neighbor, for instance. And there was Larry Wolff, whom I had not yet tried to track down. And how about —

"Hey, Matt," somebody called. "Yo! Simmons!"

Matt Simmons? The name rang a bell, and

I turned. A tall, strongly built guy in his early twenties — brown hair, rugged good looks — was striding along the walk in front of the central building. He was wearing jeans, a T-shirt that shouted OAXACA! in multicolored letters dancing around a big sombrero, and leather sandals.

Simmons stopped, and the kid who had hailed him bounced a basketball on the pavement. "A bunch of us are going over to the court," the kid said. "Got a half hour for a pickup game?"

Matt Simmons. This was the guy who was doing the research on ololiuqui — morning glory seeds — and supplying Lucy LaFarge with the raw ingredients for the street drug she was cooking up in her kitchen. According to Shannon, he had been one of the male students on Laughton's field trip to Oaxaca back in November. And then I remembered something else Shannon had said. Matt Simmons had been outside with Gloria in the parking lot of that hamburger joint when she unloaded her "tourist pottery."

Matt Simmons. He lived *here?* In the same complex where Gloria lived?

Yes, apparently. "Sorry," he said to the kid with the basketball. "Gotta study for a quiz tomorrow. Catch ya later. Okay?" He lifted a hand, went inside, and crossed the nicely decorated foyer to the elevator. As I watched, he stepped inside. The lighted indicator above the elevator showed that it was stopping at the second floor. The second floor — and Gloria had lived on the second floor. I was beginning to see some connections.

Blackie had already headed toward the manager's office, and I was still processing this information as I turned to follow him. The office was even more nicely decorated than the foyer, with a handsome walnut desk, a plush, comfy-looking sofa, several obligatory potted plants, and an array of photographs of luxury apartments, the club room, the gym, and the spa. The photos featured the young and lovely and well-heeled residents the Villa was designed to attract, all of them engaged in various fun-loving activities.

Blackie was holding up his official identification for the skeptical consideration of a dark-haired woman dressed in a peach-colored power suit with a matching camisole and three-inch heels — Ms. Sternfeld, I presumed. A pair of reading glasses hung around her neck on a gold chain.

She examined his identification as she listened to his announcement that he was here to check out the apartment of a woman who might have been the victim in an arson fire the previous Saturday. Frowning, she said, "I find it hard to believe that one of our residents would have put herself into such a situation." Her tone implied that their luxury apartments were never occupied by riffraff who might die in a house trailer, and her glance at the holster on Blackie's belt suggested that weapons were both unwelcome and unnecessary in such an exclusive enclave.

"She might not have had a choice," Blackie replied evenly. "We're still in the process of making an identification of the body. I'm afraid it's not an easy task. The victim was burned beyond recognition. However, we have probable cause to believe that it is indeed Ms. Graham, and we're proceeding under that assumption, at least for the moment."

Probable cause should have tipped her off, but apparently Ms. Sternfeld didn't watch cop shows on TV. "I really don't think I should permit —" she began in an officious tone.

"I have a search warrant," Blackie said. He pulled a folded document out of his shirt pocket and handed it to her. "Your consent to the search is unnecessary, however. I am notifying you as a courtesy. I would appreciate it if you would either unlock Ms. Graham's apartment for me or provide me with a key." It was also true that she could not have given consent to the search in any circumstances, since a landlord, or his representative, lacks the authority to do so. I wondered if she knew that.

Ms. Sternfeld put on her reading glasses, unfolded the warrant, and scanned it. Then she handed it back with the tips of her fingers, as if it were loaded with germs. "Really, Sheriff, this sort of thing is highly irregular. Our residents simply do not —"

"Irregular, yes," Blackie said. "Murder is a highly irregular event. Most people do not intend to burn to death." He put the warrant on her desk, walked to the wall, and looked pointedly at a photo that showed a young boy and girl mounted on side-by-side stationery bicycles, gazing at a television set while they listened to their iPods.

"Of course, I wouldn't want to cause any more disruption to your tenants than necessary," he went on. "Your tenants and their parents, that is. The last thing you need is a half-dozen sheriff's cars parked outside your door. But perhaps that won't be necessary. At this point, I only intend to have a preliminary look. I hope you will agree to unlock the door, so I won't have to make a forcible entry."

The manager gave an involuntary shudder. "Well, I suppose we could go up there together, and see if Ms. Graham answers the door. Let me check for the telephone number, and I'll call ahead." Furrowing her brow, she bent over a computer, looked up a number, then punched it into a phone. While she was waiting, she glanced up and saw me for the first time, standing just inside the door. "May I help you?"

"Ms. Bayles is with me," Blackie said.

"Oh," Ms. Sternfeld said, and went back to listening to the ringing on the other end of the line. Finally she put the phone down. "No answer," she said unnecessarily, and reached for a set of keys. "Well, I suppose we'd better go up there. Ms. Graham might be sick or something."

Sick or something, I thought dryly. How about dead?

But I was still thinking about Matt Simmons. As the three of us went to the elevator for the ride to the second floor, I spoke to Blackie in a chatty, isn't-this-a-small-world tone.

"What a coincidence, Sheriff. As we were coming in, I ran into Matt Simmons. Shannon Fisher may have mentioned his name to you this morning. He was on the field trip to Oaxaca with Gloria Graham. Thinking about it now, I wonder if maybe he shared her connections."

Blackie nodded. He was expressionless, but he flicked me a glance. He understood what I was saying.

"Mr. Simmons?" Ms. Sternfeld asked brightly. "He's a friend of yours? Actually, he lives across the hall from Ms. Graham, on the second floor."

"Is that right?" I asked in a friendly tone. "It was a surprise to see him. I'm sorry that we didn't have a chance to talk. I wonder — were Matt and Ms. Graham friends?"

"Actually, he moved in just a few weeks before she did. And yes, I believe they were acquainted before they both came here. He referred her to us and received a lease discount for the referral." She was looking at Blackie. "Really, Sheriff, I hope you're not right about Ms. Graham. It would be devastating if she was the one who . . ." The elevator door opened and she broke off, finding it impossible to say the words "burned to death in that house-trailer fire."

The second floor was quiet, its wide, carpeted hallway stretching from one side of the building to the other. Ms. Sternfeld rapped loudly at a door marked 204, waited a moment, then knocked again.

"Ms. Graham," she called, trying another knock. Then, with a heavy sigh and a great show of reluctance, she pushed a key into the door and turned it.

We stepped into the apartment, leaving the door partially open behind us. We had entered an elegant living room, with an off-white carpet, white leather sofa and chair, glass coffee table, and an entertainment center with a flat-screen TV the size of my dining room tabletop. The walls were covered with Mexican woven hangings, there was a large Mexican area rug under a dining table, and several pieces of Mexican pottery were scattered around the room. I looked at them, wondering if they were the real thing — real pottery, that is, rather than the stuff that ended up on the street, killing people. The kitchen boasted stainless steel appliances, but they were so spotlessly clean that I was willing to bet that they weren't seeing much use. The bedroom was as posh as the living room, although the floor was littered with clothing, the bed was unmade, and the bathroom counter was crowded with bottles and jars and tubes of makeup. A sliding glass door looked out on a private sundeck furnished with luxury redwood loungers, pots of marigolds and cosmos, and a view of the cedar-clad hills above the campus.

"A very nice apartment," I said appreciatively, as Blackie went quickly from room to room, looking for signs of violence that might suggest that whatever had happened to Gloria Graham had begun here. My own quick glance told me that this wasn't likely, but he's the expert in such matters. His trained eye would see things I missed. "I'm sure parents must feel that their children are safe here."

"Safety is our highest priority," Ms. Sternfeld said quickly. "And of course, we're always glad to add the names of young people to our waiting list. Sometimes parents put their children on our roster when they're still juniors or seniors in high school. This is quite a desirable complex, you know." She paused. "I can give you my card when we go back downstairs, if you'd like to make a referral."

"Perhaps I would," I said. "How much would someone expect to pay for this particular apartment, for instance?"

"Our one-bedroom units are $950 a month, which includes convenient garage parking and all utilities, as well as unlimited use of our fitness facilities. We do have two- and three-bedroom apartments, as well, if your student would prefer a roommate situation. Less expensive, too." With a practiced enthusiasm, she had switched into her saleslady mode. "I might also mention that you can choose from several different designer furniture, drapery, and appliance packages. And we offer a weekly cleaning service — for an extra fee, of course."

She made a sweeping gesture that included the leather sofas. "This package is our best. We have a parking garage for tenants — the door is just at the far end of the hall, so our residents don't have to go out into the weather. And twenty-four-hour security." She smiled toothily. "We make every effort to protect the young people in our care." But her smile faded quickly, as she remembered that the sheriff had told her that something very bad may have happened to Gloria Graham.

I was thinking that a student — or her parents — had to have plenty of money to afford a place like this, with its designer furniture package and weekly cleaning service. "Is Matt Simmons' apartment similar?" I asked.

"All our one-bedroom units have an identical floor plan," she replied. "Of course, his has a different view." She gestured toward the door to the deck. "I like this one, because it looks out onto the hills."

I was about to make a response, but through the partially open door, I saw a movement in the hallway. Across the hall, the door of 205 had opened, and someone was coming out. He was carrying a large canvas duffle bag, empty, and striding swiftly down the hall in the direction of the parking garage.

I crossed to the bedroom in three quick steps. "I've just seen Matt Simmons going down the hall," I said urgently to Blackie, who was inspecting a closet. "Looks like he's headed for the parking garage. I don't want to jump to conclusions, but he's carrying an empty duffle — about the size of a body bag."

Blackie grasped the situation immediately. "Stay here," he commanded. He unsnapped the flap on his holster and stepped out into the hall. "Mr. Simmons," he called. "Adams County Sheriff's Department. Hang on a minute, please. I'd like to talk to you."

But at the sound of the sheriff's voice, Simmons broke into a run, pushing through the door that led to the stairs to the parking garage. Blackie sprinted after him. I pretended I hadn't heard his command and ran after him.

"Wait!" Ms. Sternfeld cried. She was trying her best to follow, but she was hobbled by her narrow skirt and three-inch heels. Power suits may connote clout, but that's about as far as it goes.

I turned, running backward. "Call 9-1-1," I said. "Now! Tell them to come to the parking garage."

She gave up the chase and was pulling out her cell phone by the time I hit the stairway door. I pushed through and rattled down a flight of concrete stairs. The door to the parking garage had already thudded shut behind Blackie, and I opened it and stepped into the garage.

I was standing on the lowest level of the two-level concrete structure, a few cars parked nose-in along each side. In the dim light, I could see Blackie. He had slowed down and was moving deliberately through the half-darkened garage, looking into and under every car. He held his gun in one hand. Simmons was nowhere in sight.

I listened, waiting for the sound of an engine starting up, thinking that Simmons had reached his vehicle and might try to drive out. And then, off to my left, about three or four cars up the row, I saw a door in the wall, closing itself on one of those door closers that work very slowly.

I reached it before it closed completely. It

was a gray-painted metal door with the words Storage Area stenciled across the front in brown letters. Under that, Residents Only. It had one of those key-pad security locks on it, where you punch in a number code to gain access.

I knew immediately what I was looking at. Right after I graduated from law school, I had rented an apartment in a large unit in Houston. Every resident had a walk-in storage locker in a large room adjacent to the parking garage, which was handy for stowing stuff you didn't use regularly and didn't have room for in the inadequate closets in your apartment. Sports equipment, out-of-season clothing, stuff like that. The door to the parking garage was locked. Residents put their own locks on their lockers.

Matt Simmons had just carried an empty duffle bag into the Villa's storage area — not a suspicious act, of course. But instead of turning to ask why the sheriff wanted to talk to him, he had fled. Why?

My foot still in the door, I glanced around, and spotted what I was looking for, leaning up against the wall, just within arm's reach. It was a four-foot piece of lumber that people were using to prop the door open and keep it from locking when they were moving stuff in and out. I wedged it into place, then ran to Blackie.

"I think he's in the storage area." I pointed at the door. "Over here!"

Blackie turned and strode toward the door. I was ahead of him, feeling on the wall to the right for the light switch I knew must be there. My fingers found it and I flicked the switch. The room inside was what I expected, a labyrinthine complex of closets, large enough to store a stack of boxes, a bicycle — or a dead body.

If I had thought, I might have been more prudent, but I acted purely on instinct and without thinking. "Jessica!" I cried. "Jessica, are you there?"

"Help!" I heard from a far corner of the room, the quavering sound echoing eerily. It was a young woman's voice. "Oh, help, pl— !" The last word was cut off, strangled, as if a hand had gone over her mouth.

"Shut up," a man shouted. "You hear me? Just shut up!"

Blackie shoved me to one side. "Matt Simmons!" he shouted, raising his gun to shoulder level. "Come out with your hands over your head. No weapons. I want to see both of your hands up and empty."

"No way," Simmons said. "I've got the girl, and I've got a gun. Come after me and I'll kill her."

He must have jabbed her or twisted her arm, because there was a shrill, panicked cry. "No, don't, please!"

"Hear that?" Simmons asked roughly. "I mean what I say."

"I heard." Blackie's voice was calm. "Jessica, can you confirm that he has a gun?"

I heard a low, quavering, "Yes."

"Didn't I say I had a gun?" Simmons demanded, sounding annoyed.

"Yeah," Blackie replied. "Just wanted a confirmation, that's all." His tone, calm and steady, became conversational. "Jessica, you do what Simmons says. Don't take any chances. You hear me? We've got officers out here. You'll be okay."

There was no answer, but Blackie went on as if there had been. "Good. Simmons, I'll get back to you shortly. Stay where you are for now."

Without waiting for a reply, Blackie stepped back, closing the door against the prop. To me, he said in a low, steady voice, "Go out to the parking lot, China. Tell the PSPD officer to call in backup. Tell them we've got a hostage situation here. I want them to clear the garage and the outside parking lot, and keep everybody away." He unclipped the radio from his belt. "I'll call for county backup."

I ran toward the entrance to the garage, where I saw Jerry and two other uniformed PSPD patrol officers approaching fast. "We just got a 9-1-1 call from the manager," Jerry said crisply. "What's up, China?"

I pointed to where Blackie was standing, using his radio. "The sheriff has an armed man holding a female hostage. He wants you to radio for backup from the PSPD, and keep everybody away."

Jerry's eyes narrowed. "Hostage?"

"Yes," I said. "The owner of that green Ford you've been watching. We've found Jessica Nelson."

It was like a scene out of a movie. The police were dealing with a desperate individual — in this case, a suspected killer who was holding a hostage and threatening to kill her. After a while, it became clear that the situation was in what's called the "standoff phase," when the hostage taker is holed up with the hostage and the police are in control of the possible exits — in this case, the one door to the storage room.

While the backup gathered in the parking lot, Blackie established contact with Simmons, via cell phone. Simmons seemed cool and rational, and — in return for Jessica — asked for promise of safe passage out of town. To hold the ante down, Blackie was treating this as if it were a single act, unrelated to anything else, and he didn't mention the murder of Gloria Graham, or Simmons' possible involvement with her. But both he and I were pretty well convinced that Matt Simmons had murdered Gloria, and that he had seized Jessica because she managed to follow a trail of clues that led to him.

Sheila arrived and took charge of the area outside, directing the cordoning off of the area immediately in front of the parking garage. Before long, there were a dozen patrol cars and deputies' vehicles parked around the perimeter. Two EMS ambulances were there, too, with a couple of teams of medics. I waited nervously just inside the entry to the garage, where I could see the door to the storage area.

Nearby, Blackie and Sheila had set up a command center. The sheriff was on the phone to Simmons, trying to persuade him to let Jessica come out, unharmed. Simmons was stubbornly resisting, saying he would only come out if there was a car waiting for him and a promise that he could get in it and drive off. The conversation went on until Simmons suddenly stopped talking.

"Maybe the battery on his phone has given out," Sheila said worriedly, when the silence had stretched to several minutes.

"I'm going in there and find out," Blackie said. "We can get him another phone, if that's what it takes. We need to keep him talking to us."

"No," Sheila said, putting her hand on his arm. "Hold off for a few minutes, Blackie. Maybe —"

But at that moment, the door was pushed open and Jessica stumbled through it, nearly falling. Sheila ran forward and grabbed her, pulling her off to one side, while Blackie and another officer stationed themselves at the open door.

I went quickly to Jessica, now sitting on the floor, her back to the cement wall, eyes shut. She was breathing heavily. I took her hand. "You okay?" I asked.

Her eyes flew open. "China!" she exclaimed. "Oh, I'm so glad to see you! How did you get here?" She glanced wildly around. "How did you find me?"

"Long story," Sheila said beside me. "We have some med techs here who want to check you out, but we need to know what's going on in there. Did Simmons let you go? Is he a threat to himself? What kind of arsenal does he have in there?"

I understood her questions. If Simmons had released Jessica, he might be intending to kill himself. Or he might be heavily armed, intending to take out anybody who came in after him.

"He didn't let me go," Jessica said, rubbing her wrist. "I hit him. He's out cold."

Sheila stood. "Go get him," she yelled at Blackie. "Jessica says he's out cold."

"How did you do it?" I asked Jessica.

"He'd tied me up, but I'd already managed to get loose," she said. "When he came running in, he was so stressed that he didn't notice that my hands and ankles weren't tied tight, the way he'd left them. When he was talking to the sheriff on his cell, I hit him from behind with a golf club. As hard as I could."

"A golf club?" I exclaimed. "Good lord, Jessica. Where did you get a golf club?"

But the medics took over just then, and I didn't get an answer to my question. And by the time Simmons was wheeled out, strapped to a gurney and under armed escort, Jessica was already on her way to the Adams County Hospital, where she would likely spend the night. I couldn't go with her — it was nearly four, and I had to get back to the shop.

The excitement over, the patrol officers

and county deputies were beginning to leave. There was still crime scene tape closing off the front of the garage, where a team of investigators would begin the work of going through Simmons' locker and, later, both his apartment and Gloria's.

"Sorry to leave when you guys are having so much fun," I said to Blackie and Sheila, "but I have to get to work." I smiled at Blackie. "Good job, Sheriff."

"Good timing," Blackie said, clapping me on the shoulder. "I'm not forgetting what I said about recommending you as an investigator. If you hadn't been so persistent in tracking Jessica, this business today would have had a much different conclusion."

"Actually, I think the credit goes to Jessica," I said. "She said she hit him with a golf club."

"A seven iron," Blackie said. "I saw it lying in the locker where he'd been keeping her."

"The seven-iron slugger," I mused. "The media will have fun with that."

CHAPTER TWENTY

If you've never tried them, you'll find that herbal liqueurs are delightfully mood-altering. From homemade Irish Cream to coffee liqueurs made from home-ground beans to sweet and tangy drinks from your herb garden or fruits preserved in spirits, you'll enjoy making and sharing herbal liqueurs.

China Bayles
"Mood-Altering Plants"
Pecan Springs Enterprise

When this all began, Jessica had been hoping for a big story that would carry her own byline. She got a lot more than she bargained for.

Hark ran a huge banner headline: ALERT REPORTER CAPTURES ARSON-MURDER SUSPECT. He did the reporting on that one, outlining Jessica's investigation of Gloria Graham's death and her abduction by the man who was suspected of killing Graham. In addition, Jessica wrote a special full-page feature about the experience of being captured and held, bound and gagged and in desperate fear for her life, for over forty hours. The Austin *American-Statesman* printed a page of photos showing the interior of Simmons' storage locker, the machete she had used to cut her ropes, and the golf club she had whacked her captor with. The San Antonio *Express-News* featured a two-column interview with Jessica, and the Houston *Chronicle* put her on the front page — albeit below the fold. (The space above the fold was dedicated to one of the usual local political corruption scandals.)

But Jessica's media attention wasn't just print, and it wasn't just local — partly because her experience was so sensational, and partly because Jessica herself is an attractive, vivacious young woman who knows how to tell a story.

And she had a zinger of a story to tell. The day after her release, she was interviewed on CNN, NBC, and CBS, and the day after that, on *Good Morning America.* Her interviewers loved hearing her tell how she had waited in fear in the dark, bound and gagged and wondering if Simmons was going to shoot her, as he had shot Gloria Graham before he burned her alive — as he was *alleged* to have done, Jessica was careful to add. But they loved it even more when she told how she had taken out her captor entirely by herself, armed only with a seven iron. And of course they picked up on that golf club, and before long, she was known far and wide as the Seven-Iron Slugger.

Three days later, she was contacted by a New York literary agent, urging her to write a book.

"Have you seen the newspaper yet?" Ruby asked me, late on a Saturday afternoon, two weeks after the ordeal. She grinned at Jessica. "I know *you've* seen it."

We were all three sitting at the table in Ruby's kitchen, munching on some of the leftover refreshments from the garden club program and the tour of Ruby's shamanic garden. Ruby was holding up the latest *Enterprise,* open to the page of engagement announcements. At the top of the page was a photo of Sheila and Blackie. Blackie looked smug. Sheila looked a little tense.

"Yes, I saw it," Jessica replied. "Mr. Hibler wonders whether it's really going to happen."

"They've set a wedding date," I said. "The

first Sunday in September. And Blackie and McQuaid are busy making plans to join forces in the P.I. business, after Blackie leaves office." It was still hard for me to believe that Blackie could give up the post of sheriff so easily.

"Do they know where they're going to live?" Ruby asked.

"I think that's still undecided," I replied. "Sheila's house is too small for both of them, and Blackie lives even farther outside of Pecan Springs than I do." I lifted a bottle. "Anybody want another sip?"

I had brought several different bottles of homemade herbal liqueurs so that the garden club members could each have a little taste, as well as a couple of bottles from my very private stash — Rosemary Tangerine and Lemony Mint liqueurs — for Ruby. Caitie had baked more of those tasty lemon icebox cookies, and I had brought some of those, as well. Caitie was at orchestra practice this afternoon. She'd only had two lessons with her new teacher, but she was doing so well that Sandra had put her into the orchestra immediately.

Ruby held out her glass. "I'll try the Lemony Mint," she said, helping herself to another of Caitie's cookies. She turned to Jessica. "So what's the situation with the book, Jessica?"

"It's looking like a real possibility," Jessica replied. "But first there'll have to be a conviction — and that will take some time."

Ruby tasted the liqueur. "Gosh, that's good," she said. "I think I like it even better than the other one." She paused. "Do you think Simmons is likely to get convicted, China?"

"Very likely," I said. "I understand that his parents have hired Jeff Murdock, from Houston, to handle the defense. He's good. The trial is likely to be interesting — if it goes to trial."

The charges against Matthew Simmons were piling up. For now, they included murder, arson, aggravated kidnapping, and assault with a deadly weapon. Eventually, when the federal agents finished their investigation, they would include multiple counts of drug trafficking and conspiracy charges, as well.

"Looks to me like the prosecution has a very strong case," Jessica said.

I agreed. Since Simmons had been caught in a hostage situation, the kidnapping was a slam dunk, and the case of Gloria Graham's murder was almost as strong. Among the pieces of forensic evidence that would be presented at trial was the gun Simmons had in his possession when he was taken into custody in the parking garage. Ballistics testing had matched it with the single slug taken from Gloria's burned body. A big plus for the prosecution; a challenge for the defense.

The shoe evidence was less compelling, but it would pose a problem for the defense, as well, since juries know more about shoes than they know about the rifling of gun barrels. Among the crime-scene photos the prosecution would enter into evidence was the photo of the footprint taken from the area where the accelerant had been poured. The diagonal slash I had spotted on the square-and-diamond patterned tread of the Converse shoe could be seen in the photo and in the plaster cast that had been made of the print. To clinch the argument, the prosecutor would pass around the red-and-white-striped Stars and Bars basketball shoe Simmons had been wearing when he was captured, and point out that the slash in the heel exactly matched the eighth-inch-deep scar in the cast.

Jeff Murdock might be a hot-shot defense lawyer with a quiver full of acquittals to his credit, but he was going to have a tough time developing a plausible alternative explanation for those two pieces of evidence.

If Simmons were my client, I'd advise him to plead: life without parole in what was likely to be a death penalty case.

The federal drug trafficking case that the federal investigators were piecing together would be a strong one, too. The defendant wasn't talking (what else is new?), but between Shannon Fisher and Larry Wolff (who turned out to know quite a bit about what Simmons was up to), the investigators could reconstruct what had happened, and how and why.

Matt Simmons, who grew up in Brownsville, Texas, and went to high school and junior college there, had been recruited as a mule by the local chapter of the Gulf cartel, one of the most powerful cartels in Mexico. Known as "El Gringo," he had been employed by the drug lords for over five years, working his way up through the military-style organization to the role of recruiter. In addition to his undercover life, he was a graduate student at CTSU, presumably aiming to equip himself with a degree he could use when he finally decided to go straight (which, of course, the cartel would never allow).

He had met Gloria the previous year and persuaded her that smuggling was an easy — and exciting — way to earn money. Her relationship to Laughton gave her a reason to go on the field trip, and Simmons used the opportunity to introduce her to the cartel's suppliers. He hadn't expected her to bring a load across in the van. In fact, it was a dumb stunt, since it might have landed the whole crew in jail. But the border officials had been bought off and Gloria's first carry was a success. It wasn't the only one. She made the trip twice more in the next few months, before she got frightened and decided that she needed to get out. Shannon Fisher would testify that Gloria was on the verge of going to the police, with the hope of entering the Witness Protection Program.

That was when Simmons acted, the prosecution would say, under the urging of his cartel bosses, who insisted that he silence her and instructed him on how to do it. But he'd never shot anybody before. He had never set an arson fire, either. He botched the job of killing Gloria outright, and I had happened on the fire before the evidence could be completely destroyed. And he had carelessly left that telltale shoeprint.

But even with that evidence, it's hard to see how the police would have caught up with him if it hadn't been for Jessica. As she told the media people who interviewed her, she was compelled to get involved because she had been absolutely stunned by the horrible fact of Gloria's death.

"When I learned that this young woman had been alive and conscious when the fire reached her — that she had burned to death, I couldn't get it out of my mind," she told her various interviewers. "My parents and my twin sister died in a fire. Gloria's horrific death woke the memories I had buried, the nightmares I had tried to ignore. I was possessed by it, and it possesses me still. Following Gloria's story, piecing it together, I was mourning her, in a way. But I was also mourning my sister and my mom and dad. I had to find out who killed Gloria and why."

Under the interviewers' questioning, she told how she had followed the trail, from Scott Sheridan to Lucy LaFarge, and from Lucy to Zoe Morris. After she left Zoe, she had found a list of laboratory assignments on Stuart Laughton's bulletin board. She had happened on the name of Gloria Graham, put it together with the initials on the bracelet, and concluded that Gloria might be the woman who had died in the fire. She found her address, went to her apartment, and began knocking on neighbors' doors.

"That's when I met Matt Simmons," she

told her interviewers. "He seemed interested and started asking me more and more questions. At some point, I guess he must have realized that I was beginning to piece the story together, and that I was close to finding out what he had done."

She, too, realized how close she was, and that she was in real danger. "I tried to phone my friend China Bayles for help," she said, "but Simmons discovered what I was doing and grabbed the phone." He hit her hard enough to knock her out, took her down to his storage locker, where he bound and gagged and locked her up.

"I had no idea where I was," she said, "or what time it was. Most of the time it was pitch dark and I couldn't see a thing. But once when somebody came in and turned on the main overhead light, I got a quick look around. I realized that I was being held in a storage closet — and that there was a bag of golf clubs and a machete in the corner. You know, a banana knife. I guess he'd brought it back from Mexico. I managed to scoot across the floor to the point where I could reach it, and wedged the blade into position so I could use it to cut the ropes on my wrists. After that, I was able to get the ropes off my ankles and pull the tape off my mouth. I couldn't escape, because there was a lock on the outside of the door, but I was hoping somebody would come into the storage area before he came back, and I could yell and get some help."

"And that golf club?" her interviewers would ask. (They always asked about that club, so they could work in the nickname "Seven-Iron Slugger.")

"Oh, that." She laughed. "Well, I thought I needed a weapon. The machete was kind of big, but I thought one of the golf clubs would work. I took the seven iron out of the bag and put it on the floor behind me, hoping I'd get a chance to hit him with it."

The interviewer would lean forward, wide-eyed, anticipating what was next. "And then he came back?"

Jessica would nod. "That's right. He came back with a duffle bag — for my dead body, I guess — and a gun. I don't know whether he intended to shoot me on the spot or knock me out and take me somewhere else to kill me. That's what he's accused of doing to Gloria."

"He couldn't see that you weren't tied up?"

"At that point, I guess the sheriff was already chasing him, and he was pretty scared. He just assumed that I was still tied."

"And when he was talking to the sheriff

on his cell phone . . ." the interviewer would prompt breathlessly.

"When he was talking on his cell, I whacked him." At that point, Jessica always grinned, reveling in the memory. "I grabbed the seven iron and walloped him as hard as I could, just above his right ear."

"You must have hit him pretty hard," the interviewer would say, frowning slightly. "He sustained a skull fracture."

"Good," Jessica would say. "He had it coming."

I picked up the bottle of Rosemary Tangerine liqueur. "Another sip or two?" I asked.

Ruby held out her glass. "What's happening with Stuart Laughton?" she asked. "He wasn't really involved in any criminal activity, was he?"

"Depends on how you define criminal," Jessica said, looking chagrined. "I'm ashamed of myself. Really. If I had known . . ."

Ruby patted her hand understandingly. "Been there, done that," she said softly. "Don't beat up on yourself, Jessica."

"I imagine he'll think twice before he fools around with anybody else," I said. "Donna Fletcher told me that Margie has given him an ultimatum. If he does it again, she'll divorce him. And McQuaid heard, through the faculty grapevine, that Laughton's department chair has laid down the law. If he gets involved with another student, his tenure will be revoked."

"What about the other stuff?" Ruby asked. "You know, the smuggling."

"Blackie says that the federal agents have questioned him closely," I reported, filling Ruby's glass. "They're satisfied that he had nothing to do with the drug-smuggling operation. However, his dean is not too happy. There will be no more field trips to Mexico for a while."

"The publicity isn't hurting the sales of the new book, though," Jessica said. "I understand that he and Margie are going to be on *All Things Considered.*"

"When are *you* going to be on *All Things Considered?*" Ruby asked. "When you sign the contract for your book? Or maybe when they announce the movie?"

"Gosh," Jessica said, widening her eyes. "A movie! You think?" She mused. "Maybe Amy Adams playing me? Or Alyson Hannigan?"

"I'll vote for Tom Selleck to play Blackie," I offered, although I've always thought that Selleck looks a lot more like McQuaid than Blackie.

"Who should play you, China?" Ruby

asked practically. "How about Holly Hunter?"

"Aw, gee," I said, pleased. "Really? Tell the casting director I'll go along with that." I paused. "You'll have to be in it, too, Ruby. Julia Roberts, maybe?"

"Oh, yum." Ruby rolled her eyes in ecstasy. "But we'll need to come up with a title."

"We can use the title of my book," Jessica said modestly. "I mean, if I really do get a contract to write it."

"You will," Ruby said with a confident smile. "It's a slam dunk. What's the title?"

"Mourning Gloria," Jessica replied.

Ruby frowned. "I'm not sure I understand that."

But I did.

RECIPES

KATE'S GRILLED HERB-BUTTERED SWEET CORN

8 ears fresh corn
Hot water to cover the corn
2 tablespoons butter, softened
3 tablespoons grated Parmesan cheese
2 tablespoon chopped fresh herbs: basil, parsley, oregano, dill, or thyme
Salt and pepper, to taste

Preparing the Ears

Pull the corn husks down but don't remove them. Remove the silks, and pull up the husks around the ears. Put the ears into a large pan and cover with hot (not boiling) water. Soak for 15 minutes to saturate the husks. Drain the ears, leaving them wet.

Grilling the Ears

Combine the butter, cheese, herbs, salt, and pepper. Divide the mixture into eight equal portions. Pull down the wet husks and rub one-eighth of the butter mixture onto each ear of corn. Pull the husks up to cover. Tightly wrap each ear in aluminum foil and place on a hot grill. Steam for 10 minutes. Remove the foil and grill the ears (still wrapped in the husks) 5–7 minutes longer, turning several times. Serve with additional herb butter.

CHINA'S CARROT CUPCAKES

2 cups flour
1 teaspoon cinnamon
1/4 teaspoon nutmeg
Pinch of cloves
1 teaspoon salt
1 teaspoon baking soda
1 teaspoon baking powder
4 eggs
2 cups sugar
3/4 cup vegetable oil
3 cups washed, grated carrots (about 1 pound)
1 teaspoon vanilla
1 cup chopped pecans or walnuts

Preheat oven to 325°. Grease a muffin tin or line with paper cupcake cups. Sift the flour, cinnamon, nutmeg, cloves, salt, baking soda, and baking powder together. In a large bowl, beat the eggs with the sugar. Add the oil, grated carrots, and vanilla and mix well. Add the flour mixture and nuts. Blend until just mixed. Fill the cups 3/4 full. Bake about 25 minutes. Cool and frost.

Frosting
1/3 cup cream cheese
1/4 cup butter (1/2 stick) or margarine
1 teaspoon vanilla
2 cups confectioners' sugar
Edible flowers for decoration

Bring the cream cheese and butter or margarine to room temperature. Add the vanilla and blend, then beat in the sugar. Separate into three small dishes and add food coloring, if desired. If the frosting is still too stiff, add a few drops of milk. Frost.

Decorate the cupcakes with edible flowers (unsprayed!) from your garden: blossoms of lavender, thyme, chives, basil, nasturtiums, bachelor's buttons, clover, chrysanthemum, calendula, and squash.

MARGIE LAUGHTON'S SECRET RECIPE PIZZA SAUCE
2 pounds ripe tomatoes
3 tablespoons olive oil
1 large onion, chopped

1 green bell pepper, chopped
1 carrot, grated
1 zucchini, grated
5 cloves garlic, minced
1/4 cup chopped fresh basil
2 teaspoons fresh thyme, minced, or 1/2 teaspoon dried
2 teaspoons fresh oregano, minced, or 1/2 teaspoon dried
2 teaspoons fresh dill weed, or 1/2 teaspoon dried
1/2 teaspoon celery seed
1/3 cup Burgundy or other hearty red wine
1 bay leaf
2 tablespoons tomato paste

Preparing the Tomatoes

In a large bowl, add ice cubes to cold water. Bring a pot of water to a boil. Drop whole tomatoes in the boiling water. When the skin is loosened (about 1 minute), remove the tomatoes with a slotted spoon and drop them into the bowl of ice water. When cool, remove the skin, cut each tomato in half, and remove the seeds. Chop and set aside two tomatoes. Chop the rest and puree in a blender, food processor, or ricer.

Making the Sauce

In a large pot over medium heat, heat the oil and sauté the onion, bell pepper, carrot, zucchini, and garlic about 5 minutes. Pour in the pureed tomatoes. Stir in the chopped tomatoes, herbs, and wine. Add the bay leaf and bring to a boil. Reduce the heat, cover, and simmer 2 hours. Stir in the tomato paste and simmer an additional hour. Discard the bay leaf. Cool and spread over unbaked pizza. Add toppings and bake.

BOB GODWIN'S CABRITO KABOBS

3/4 cup vegetable oil
Juice of three limes
3 teaspoons soy sauce
4 cloves garlic, chopped
2 teaspoons fresh cilantro, chopped (if desired)
1 teaspoon dried cumin
2 pounds cabrito (goat meat), cut into 2-inch cubes
Cherry tomatoes
Chunks of onion, pineapple, green peppers

Mix the oil, lime juice, soy sauce, garlic, cilantro, and cumin. Place the meat in a zip-top bag and pour the marinade mixture over it, making sure that all the meat is covered. Marinate for 8 hours. Skewer the meat, alternating with tomatoes, onion, pineapple, and green peppers. Brush with the marinade. Grill over hot coals for about 10 minutes. Turn, repeat. Serve hot.

CAITLIN'S LEMON ICEBOX COOKIES

1 cup shortening, room temperature
1 cup granulated sugar
1 cup light brown sugar, firmly packed
2 large eggs
1 teaspoon grated lemon rind
2 tablespoons fresh lemon juice
3 1/2 cups flour
1 teaspoon baking soda
1/2 teaspoon salt
2 tablespoons finely minced lemon herbs: lemon balm, lemon verbena, or lemon thyme

In a large bowl, beat the shortening and sugars at medium speed with an electric mixer until fluffy. Add the eggs, separately, beating well after each addition. Add the grated lemon rind and lemon juice, and beat until blended. In a separate bowl, combine the flour, baking soda, salt, and herbs. Add by thirds to the butter mixture, beating just until blended. Divide the dough into thirds. On wax paper, form each third into a 12-inch log. Wrap in wax paper and chill 4–6 hours. Slice each log into 1/2-inch slices (about 28), and place on parchment-covered or lightly greased baking sheets. Bake at 350° for 12–14 minutes or until the edges are lightly browned. Remove the cookies to wire racks to cool. Store in an airtight container, or freeze.

YAUPON TEA
Preparing the Leaves
Gather several cups of young and older leaves. (Young green leaves have the most caffeine.) Roast the leaves at 200° for 1–2 hours, or toast in a hot skillet until they are dry and brittle. (Euell Gibbons, in *Stalking the Blue-Eyed Scallop,* writes that the darker the leaves, the stronger the caffeinated effect.) Use immediately or store in a tightly lidded jar.

Making the Tea
Pour boiling water over crushed leaves in a mug or teacup. Use about 1 tablespoon per cup of boiling water. Allow to steep for 4–6 minutes.

Serve either hot or iced. May be flavored with mint or lemon herbs.

GINA'S SAVORY SALT-FREE SEASONING BLEND

3 dried bay leaves, broken
3 tablespoons dried parsley
2 tablespoons dried rosemary leaves
1 tablespoon dried basil
1 teaspoon dried sage
1 teaspoon dried thyme
1 tablespoon dried lemon zest*
2 tablespoons onion powder
1 teaspoon garlic powder
1 teaspoon cayenne powder

In a blender or grinder, pulverize all the herbs, dried zest, and powders. Place in a large-holed shaker. Excellent on poultry, fish, meat, vegetables, and salads.

*Lemon zest is the yellow peel, without the white pith. You can use a potato peeler to peel the lemon. Slice or chop fine and dry thoroughly before using.

ROSEMARY TANGERINE LIQUEUR

3 tangerines
1 cup sugar
2 cups water
3/4 cup fresh rosemary leaves, loosely packed
1/4 teaspoon ground coriander
1 cup 80-proof vodka

1/2 cup brandy

Preparing the Tangerines

Remove the peel from the tangerines and scrape and discard the bitter white pith from the inside. (Save the peeled tangerines for another use.) Chop the peel and place in a pan in a 200° oven for 2 hours. Turn off the oven, open the door slightly, and leave the peels in overnight.

Making the Liqueur

Bring the sugar and water to a boil over medium-high heat, stirring constantly until the sugar dissolves. Add the rosemary leaves and simmer for 5 minutes, stirring frequently. Strain and discard the leaves, using a fine-mesh strainer. Add the dried tangerine peel and coriander and pour into a clean 1-quart container with a tight-fitting lid. Let cool for 20 minutes. Add the vodka and brandy. Cover and let stand in a cool, dark cupboard for 1 month. Strain through a coffee filter into another container, cover, and allow to age for 1 month before serving. Makes about a quart.

LEMONY MINT LIQUEUR

1 lemon
1 cup sugar

2 cups water
3/4 cup mint leaves, loosely packed
1/2 cup lemon balm leaves
1/3 cup lemon thyme leaves
1/3 cup lemongrass, chopped
2 cups light rum

Preparing the Lemon

Follow the directions for preparing tangerine peels for Rosemary Tangerine Liqueur.

Making the Liqueur

Bring the sugar and water to a boil over medium-high heat, stirring constantly until the sugar dissolves. Add the mint and simmer for 5 minutes, stirring frequently. Strain and discard the leaves, using a fine-mesh strainer. Pour into a clean 1-quart container with a tight-fitting lid. Add the lemon balm, lemon thyme, lemongrass, and dried lemon peel. Let cool for 20 minutes. Add the rum. Cover and let stand in a cool, dark cupboard for 1 month. Strain through a coffee filter into another container, cover, and allow to age for 1 month before serving. Makes about a quart.

CHINA'S COSMETIC VINEGAR

Cosmetic vinegar helps to tone, refresh, and restore the skin's natural acidity. For each kind of vinegar you want to make, you'll need 4 cups of high-quality apple cider vinegar and 2 cups fresh (or 1 cup dried) herbs, as suggested below. Steep the herbs in the vinegar for several weeks, then strain into pretty bottles. For a gift, add a raffia tie and this instruction: *To use, mix 1/2 cup vinegar with 3 cups water, and spritz or splash it on your face after washing.*

Herbal Combinations

- Minty Vinegar: equal amounts of spearmint, sage, thyme, and rosemary.
- Sweet Floral Vinegar: equal amounts of rose petals and hips, willow bark, chamomile flowers, and dried orange peel. To use, mix with rosewater.
- Lovely Lavender Vinegar: lavender flowers, rosemary, and thyme.

RUBY'S CALMING FRAGRANCE BLEND
6 drops sandalwood essential oil
4 drops clary sage essential oil
4 drops myrrh essential oil
4 drops frankincense essential oil
3 drops clove essential oil
2 drops rose essential oil

Combine and mix the oils. Store in a small dark-colored bottle. Use in a diffuser.

ABOUT THE AUTHOR

Susan Wittig Albert grew up on a farm in Illinois and earned her Ph.D. at the University of California at Berkeley. A former professor of English and a university administrator and vice president, she now lives with her husband, Bill, in the country outside of Austin, Texas. In addition to the China Bayles mysteries, she writes a Victorian mystery series with her husband under the pseudonym of Robin Paige.

We hope you have enjoyed this Large Print book. Other Thorndike, Wheeler, Kennebec, and Chivers Press Large Print books are available at your library or directly from the publishers.

For information about current and upcoming titles, please call or write, without obligation, to:

Publisher
Thorndike Press
295 Kennedy Memorial Drive
Waterville, ME 04901
Tel. (800) 223-1244

or visit our Web site at:

http://gale.cengage.com/thorndike

OR

Chivers Large Print
published by BBC Audiobooks Ltd
St James House, The Square
Lower Bristol Road
Bath BA2 3SB
England
Tel. +44(0) 800 136919
email: bbcaudiobooks@bbc.co.uk
www.bbcaudiobooks.co.uk

All our Large Print titles are designed for easy reading, and all our books are made to last.